MACABRE MASTERPIECES . . .

A cunning American solves a chilling puzzle in "An Agent Named Riddle" . . .

A determined policeman employs an unusual weapon in "Cop Killer" . . .

A gifted medium picks up a deadly message in "Just Curious" . . .

A beautiful woman takes a cross-country trip with death at her side in "Homicide En Route" . . .

A hungry swindler bites off more than he can chew in "The Death of Autumn" . . .

D0828012

DEATH CAN BE BEAUTIFUL

ALFRED HITCHCOCK

A DELL BOOK

Published by
Dell Publishing Co., Inc.
1 Dag Hammarskjold Plaza
New York, New York 10017

ISBN: 0-440-11755-0

Printed in the United States of America
One Previous edition
New edition
First printing—March 1982

Acknowledgments

Day of the Tiger by JACK WEBB. Copyright © 1966 by H. S. D. Publications, Inc. Reprinted by permission of the author and the author's agents, Scott Meredith Literary Agency, Inc.

The Fanatical Ford by ARTHUR PORGES. Copyright © 1960 by H. S. D. Publications, Inc. Reprinted by permission of the author and the author's agents, Scott Meredith Literary Agency, Inc.

The Sound of Murder by DONALD E. WESTLAKE. Copyright © 1962 by H. S. D. Publications, Inc. Reprinted by permission of the author and the author's agents, Scott Meredith Literary Agency, Inc.

An Agent Named Riddle by H. A. DeRosso. Copyright © 1960 by H. S. D. Publications, Inc. Reprinted by permission of the author's agents, Scott Meredith Literary Agency, Inc.

Homicide En Route by C. B. GILFORD. Copyright © 1960 by H. S. D. Publications, Inc. Reprinted by permission of the author and the author's agents, Scott Meredith Literary Agency, Inc.

The Listening Cone by ED LACY. Copyright © 1966 by H. S. D. Publications, Inc. Reprinted by permission of the author and the author's agent, Howard Moorepark.

Cop Killer by JAMES HOLDING. Copyright © 1962 by H. S. D. Publications, Inc. Reprinted by permission of the author and the author's agents, Scott Meredith Literary Agency, Inc.

The Death of Autumn by HAL ELLSON. Copyright © 1968 by H. S. D. Publications, Inc. Reprinted by permission of the author and the author's agents, Scott Meredith Literary Agency, Inc.

Of Men and Vengeance by DONALD HONIG. Copyright © 1958 by H. S. D. Publications, Inc. Reprinted by permission of the author and the author's agent, Theron Raines.

Just Curious by JAMES H. SCHMITZ. Copyright © 1968 by H. S. D. Publications, Inc. Reprinted by permission of the author and the author's agents, Scott Meredith Literary Agency, Inc.

Beyond the Wall by NEDRA TYRE. Copyright © 1968 by H. S. D. Publications, Inc. Reprinted by permission of the author and the author's agents, Scott Meredith Literary Agency, Inc.

What If I Had Taken The Train? by ROBERT COLBY. Copyright © 1968 by H. S. D. Publications, Inc. Reprinted by permission of the author and the author's agents, Scott Meredith Literary Agency, Inc.

Contents

I wonder if we're not on the verge of carrying truth, normally a good thing, too far. I pose the question due to the fact that my attention has recently been called to a thing called Truth in Lending. As I understand it, the people who lend us money are now bound to tell us exactly, no beating around the bush, how much they are charging us for taking advantage of the privilege of borrowing from them.

All well and good, I suppose, in theory. The truth, according to one old saw, never hurt anyone. But let's take a closer look. What will happen when we find out what we've been paying all along in finance charges? If we have any sense, after we emerge from the slough of despond into which we've sunk, we'll stop buying on time. But what young bachelor with his eye on an MG, or head of the family in need of an addition to the house, ever let sense stand in the way of borrowing?

The real consequence of Truth in Lending, I fear, will be a rash of nervous breakdowns. We won't stop borrowing. We'll simply realize what fools and weaklings we are for doing it, considering that, over the long run, we'll probably be paying something like twice for what we buy. Previously, we thought there was something astute, even, to an extent, patriotic, about dealing with the moneylenders. We were keeping the economy churning, we thought. But the truth, more than likely, will destroy us. We'll realize that not only have we been patsys all those years, but, now that we know it, we're much too irresolute to break the habit.

I wouldn't be surprised to hear about a movement toward Truth in Advertising next. Madison Avenue is always the reformers' favorite target. And, sooner or later, they'll undoubtedly achieve their goal, with the result that we'll be hearing television commercials such as: "Ladies, this outlandishly overpriced scent won't take six inches off your hips, restyle your hair, and photograph you in a more flattering light. At the most, it will make you smell a little strange, something like an Irish bog." Or: "Men, this sleek new automobile won't make you look twenty years younger when you're at the wheel. But it will probably hustle you along toward your first heart attack when, a week after you buy it, the engine drops out and you have to send it back to the factory for rebuilding." I ask you, though, is this what we want to hear? Or would we prefer our fantasies?

Once Truth gets a foothold, there will be no stopping it. We'll find ourselves trying to cope with, for example:

Truth in Courtship. Our hero, Harold, having asked our heroine, Gwendolyn, for her hand, will get a question in response. Will Harold, she will want to know, love her in the future as he does in the present? He will be forced to reply: "It hardly seems likely. It's the nature of the male, after a time, to become bored with his mate. I will undoubtedly reach a point, along about the age of forty, when I will detest your cooking, cringe at your cliché-ridden conversation, and, after you have become as overweight as your mother, shudder at the sight of you in a negligee." With a truth like that to contend with, it is unlikely that Harold and Gwendolyn will ever get to the altar.

Or Truth in Medicine. We go to doctors because we believe subconsciously that they practice a magic that can cure us of all our ills. How will we feel, though, when, under the new system, the doctor gives us a pill, but adds that it won't do us one bit of good. "I'd like to help you," he'll say. "Frankly, however, your recurring headaches could mean a thousand and one things, and by the time I gave you all the tests required to isolate the single cause, you'd be too old to save, anyway." How much better to have a false diagnosis and a sugar pill. They at least stopped the headaches temporarily.

Truth in Politics, I imagine, will probably do us the most harm. We will soon discover that there isn't one honest man among us. Consequently, we will have to accept admitted scoundrels as our leaders or go entirely without. It will probably mean the end of civilization as we now know it.

Fortunately, we do not yet have to put up with the whole truth. There is plenty of fiction to fall back on. For example, the stories which follow. And the situation, I venture to say, is to our advantage. For you are undoubtedly here to be entertained. And, to quote another old saw: Fiction is stranger than Truth.

—ALFRED HITCHCOCK

DAY OF THE TIGER

by Jack Webb

The third shot fired by Officer Shelby struck Dandy Fornos in the calf of his left leg. It was a slight wound, cutting through the edge of the flesh, slashing twice through the cheap wool of his charcoal slacks, but it put the fear of the devil in his heart and wings on his heels. He did not drop the briefcase which was all that was left of the shambles behind him: the car with its engine block smashed by a .357 Magnum slug; Ronnie and Joe, dead; the cop crumpled behind the wheel of the black and white sedan, and the other on his stomach in the road, shooting, shooting.

Away to the right was a line of thick shrubs along a high steel mesh fence. Dandy turned and fled toward them.

Shirley Duff braked her car hard and fast and pressed the horn. What was the crazy fool doing, rushing blindly across this sidestreet, sportcoat flying, clutching that silly briefcase with both hands?

North from the way she was driving, more sirens than before were wailing. She was glad she had come into the park over the bridge from the south. She was in no mood to be stopped by a fire or an accident, however grim it might be.

She parked the small sport coupe competently a little way from the entrance of the zoo. What a foolish place to meet, but it was safe. Tom was clever about such things, almost too clever.

Her long legs were elegant as they reached from the edge of the seat to the pavement. Her blue silk suit was freshly pressed, and her soft brown hair shone in the sunlight. She was quite young, pretty, and in love. It showed in the way she walked and in the proud way she carried her shoulders as she hastened toward a destiny where all birds sang.

At the turnstile to the zoological gardens, she had to wait while the man ahead of her received his change.

He was a slim individual, neither much older, nor much taller than she. His thin, blond hair was sparse at the temples, and his gray flannel, although it had been a good suit once, was shabby now, not so much with wear but as though he no longer cared about his personal appearance— like his shoes, good leather, well-shaped, but desperately needing a polish.

Tom would never become like that, she thought. Vaguely, Shirley felt a little sorry for the unhappy young man. But this was no day for that! This was a day for casting away all regrets, all fears . . .

Not so for Allen Trask. He hurried away from the pretty girl behind him at the turnstile, for there had been something in the tilt of her chin, the directness of her brown eyes, that had reminded him of Anne—not much, but enough. Now Anne was dead, and he had killed her as surely as though he had held a knife, taken a gun . . .

He did not pause at the reptile house which came first along the road to the exhibits. Snakes were dreadful things, death in a coil, death in a shady corner, and he had had enough of death.

Then, coming to the zoo, there had been the siren, and now there were more, running closer, and it was all beginning again—the dread cry that had been there in the night, the first sound he had heard after smashing through the guardrail; seeing the lights askew where the car had crashed, hearing the scream, the terrible cry of the sirens coming, focusing on the distorted ring of faces about him, finding awful words to ask and no one to tell him of Anne, of Anne who had been on the seat beside him . . .

At a cage of macaws, he paused. With their wise, sober eyes, they regarded him from clown faces. Each bird was clothed in bright feathers, blue and yellow, red and green; glorious birds. One, with a bright yellow breast and long banners of blue for wings, hooked its way down the tall side of steel mesh until it hung opposite him. "Pretty Polly," it rasped at Allen Trask.

"Pretty Polly," Allen said bleakly.

The girl went by, her tall heels clicking. The gaudy parrots watched the girl.

"Pretty Polly," Allen repeated.

The blue and yellow macaw grumbled.

Through the glass door marked "Director," John Krueger saw the boy with the briefcase fumble for the price of admission, enter the zoo and hurry out of sight down the road toward the reptile house. It was a warm day, but not so warm that beads of perspiration should stand out on the boy's forehead, and why did he hurry so much with such a difficult limp? Krueger's eyes crinkled thoughtfully. He would not admit to his premonitions, yet the very business he was in depended upon them. Take those two cocky sailors last week—something about the way they had laughed. They had bothered him so much he had followed them later, and found them heating pennies with a cigarette lighter to toss into a cageful of inquisitive monkeys.

The phone rang on his desk. He lifted it and listened. "Sheba's begun," Pete told him. His tone was excited. "Doc Chapman thought you would want to come."

"You bet," Krueger said to the cat keeper. "Take care of things till I get there."

At the door to his office, Krueger paused to speak to the girl at the switchboard. "I'm going to be busy, Marge. The tiger's cubs are coming."

"Yes, Mr. Krueger."

He went out the door and climbed into his car. Last year, they had lost Sheba's litter. This time . . . He started the car and swung it around onto the road. There was a spot of color, and another, and another, shining dark in the sunlight against the pavement top. Krueger slowed and stared at the road. Blood! Not much, but certainly blood. The young man with the limp? He recalled hearing sirens.

He thought of phoning the police, but rejected the idea. He wanted no troop of policemen tramping about the park, not until Sheba's cubbing was over. The slightest unnatural movement, sudden sound, unknown voice could wreck everything.

If the boy *were* a fugitive, he would remain quiet, unobtrusive. Krueger frowned and drove on. Perhaps he was letting his mind run away, but in a zoo you become so conscious of a spot or two of blood, of the trouble it could mean inside a cage, that you never see it without translating those blots into a dangerous possibility.

The limping young man was not in sight as he drove down the road into the canyon.

The small, open amphitheater where the trained seals performed each afternoon was empty. Slowly, painfully, Dandy Fornos made his way among the tiers of seats until he was out of sight from the rim of the bowl. There he sat upon a step, stretching his left leg stiffly before him. The pain blossomed up from the calf and shook his whole body. Every nerve was still taut with the near thing, the real. Not yet twenty, slight of build and dark, he would have been handsome except for his eyes which were like those of the lean gray wolf in the canyon below.

He set the briefcase down beside him. *What a lousy price for Ronny and Joe, for the wrecked car and the dead cop;* for the hurt pulsing through him only a slow pace behind the beat of his heart.

Dandy found his handkerchief and carefully pulled up his left trouser leg. He thought about the car which had nearly run him down, of it being parked before the zoo. *If she were here!*

A sudden, hard thump hit the rail at the top of the amphitheater behind his back. Dandy swung around, his hand sliding under his coat.

The big blue peacock settled on the rail, arched its neck, tilted its head from one side to the other and examined him with beady eyes before it stretched a striped wing to peck unconcernedly at a loose feather.

Dandy Fornos swore. He would have to get out of this damned fishbowl.

Shirley Duffy glanced at her watch. It was almost a quarter till eleven. Tom had said ten. So often she had had to wait for Tom in these hidden places, but not after to-day. This was to be the end of that sort of thing. Tom had promised.

Down the line, the shabby young man who had preceded her into the zoo was leaning against the rail and smiling. Something in that particular monkey cage was amusing him. She was glad he was happy even for a moment. He had looked so beaten, so nondescript. Now that he was smiling, he was almost attractive. Of course, he could not be handsome, not with his scalp shining through his thinning hair. Tom had a wonderful head of hair, dark, just beginning to fleck with gray, perfectly groomed. Tom was distinguished. Women looked at Tom Connors and envied her. Men liked him. Tom should have been in the diplomatic corps, but he had been waiting for her—in spite of the mistake of his marriage. Shirley sighed and it was almost like the pleasure of his touch.

The man in the shabby flannels laughed aloud. It was so unexpected that Shirley strolled down the line of cages to see what had caused his good humor. The sign on the cage front read:

DIANA MONKEY
(Cercopithecus diana roloway)
West Africa

Behind the steel mesh, a dark, triangular-faced monkey with a black Vandyke and a snowy chest was meticulously examining a scrawny baby. The little old man looked so much like a proud grandfather inspecting his first grandson that Shirley smiled, too. A female monkey beside the pair chattered nervously while three others watched in attitudes of bright expectancy.

"Mama's worrying about Gramp," Shirley said.

When she spoke, the man turned. "Yes," he said, "isn't she?" Most of the good humor fled his face.

"I'm sorry," Shirley said tartly, "I didn't mean to intrude."

"Please, you didn't. Believe me . . ."

"Ah, there you are."

They both turned and Shirley exclaimed, "Tom!" She ran to the handsome, middle-aged man, her hands extended.

Allen Trask returned to the cage full of Diana monkeys. There were no complications in monkeys, only a full-of-lifeness, only an entertainment.

Down in the canyon, Sheba was moaning; it was low and full-bodied and almost human. Crouched in a corner behind the tall rear wall of the cat grotto, almost out of sight, Krueger, Pete the keeper, and Doctor Chapman the veterinarian, watched and listened. Krueger had parked his car and walked down to join the two men.

Gently, almost secure in her time of pain, the tigress began to work at the tenuous sheath surrounding the first of her newborn.

"Sheba," Pete called softly, "Sheba, Sheba-girl." It was as though there were a communion between the keeper and the cat. Dr. Chapman raised a warning finger. Then he saw that the cat had heard and was not afraid. There was nothing about this in all the books he had ever read on veterinary medicine—except where house pets were concerned, of course—but this was a tiger, savage, neurotic and unpredictable.

"Sheba," the stocky keeper chanted, "Sheba, Sheba," and the miracle in the cave went on.

It went on without Sultan, for the big male Amurian tiger was in a strange place. Yesterday morning, after a full day of fasting, he had been trapped in a carrying cage pushed against the rear door of the grotto where he had spent five years with Sheba, and moved to a circus wagon which stood in the OFF LIMITS area on the side of the hill above.

For more than a day and a night now, he had carried his

ears flat against the golden orange velvet of his mammoth skull, his tail twitching at the slightest sound, and the snarl in his throat was a constant anger. All the tameness of his captivity was gone, all the security, as he paced the narrow cage, feeling strength in the steel-spring quiet of his footsteps and the coil of muscles beneath the black and gold of his shoulders.

It was an old cage on wheels, a cage that had rattled and rumbled across the country a hundred times and more. With plumed horses before it, it had paraded the streets from Portland, Oregon, to Portland, Maine, from 'Frisco to St. Augustine. A great hulk of teak and iron and oak, of peeling gilt and shining memories, Krueger had bought it for the zoo when a shoestring circus had folded in town. No one had thought it would not hold a tiger.

"Strongest cage I ever seen," Pete had said. Nor had anyone doubted or even taken the time to look closely at all the bolts and nuts and hinges.

A peahen came out of the bush before the cage and paused to peck at a tuft of weed. Behind her, swift and driving, came a male. When he discovered they were in the open, the peacock halted his plunging run, fanned his tail rigid and forced upward the spectacular three-quarter circle of his train, a shimmering arch of green and blue. His bulky body quivered, and the stiff quills of his feathers rattled.

The drab peahen paid him no attention.

Sultan did. Flat on his belly, his eyes shaded to black and light slits, the tiger felt his muscles grow with tension. The tip of his tail beat like a metronome.

The peacock continued to strut and shake and bow with quick, vibrant, excited movements.

Suddenly, the alchemy of his rage and his instincts becoming one overwhelming wave, Sultan charged. He was three feet off the floor when he hit the heavy bars of the cage door. The tremendous impact knocked him flat.

The birds fled.

Through the somber furnace of his eyes, Sultan saw the door at the end of the cage swing open, smashed from the rusted hinge bolts of almost a century, to dangle by the new lock and hasp. As softly as a domestic cat going down

an alley in the night, the great Amurian tiger slipped from
the cage and vanished beneath a bloom of white oleanders.

Nor was Sultan the only one who had gone into hiding.

Under the luxuriant leaf-fall of a weeping willow, Dandy
Fornos lay with his head on his briefcase to wait out the interminable hours of daylight. In the seclusion of his green
bower, Dandy had opened the briefcase and counted its contents. Twenty grand and some odd green. What a hell of a
poor haul that would have been to split three ways. Tonight
he would cross the wires on some car, some little, un-
noticeable car, before one of the big apartments off Twelfth
Avenue and head south—not directly to Tijuana, but on a
road that angled east from Chula Vista, farther east than the
tall, barbed border fence extended. There was a girl in the
Midnight Cabaret who would put him up, take care of
him. His left leg throbbed steadily.

On the bench beyond the last long droop of willow boughs
were a man and a girl—the girl who had been behind the
wheel of the coupe that had almost driven him down. He
did not worry anymore about her. This chick had troubles
of her own. Foolish troubles, silly troubles, but they helped
pass the time. Dandy cocked his head and listened.

"But I feel like such a fool!" Shirley said. Her voice was
cold, and hurt, and trembling a little. "No more than a
cheap affair. I'm no more than a tramp! A tramp!"

"Shirley, Shirley." The dapper man with flecks of gray in
his hair held to her hand and stroked it gently. "Surely you
understand it is better to do these things without a scene,
without unnecessary noise and confusion. You know how I
hate scenes!"

She pulled herself together, her hair still shining in the
sunlight that filtered through the tall gray trees, her eyes
suspiciously puffy as though she had been crying.

"After all," Tom said evenly, "there is my wife, Helen,
to be considered."

"Helen," Shirley repeated after him. "Helen!"

For three years it had been Helen. *From that very first
not-quite innocent luncheon there always had been Helen,*
Shirley thought. Once, she had believed, *If not me, then*

some other, some other who might hurt him. From her safe, sacrosanct cubbyhole beside the vice president's office, she had looked down the line of desks to Accounting, and Tom, so sweet, so vulnerable . . . He did have such hell at home— so many times he had told her.

"Helen," Shirley repeated aloud, breaking the spell of her lost enchantment.

"After all," he said uneasily, "she is my wife."

"I know. I know. I know. I know." She began to cry.

This was the nuts, Dandy Fornos thought, *better than TV, better than the movies. What a racket this joe had had.* He almost forgot the throb in his leg, the ache that was reaching up through his thigh like a knife.

Allen Trask had not meant to see her again. The zoo was a big place. He had let the girl go to her tryst. Now, coming down the canyon road from the opposite direction, he was running into her again, her with tears on her face, her and that sleek bum. Resolutely, he turned his back and stared into the lion pit:

LION
Panthera leo
Africa

The big lion lolled in the mid-morning sun. His shaggy mane was thick and dark and ragged at the edges as though it needed a good brushing. He did not look fierce. In fact, Allen Trask smiled, he looked more like the *Cowardly Lion of Oz*. In spite of the girl, the zoo had been good to Allen. It had taken him back before Anne, before that awful night; it had taken him back to himself.

Only now the girl was here once more, and though he had smiled at the lion, he could feel the tears shining on his cheeks. What good were tears? *You should not brood so much, Allen,* Dr. Bruce had said. *It isn't natural.* Then, a month or two ago, *Do you mind if I suggest another doctor?*

The lion yawned. Allen watched, unseeing.

He had taken the card Dr. Bruce had scribbled and gone

up a flight of stairs in the Professional Building, turned right, gone down the long corridor and stood before the door. Like the signs here in the zoo:

Dr. Anthony B. Connors
PhD., MD.
Psychiatrist

He had not gone through the door. He wasn't insane. It was only that he must pay for the accident. *One way or another you paid for everything you did in this life.* And he was paying. God knew he was paying—God, and Anne!

Shirley whispered, "You're cheating us, Tom. You're cheating all of us. You, Helen, me . . ."

"Shirley!" The man was rubbing his hands together.

For cripe's sake, Dandy Fornos thought. The pain in his leg made his muscles jerk. Uncomfortably, he rearranged himself, turned his head from the couple on the bench and gazed into the terrifying black, orange and white mask of a living tiger.

Allen Trask walked on to the sign that read: AMURIAN TIGERS. No cats were in sight, and he did not notice the group across the way.

On the other side of the empty grotto, Krueger whispered excitedly, "That's her fourth, that should be the lot of them!"

The veterinarian nodded, grinning. Impulsively, the keeper squeezed the elbow of his boss. Krueger smiled. Inside the cave, Sheba began to work on the thin envelope surrounding the furry, squirming weight of her fourth-born.

Sultan knew that he had come home. With that driving, constant instinct which is the birthright of every cat, Sultan had found his way back to the grotto. And now, under the leafy bower that led toward his mate, lay this human being exuding the scent of fear. Sultan bared his fangs and snarled.

Dandy Fornos scrambled backwards, his hand sliding under his coat, the briefcase left behind.

"Tiger!" he screamed. "Tiger!"

He came around the bench running, paying no attention to the ramming pain of every pounding stride. Tom Connors saw the tiger, and ran ahead of the boy, leaving Shirley. She stood before the bench, seeing the soft velvet of black and gold through a tracery of shadows, seeing the great yellow eyes with their bright shining centers as the big cat crept forward. She was unable to move, unable to take a step.

Then a man's body crashed into hers, knocking her down, covering her. She tried to struggle.

"For the love of heaven, be still," he whispered hoarsely.

She could feel the fear consuming his slender body, and beyond the fear, the courage that held him there, the two of them one and together on the other side of a flimsy wooden bench from the creeping tiger.

Sultan sprang, following the runners, pursuing the moving enemy who had come between him and his own.

Dandy Fornos, rocking unevenly on his bad leg, turned his head and saw the tiger coming, one seven-league leap and then another. He knew where the next would be. Instantly, Dandy swung and stood steady, the big automatic bucking as he squeezed the trigger. The last shot was almost in the tiger's throat. They died together, each with the same wild, desperate valor.

Then Allen Travers came to his feet and went down the road to see if there were anything he could do. Tom Connors stood beyond all of them, wiping his brow, while Shirley pulled herself unsteadily onto the bench and watched.

At the first shot, Sheba had risen from her litter. At the second, she had gone snarling into the open air of the grotto beyond her cave. Before the third explosion, the last, Dr. Chapman had pulled the lever that let the steel grate slide down to separate Sheba from her cubs.

It was all over finally. What was left of the boy and the tiger were removed from the canyon, the briefcase was found, the questions asked, Shirley's elegant Tom disappearing before the interrogation. Dr. Chapman and Pete removed the cubs, carrying them all in a wicker basket, incubator babies now.

Left alone, Shirley Duffy and Allen Trask walked up a path shady with trees, each a stranger not so much to each other as to themselves.

"Why did you do it?" she asked.

He shrugged. "It was the only way."

"But you ran toward the tiger." Her brown eyes regarded him soberly.

"You were there. If I could knock you down, if the cat jumped the bench . . ." He let it go.

"The others were running," she said.

"I thought of that," he admitted, "but so was I, and if the cat had to take somebody . . ."

She reached then and touched his hand. "You were willing?"

"It would not have made much difference. For a long time, it wouldn't have made much difference."

Still, she thought, *it was for me he did it.* "Will you take me home? she asked.

"I don't have a car."

"I do."

"I haven't driven for a long time," Allen said.

"I can drive."

"No," he said, "you shouldn't."

They turned and retraced their steps toward the entrance to the zoo. As they strolled, Allen began to talk, starting slowly at first, and then letting the words spill like waters loosed from a dam.

Shirley took his hand finally and held it in her own. There was fear there, all his nerves screaming from the fingertips, but beyond that was the courage—and the pent-up longing of a man who had been in the prison of his own soul. Shirley still held his hand as they went out the gate.

Krueger saw them go from the glass pane in his office door. *Well, now,* he thought. *Well, now, and what do you make of that?* But he had no time to make anything of it. Zoos are too busy for that sort of thing.

THE FANATICAL FORD

by Arthur Porges

"Fords is the worst," the old man quavered, fixing the reporter with an indignant eye of watery blue. "They stick together like—like them hillbillies that are all relatives, even though they're scattered to hell and gone over Kentucky. You be sure to put that down, young man: the others is bad, but them Fords is the worst. Family pride, by God!"

The reporter nodded, scribbling expert shorthand in his notebook. Quite a character, this old boy. A brand new approach to insanity. Too bad this wasn't a TV assignment; it would be nice to get a salty tape of that voice. Reminded him of Walter Brennan.

He wrote: "Fred Marer, a leather-faced, gimlet-eyed veteran, is being persecuted—" No. Better: "—claims to be a victim of the oddest persecution—"

Marer broke into this train of thought. "I know just how it started. Back in 1913, it was. Before you were born, likely. I made my Pa's Model T real mad. I was only a kid then, but I had a nasty mouth—You getting all this?"

"You bet I am, Mr. Marer. It's a remarkable story."

"And a whole pack of lies, you're thinking," the old man said shrewdly.

"It's not my business to decide that," the reporter replied in a bland voice. "I just report the facts. There may be good reason for your belief. Now, about this Model T you —ah—antagonized. I didn't know"—he smiled—"that they were so touchy. My grandfather called his names any decent mule wouldn't have tolerated. Once, I remember he even gave it a good boot in the radiator. About a quart of bolts and things flew off, but that didn't seem to matter; the car still ran—when it had a mind to." He paused, flushing. He was talking too much, and personalizing the old car as foolishly as Marer.

"That's right," the hermit agreed ruefully. "They wasn't easy to insult. Not a whole lot of pride when you're turned out on an assembly line. Not like a Rolls. But you see, Mr.—ah—"

"Nelson."

"—Nelson—most people abused their Fords in a kinda half-affectionate way. Oh, the owners got mad enough—stuck in mud, or engine dead on a cold morning, or gears wouldn't mesh—but it was like quarreling between husband and wife. When they really love each other, it doesn't go deep and fester. But I had a lippy mouth, and maybe too it was one of these here natural enemy things. I'd had my heart set on a bigger, better car, and took it out on this one.

"Don't ask me what I said, because it's too far back. Wasn't one thing, anyhow—more the last straw in a heap of insults. Know when it happened, though. I was cranking her one cold morning—real winters there—not like California—and she just wouldn't start."

"Why 'she?' "

"Dunno. But it was a 'she' all right. Nobody can hold a grudge like a female. You know about a woman scorned; you ain't that young, I reckon. Anyhow, like I'm saying, you remember—guess you wouldn't, a kid like you—how a Model T'd go 'er-rah! er-rah! er-er-er!,' when she was cranked. A sort of sneer it seemed that morning, with me late for work and colder'n Eskimo's nose in Alaska." He paused to spit reflectively. Overhead two ravens flapped, calling harshly; and high above the clouds there was the hissing scream of a jet cargo plane, Los Angeles bound.

"It was something in her tone that riled me up, and I cussed her out good. And that wasn't all. I hauled off and hit her a terrible clout with the jack handle. Made a big dent in the hood, and just ruined a headlight. Knocked it out of kilter." He nodded knowingly. "That Model T never looked right again. She was like a purty gal with a cast in one eye. When you spoil a woman's looks, watch out—that's all! After all our other fighting, this was the finish. She really hated me. And it wasn't just her; she passed the word along. Them Fords was like a family, and stuck together. You hurt one, you hurt 'em all. It was as if I'd belted the whole cussed tribe, instead of just one female. And that wasn't all; the other cars—different makes—joined in soon enough. Maybe an Olds didn't like a Ford, but I was a common enemy to 'em all."

"When was the first—ah—attack?"

"Why, that there very Model T tried to kill me a dozen times before we got rid of her. Once I started to crank her up and, mind you, I *know* she was in neutral. But the minute she turned over, she got into gear somehow. I jumped aside just in time. Damned if she didn't chase me over a field, turning when I did. And the proof is that when I jumped a gully, instead of her going on, like a car would if it was really out of control, she stopped and went back to neutral. *She* wasn't a-going to smash herself up! Doesn't that prove it?" he demanded belligerently. "No car that ain't chuck full of spite behaves that way."

"Sounds reasonable," Nelson agreed, wooden-faced.

"Well, I finally persuaded my dad to sell the car. Then we bought an Olds. And it was just as bad. Nothing merry about that durned heap. Twice it backed up on me suddenlike when Pa was driving. He swore he didn't touch the reverse, and I believe him. Pa was a good driver. Naturally, I wouldn't ride in the thing at all after that, but it was always trying to get me anyhow by backing, swerving, or speeding up without no warning. Pa used to say I was a jinx— 'cause that there Olds didn't act normal when I was around. You just bet it didn't! I tried to tell him about how I was in bad with Fords, and how they was pizening the other cars against me, but Pa just laughed. Ma kinda believed me—she was afraid of most machinery and hated to see horses disappear—but Pa never paid no mind to her.

"It got so I wasn't safe on the street. You saw them clippings. Does it seem natural to you that one man could of been in so many auto accidents? Looky here." He thumbed a fistful of yellow papers. "In 1920 I was almost killed three times by cars that just went wild, running up on sidewalks and things. Usually the driver had a clean record, too. I've had both legs broken eight times, my collarbone five, and ribs moren'n you can count. Here! In 1932 a dump truck that was parked by the curb—no driver, even—suddenly let go with five tons of gravel. Cut my legs up something fierce. You should see the scars. Now if that don't show—"

"It's certainly a remark—" No; he'd said that once. "Extremely interesting. What happened after that?"

"What d'you expect? Nothing but more of the same, and oftener, as cars increased. Busses, trucks, taxis—even a tractor, but it was too slow. They were all after me. And how about this, young feller? Twice the house I lived in was pretty near wrecked by big interstate trucks running wild off the highway. Bruises—the bed saved me the first time. And then a broken ankle. After that I stayed on the little back roads. Think that solved the problem? Not on your life! First thing you know there was motorcycles and jeeps." He rubbed a thin, white scar on his stubbled chin. "Fellow with a motorcycle did that in forty-five. Claimed the machine went wild. I was a good fifty yards off the dirt road, hunting mushrooms. If it'd hit me square, I wouldn't be here. When that kid looked at his steering gear, wasn't a blamed thing wrong."

"You must have collected a fortune in damages or insurance."

"What if I did!" the old man flared. "I had it coming, didn't I? Even if the drivers wasn't to blame, somebody had to pay my doctor bills. Why should I tell 'em it was the autos—them cussed Fords mostly—and not me. Who'd believe me? It's only my lawsuit money that lets me live in a safe place like this." He waved one gnarled hand. From their bench outside the mountain cabin, they could see for miles over the rolling California hills, already seared by the dry summer. Nowhere another human to be seen—only a few sleek brown and white steers.

"Couldn't even get no insurance after a while," the old man said querulously. "So I'd just collect my damages. They tried to prove I was causing accidents deliberately, but most of the drivers was honest about it, and there was witnesses, anyhow. They always said how the cars went out of control.

"Then after they got to building them cars with the hoods like big mouths. They—what're you snickering at? Young whippersnapper—you don't—"

"Sorry," Nelson said, gravely contrite. "It wasn't at anything you said. Just reminded me of a cartoon. Please go on, Mr. Marer; this is quite a story. I mean, quite fascinating. Valuable, too," he added hastily.

The old man gave him a suspicious glance. "I'm telling the gospel truth, exactly like it happened. Ain't nothing wrong with my memory. Right now I could tell you the serial number of the Model T that started the whole thing. And that there car musta been junked before you were born." He paused triumphantly. "Twelve thousand and twelve, it was—easy to remember."

"One of the early ones, all right. But about those new hoods. You were saying—"

"Yeah, lemme tell you about that. You'd think I'd have the sense to keep away, but those cars looked so different. They didn't seem like the same tribe. No reason for *them* to carry on the grudge. That Model T had been rust for thirty years or more. After all that hiding out in the back country, I figured maybe them Fords had forgotten me." He glowered into space, savoring his grievance. "Damn hood snapped down just like big jaws. All I wanted was a little peek at the motor; hadn't seen one close up since twenty-nine." His shoulders flexed reminiscently. "Lucky I had on a padded jacket. But my back ain't been right since."

"What about foreign cars? You could have lived abroad."

"That's what you think! Teach your grandmother to suck eggs. I tried that, just once. Took my $5000 damages when a motor scooter knocked me into a gully, and went to Europe for a year. In the first place, there's a lot of American cars there. They was made here, and got tipped off in the factory. The ones made in Europe, like the British Fords, soon caught on. It's a system like that there Mafia. They all hung together. I was chased by M. G.'s, Jaguars, Dauphines, and Volkswagens. Sure, I could live in Ethiopia or Libya where there ain't but a few cars in the whole country, but I'd sooner take my chances." He shook his head in disgust. "They don't ever pay good damages in Europe."

"Well," the reporter said, pocketing his notebook, "you've finally licked the problem, I see. No car can get up here, that's for sure. But what do you do about supplies?"

"Mule pack up the trail. It's not too bad a walk, but nothing on wheels can make it."

"And you've lived here—how long?"

"Eight years. I'm almost seventy. Down there I couldn't move fast enough for them new models. The 1953 bunch was bad enough! I ain't hankering to tangle with no 1960 Ford."

"You're safe. Not even the new Army scout-cars could get up here. Seems to me you've won in the end."

"I ain't so sure. Them Fords don't give up easy. They'll never rest till I'm dead. It was a Ford I insulted, and it's a Ford that'll kill me. But by God, at least it won't be a Model T—they ain't many of them around these days. You'll send me a copy of the paper—make it a couple?"

"Sure thing," Nelson promised, knowing that he wouldn't. Better to forget than offend the old guy; and the old guy was certain to resent any objective treatment of his story. A typical paranoiac, but what an imagination!

"Now, if you'll let me take those pictures . . ." Nelson went to the gadget bag, and took out the press camera. "On the bench first. That's it."

The old man sat there stiffly erect, his wrinkled, tanned face sternly dignified. The reporter snapped the shutter with the easy confidence of a man who never doubts the quality of his negatives.

"Now let's do one with you shaking your fist as if—ah—cursing that Model T of yours."

Marer looked doubtful. "It'll make a silly picture," he objected. "You ain't got the right idea. This is a serious business."

"Come on," Nelson urged. "You want people to hear your side of the thing, don't you? They seem to think you're either a clever insurance swindler or a bit—see what I mean?

Look, if the photo's a little unfair, what of it? That makes people read your story, and that's what you're after."

"All right," Marer said reluctantly. "Where'll I stand?"

"Right here in the clearing. Good. Now shake your fist. No, harder—up at the sky, like an angry prophet. That's the idea—hold it."

He was just visualizing the caption: "CURSES MODEL NEMESIS," when there was a whistling scream and an earth-jarring impact that flung him dazed to the hard ground. When he recovered his senses, some moments later, and shoved a heavy plank from his bruised body, he saw that where the old man had stood there lay a jumble of wood and metal fragments, many of them bloody.

It took him some time, shaken as he was, to identify their origin. The wood must have come from a large packing case; and the crumpled wheels, battered radiator, and assorted engine parts placed the contents. Above all, there was the famous old black, shiny finish on the metal.

He learned later that the reconditioned Model T was on its way by air cargo to Los Angeles, when it had fallen, in mysterious circumstances, through the hatch.

But what bothered him most was its serial number: twelve thousand and twelve.

THE SOUND OF MURDER

by Donald E. Westlake

Detective Abraham Levine of Brooklyn's Forty-third Precinct sat at his desk in the squadroom and longed for a cigarette. The fingers of his left hand kept closing and clenching, feeling awkward without the paper-rolled tube of tobacco. He held a pencil for a while but unconsciously brought it to his mouth. He didn't realize what he was doing till he tasted the gritty staleness of the eraser. Then he put the pencil away in a drawer, and tried unsuccessfully to concentrate on the national news in the news magazine.

The world conspired against a man who tried to give up smoking. All around him were other people puffing cigarettes casually and unconcernedly, not making any fuss about it at all, making by their very nonchalance his own grim reasons for giving them up seem silly and hypersensitive. If he isolated himself from other smokers with the aid of television or radio, the cigarette commercials with their erotic smoking and their catchy jingles would surely drive him mad. Also, he would find that the most frequent sentence in popular fiction was, "He lit another cigarette." Statesmen and entertainers seemed inevitably to be smoking whenever news photographers snapped them for posterity, and even the news items were against him: He had just reread for the third time an announcement to the world that Pope John XXIII was the first Prelate of the Roman Catholic Church to smoke cigarettes in public.

Levine closed the magazine in irritation, and from the cover smiled at him the Governor of a Midwestern state, cigarette in FDR cigarette-holder at a jaunty angle in his mouth. Levine closed his eyes, saddened by the knowledge that he had turned himself at this late date into a comic character. A grown man who tries to give up smoking *is* comic, a Robert Benchley or a W. C. Fields, bumbling along, plagued by trivia, his life an endless gauntlet of minor crises. *They could do a one-reeler on me,* Levine thought. *A great little comedy. Laurel without Hardy. Because Hardy died of a heart attack.*

Abraham Levine, at fifty-three years of age, was twenty-four years a cop and eight years into the heart-attack range. When he went to bed at night, he kept himself awake by listening to the silence that replaced every eighth or ninth beat of his heart. When he had to climb stairs or lift anything heavy, he was acutely conscious of the labored heaviness of his breathing and of the way those missed heartbeats came closer and closer together, every seventh beat and then every sixth and then every fifth—

Some day, he knew, his heart would skip two beats in a row, and on that day Abraham Levine would stop, because there wouldn't be any third beat. None at all, not ever.

Four months ago, he'd gone to the doctor, and the doctor had checked him over very carefully, and he had submitted to it feeling like an aging auto brought to a mechanic by an owner who wanted to know whether it was worthwhile to fix the old boat up or should he just junk the thing and get another. (In the house next door to his, a baby cried every night lately. The new model, crying for the old and the obsolete to get off the road.)

So he'd gone to the doctor, and the doctor had told him not to worry. He had that little skip in his heartbeat, but that wasn't anything dangerous, lots of people had that. And his blood pressure was a little high, but not much, not enough to concern himself about. So the doctor told him he was healthy, and collected his fee, and Levine left, unconvinced.

So when he went back again three days ago, still frightened by the skip and the shortness of breath and the occasional chest cramps when he was excited or afraid, the doctor had told him the same things all over again, and had added, "If you really want to do something for that heart of yours, you can give up smoking."

He hadn't had a cigarette since, and for the first time in his life he was beginning to really understand the wails of the arrested junkies, locked away in a cell with nothing to ease their craving. He was beginning to be ashamed of himself, for having become so completely dependent on something so useless and so harmful. Three days now. Comic or not, he was going to make it.

Opening his eyes, he glared at the cigarette-smoking Governor and shoved the magazine into a drawer. Then he looked around the squadroom, empty except for himself and his partner, Crawley, sitting over there smoking contentedly at his desk by the filing cabinet as he worked on a report. Rizzo and McFarlane, the other two detectives on this shift, were out on a call but would probably be back soon. Levine longed for the phone to ring, for something to happen to distract him, to keep mind and hands occupied and forgetful of cigarettes. He looked around the room, at a loss, and his left hand clenched and closed on the desk, lonely and incomplete.

When the rapping came at the door, it was so faint that Levine barely heard it, and Crawley didn't even look up. But any sound at all would have attracted Levine's straining attention. He looked over, saw a foreshortened shadow against the frosted glass of the door, and called, "Come in."

Crawley looked up. "What?"

"Someone at the door." Levine called out again, and this time the doorknob hesitantly turned, and a child walked in.

It was a little girl of about ten, in a frilly frock of pale pink, with a flared skirt, with gold-buckled black shoes and ribbed white socks. Her hair was pale blonde, combed and brushed and shampooed to gleaming cleanliness, brushed back from her forehead and held by a pink bow atop her head, then cascading straight down her back nearly to her waist. Her eyes were huge and bright blue, her face a creamy oval. She was a little girl in an ad for children's clothing in the Sunday *Times*. She was a story illustration in *Ladies*

Home Journal. She was Alice in Blunderland, gazing with wide-eyed curious innocence into the bullpen, the squad-room, the home and office of the detectives of the Forty-third Precinct, the men whose job it was to catch the stu-pid and the nasty so that other men could punish them.

She saw, looking into this brutal room, two men and a lot of old furniture. One of the men, Jack Crawley, clearly be-longed to this room. A big and bulky man in his middle forties, he was square-faced and heavy-jowled, with lines of toughness and distrust around cold eyes and grim mouth. He looked the part of the tough cop, and played the part well, and was nearly as tough as he looked.

The other man, Levine, looked out of place here. He was short and chunky, the lines of his body all softened within his brown suit, his face round, soft-eyed, sensitive-lipped, lined by worry and doubt and frailty. His graying hair, clipped stiff and short in a harsh military crewcut, only em-phasized the softness of the rest of him. An unsuccessful small businessman, a friendly but poor uncle, that was Le-vine. Not a harness bull in a squadroom.

It was inevitably to Levine that the little girl spoke: "May I come in?" Her voice was as faint as her tapping on the door had been. She was poised to flee at the first loud noise.

Levine automatically lowered his own voice when he an-swered. "Of course. Come on in. Sit over here." He mo-tioned at the straightbacked wooden chair beside his desk.

The girl crossed the threshold, carefully closed the door again behind her, and came on silent feet across the room, glancing sidelong at Crawley, then establishing herself on the edge of the chair, her toes touching the floor, still ready for flight at any second. She studied Levine. "I want to talk to a detective," she said. "Are you a detective?"

Levine nodded. "Yes, I am."

"My name," she told him solemnly, "is Amy Thornbridge Walker. I live at 717 Prospect Park West, apartment 4-A. I want to report a murder, a quite recent murder."

"A murder?"

"My mother," she said, just as solemnly, "murdered my stepfather."

Levine glanced over at Crawley, who screwed his face up

in an expression meant to say, "She's a nut. Hear her out, and then she'll go home. What else can you do?"

There was nothing else he could do. He looked at Amy Thornbridge Walker again. "Tell me about it," he said. "When did it happen?"

"Two weeks ago Thursday," she said. "November 27th. At two-thirty P.M."

Her earnest calm called for belief. But children with wild stories were not unknown to the precinct. Children came in with reports of dead bodies in alleys, flying saucers on rooftops, counterfeiters in basement apartments, kidnappers in black trucks—And once out of a thousand times what the child reported was real and not the product of a young imagination on a spree. More to save the little girl's feelings than for any other reason, therefore, Levine drew to him a pencil and a sheet of paper and took down what she told him. He said, "What's your mother's name?"

"Gloria Thornbridge Walker," she said. "And my stepfather was Albert Walker. He was an attorney."

To the side, Crawley was smiling faintly at the girl's conscious formality. Levine solemnly wrote down the names, and said, "Was your father's name Thornbridge, is that it?"

"Yes. Jason Thornbridge. He died when I was very small. I think my mother killed him, too, but I'm not absolutely sure."

"I see. But you *are* absolutely sure that your mother killed Albert Walker."

"My stepfather. Yes. My first father was supposed to have drowned by accident in Lake Champlain, which I consider very unlikely, as he was an excellent swimmer."

Levine reached into his shirt pocket, found no cigarettes there, and suddenly realized what he was doing. Irritation washed over him, but he carefully kept it from showing in his face or voice as he said, "How long have you thought that your mother killed your rea—your first father?"

"I'd never thought about it at all," she said, "until she murdered my stepfather. Naturally, I then started thinking about it."

Crawley coughed, and lit a fresh cigarette, keeping his

hands up in front of his mouth. Levine said, "Did he die of drowning, too?"

"No. My stepfather wasn't athletic at all. In fact, he was nearly an invalid for the last six months of his life."

"Then how did your mother kill him?"

"She made a loud noise at him," she said calmly.

Levine's pencil stopped its motion. He looked at her searchingly, but found no trace of humor in her eyes or mouth. If she had come up here as a joke—on a bet, say, from her schoolmates—then she was a fine little actress, for no sign of the joke was on her face at all.

Though how could he really tell? Levine, a childless man with a barren wife, had found it increasingly difficult over the years to communicate with the very young. A part of it, of course, was an envy he couldn't help, in the knowledge that these children could run and play with no frightening shortness of breath or tightness of chest, that they could sleep at night in their beds with no thought for the dull thudding of their hearts, that they would be alive and knowing for years and decades, for *decades,* after he himself had ceased to exist.

Before he could formulate an answer to what she'd said, the little girl jounced off the chair with the graceful gracelessness of the young and said, "I can't stay any longer. I stopped here on my way home from school. If my mother found out that I knew, and that I had told the police, she might try to murder me, too." She turned all at once and studied Crawley severely. "I am not a silly little girl," she told him. "And I am not telling a lie or making a joke. My mother murdered my stepfather, and I came in here and reported it. That's what I'm supposed to do. You aren't supposed to believe me right away, but you are supposed to investigate and find out whether or not I've told you the truth. And I have told you the truth." She turned suddenly back to Levine, an angry little girl—no, not angry, *definite*—a definite little girl filled with stern formality and a child's sense of rightness and duty. "My stepfather," she said, "was a very good man. My mother is a bad woman. You find out what she did, and punish her." She nodded briefly, as though to punctuate what she'd said, and marched to the door, reaching it as Rizzo and McFarlane came in. They looked down at her in surprise, and she stepped past them and out to the hall, closing the door after her.

Rizzo looked at Levine and jerked his thumb at the door. "What was that?"

It was Crawley who answered. "She came in to report a murder," he said. "Her Mommy killed her Daddy by making a great big noise at him."

Rizzo frowned. "Come again?"

"I'll check it out," said Levine. Not believing the girl's story, he still felt the impact of her demand on him that he do his duty. All it would take was a few phone calls. While Crawley recounted the episode at great length to Rizzo, and McFarlane took up his favorite squadroom position, seated at his desk with the chair canted back and his feet atop the desk, Levine picked up his phone and dialed the *New York Times*. He identified himself and said what he wanted, was connected to the proper department, and after a few minutes the November 28th obituary notice on Albert Walker was read to him. Cause of death: a heart attack. Mortician: Junius Merriman. An even briefer call to Merriman gave him the name of Albert Walker's doctor, Henry Sheffield. Levine thanked Merriman, assured him there was no problem, and got out the Brooklyn yellow pages to find Sheffield's number. He dialed, spoke to a nurse, and finally got Sheffield.

"I can't understand," Sheffield told him, "why the police would be interested in the case. It was heart failure, pure and simple. What seems to be the problem?"

"There's no problem," Levine told him. "Just checking it out. Was this a sudden attack? Had he had any heart trouble before?"

"Yes, he'd suffered a coronary attack about seven months ago. The second attack was more severe, and he hadn't really recovered as yet from the first. There certainly wasn't anything else to it, if that's what you're getting at."

"I didn't mean to imply anything like that," said Levine. "By the way, were you Mrs. Walker's first husband's doctor, too?"

"No, I wasn't. His name was Thornbridge, wasn't it? I never met the man. Is there some sort of question about him?"

"No, not at all." Levine evaded a few more questions, then hung up, his duty done. He turned to Crawley and shook his head. "Nothing to—"

A sudden crash behind him froze the words in his throat. He half-rose from the chair, mouth wide open, face paling as the blood rushed from his head, his nerves and muscles stiff and tingling.

It was over in a second, and he sank back into the chair, turning around to see what had happened. McFarlane was sheepishly picking himself up from the floor, his chair lying on its back beside him. He grinned shakily at Levine. "Leaned back too far that time," he said.

"Don't do that," said Levine, his voice shaky. He touched the back of his hand to his forehead, feeling cold perspiration slick against the skin. He was trembling all over. Once again, he reached to his shirt pocket for a cigarette, and this time felt an instant of panic when he found the pocket empty. He pressed the palm of his hand to the pocket, and beneath pocket and skin he felt the thrumming of his heart, and automatically counted the beats. Thum, thum, *skip,* thum, thum, thum, thum, thum, *skip,* thum, thum—

On the sixth beat the *sixth* beat. He sat there listening, hand pressed to his chest, and gradually the agitation subsided and the skip came every seventh beat and then every eighth beat, and then he could dare to move again.

He licked his lips, needing a cigarette now more than at any other time in the last three days, more than he could ever remember needing a cigarette at any time in his whole life.

His resolve crumbled. Shamefacedly, he turned to his partner, "Jack, do you have a cigarette?"

Crawley looked away from McFarlane, who was checking himself for damage. "I thought you were giving them up, Abe," he said.

"Not around here. Please, Jack."

"Sure." Crawley tossed him his pack.

Levine caught the pack, shook out one cigarette, threw

the rest back to Crawley. He took a book of matches from the desk drawer, put the cigarette in his mouth, feeling the comforting familiarity of it between his lips, and struck a match. He held the match up, then sat looking at the flame, struck by a sudden thought.

Albert Walker had died of a heart attack. "She made a loud noise at him." "The second attack was more severe, and he hadn't really recovered as yet from the first."

He shook the match out, took the cigarette from between his lips. It had been every sixth beat there for a while, after the loud noise of McFarlane's backward dive.

Had Gloria Thornbridge Walker *really* killed Albert Walker?

Would Abraham Levine *really* kill Abraham Levine?

The second question was easier to answer. Levine opened the desk drawer and dropped the cigarette and matches into it.

The first question he didn't try to answer at all. He would sleep on it. Right now, he wasn't thinking straight enough.

At dinner that night, he talked it over with his wife. "Peg," he said, "I've got a problem."

"A problem?" She looked up in surprise, a short solid stout woman three years her husband's junior, her iron-gray hair rigidly curled in a home permanent. "If you're coming to me," she said, "it must be awful."

He smiled, nodding. "It is." It was rare for him to talk about his job with his wife. The younger men, he knew, discussed their work with their wives as a matter of course, expecting and receiving suggestions and ideas and advice. But he was a product of an older upbringing, and still believed instinctively that women should be shielded from the more brutal aspects of life. It was only when the problem was one he couldn't discuss with Crawley that he turned to Peg for someone to talk to. "I'm getting old," he said suddenly, thinking of the differences between himself and the younger men.

She laughed. "That's your problem? Don't feel lonely, Abe, it happens to all kinds of people. Have some more gravy."

"Let me tell you," he said. "A little girl came in today, maybe ten years old, dressed nicely, polite, very intelligent. She wanted to report that her mother had killed her step-father."

"A little girl?" She sounded shocked. She too believed that there were those who should be shielded from the more brutal aspects of life, but with her the shielded ones were children. "A little girl? A thing like that?"

"Wait," he said. "Let me tell you. I called the doctor and he said it was a heart attack. The stepfather—Mr. Walker—he'd had one attack already, and the second one on top of it killed him."

"But the little girl blames the mother?" Peg leaned forward. "Psychological, you think?"

"I don't know. I asked her how her mother had done the killing, and she said her mother made a loud noise at her father."

"A joke." She shook her head. "These children today, I don't know where they get their ideas. All this on the TV—"

"Maybe," he said. "I don't know. A man with a bad heart, bedridden, an invalid. A sudden shock, a loud noise, it might do it, bring on that second attack."

"What else did this little girl say?"

"That's all. Her stepfather was good, and her mother was bad, and she'd stopped off on her way home from school. She only had a minute, because she didn't want her mother to know what she was doing."

"You let her go? You didn't question her?"

Levine shrugged. "I didn't believe her," he said. "You know the imagination children have."

"But now?"

"Now, I don't know." He held up his hand, two fingers extended. "Now," he said, "there's two questions in my mind. First, is the little girl right or wrong. Did her mother actually make a loud noise that killed her stepfather or not? And if she did, then question number two: Did she do it on purpose, or was it an accident?" He waggled the two fingers and looked at his wife. "Do you see? Maybe the little girl is right, and her mother actually did cause the death, but not intentionally. If so, I don't want to make things worse for the mother by dragging it into the open. Maybe the little girl is wrong altogether, and if so it would be best to just let the whole thing slide. But maybe she's right, and it *was* murder, and then that child is in danger, because if I don't do anything, she'll try some other way, and the mother will find out."

Peg shook her head. "I don't like that, a little girl like that. Could she defend herself? A woman to kill her husband, a woman like that could kill her child just as easy. I don't like that at all, Abe."

"Neither do I." He reached for the coffee cup, drank. "The question is, what do I do?"

She shook her head again. "A child like that," she said. "A woman like that. And then again, maybe not." She looked at her husband. "For right now," she said, "you eat. We can think about it."

For the rest of dinner they discussed other things. After the meal, as usual, the craving for a cigarette suddenly intensified, and he was unable to concentrate on anything but his resolution. They watched television during the evening, and by bedtime he still hadn't made a decision. Getting ready for bed, Peg suddenly said, "The little girl. You've been thinking?"

"I'll sleep on it," he said. "Maybe in the morning. Peg, I am longing for a cigarette."

"Nails in your coffin," she said bluntly. He blinked, and went away silently to brush his teeth.

The lights turned out, they lay together in the double bed which now, with age, had a pronounced sag toward the middle, rolling them together. But it was a cold night out, a good night to lie close together and feel the warmth of life. Levine closed his eyes and drifted slowly toward sleep.

A sudden sound shook him awake. He blinked rapidly, staring up in the darkness at the ceiling, startled, disoriented, not knowing what it was. But then the sound came again, and he exhaled, releasing held breath. It was the baby from next door, crying.

Move over, world, and give us room, he thought, giving words to the baby's cries. *Make way for the new.*

And they're right, he thought. *We've got to take care of them, and guide them, and then make way for them. They're absolutely right.*

I've got to do something for that little girl, he thought.

In the morning, Levine talked to Crawley. He sat in the client's chair, beside Crawley's desk. "About that little girl," he said.

"You, too? I got to thinking about it myself, last night."

"We ought to check it out," Levine told him.

"I know. I figure I ought to look up the death of the first father. Jason Thornbridge, wasn't it?"

"Good," said Levine. "I was thinking of going to her school, talking to her teacher. If she's the kind of child who makes up wild stories all the time, then that's that, you know what I mean?"

"Sure. You know what school she's in?"

"Lathmore Elementary, over on Third."

Crawley frowned, trying to remember. "She tell you that? I didn't hear it if she did."

"No, she didn't. But it's the only one it could be." Levine grinned sheepishly. "I'm pulling a Sherlock Holmes," he said. "She told us she'd stopped in on her way home from school. So she was walking home, and there's only three schools in the right direction—so we'd be between them and Prospect Park—but they're close enough for her to walk." He checked them off on his fingers. "There's St. Aloysius, but she wasn't in a school uniform. There's PS 118, but with a Prospect Park West address and the clothing she was wearing and her good manners, she doesn't attend any public school. So that leaves Lathmore."

"Okay, Sherlock," said Crawley. "You go talk to the nice people at Lathmore. I'll dig into the Thornbridge thing."

"One of us," Levine told him, "ought to check this out with the Lieutenant first. Tell him what we want to do."

"Fine. Go ahead."

Levine scraped the fingers of his left hand together, embarrassment reminding him of his need for a cigarette. But this was day number four, and he was going to make it. "Jack," he said, "I think maybe you ought to be the one to talk to him."

"Why me? Why not you?"

"I think he has more respect for you."

Crawley snorted. "What the hell are you talking about?"

"No, I mean it, Jack." Levine grinned self-consciously. "If I told him about it, he might think I was just dramatizing it, getting emotional or something, and he'd say thumbs down. But you're the levelheaded type. If you tell him it's serious, he'll believe you."

"You're nuts," said Crawley.

"You *are* the level-headed type," Levine told him. "And I *am* too emotional."

"Flattery will get you everywhere. All right, go to school."

"Thanks, Jack."

Levine shrugged into his coat and plodded out of the squadroom, downstairs, and out to the sidewalk. Lathmore Elementary was three blocks away to the right, and he walked it. There was a smell of snow in the air, but the sky was still clear. Levine strolled along sniffing the snow-tang, his hands pushed deep into the pockets of his black overcoat. The desire for a smoke was less when he was outdoors, so he didn't hurry.

Lathmore Elementary, one of the myriad private schools which have sprung up to take the place of the enfeebled public school system long since emasculated by municipal politics, was housed in an old mansion on one of the neighborhood's better blocks. The building was mainly masonry, with curved buttresses and bay windows everywhere, looming three ivy overgrown stories to a patchwork slate roof which dipped and angled and rose crazily around to no pattern at all. Gold letters on the wide glass pane over the double-doored entrance announced the building's new function, and just inside the doors an arrow on a wall was marked OFFICE.

Levine didn't want to have to announce himself as a policeman, but the administrative receptionist was so officious and curious that he had no choice. It was the only way he could get to see Mrs. Pidgeon, the principal, without first explaining his mission in minute detail to the receptionist.

Mrs. Pidgeon was baffled, polite, terrified and defensive, but not very much of any of them. It was as though these four emotions were being held in readiness, for one of them to spring into action as soon as she found out just exactly what it was a police officer could possibly want in Lathmore Elementary. Levine tried to explain as gently and vaguely as possible:

"I'd like to talk to one of your teachers," he said. "About a little girl, a student of yours."

"What about her?"

"She made a report to us yesterday," Levine told her. "It's difficult for us to check it out, and it might help if we knew a little more about her, what her attitudes are, things like that."

Defensiveness began to edge to the fore in Mrs. Pidgeon's attitude. "What sort of report?"

"I'm sorry," said Levine. "If there's nothing to it, it would be better not to spread it."

"Something about this school?"

"Oh, no," said Levine, managing not to smile. "Not at all."

"Very well." Defensiveness receded, and a sort of cold politeness became more prominent. "You want to talk to her teacher, then."

"Yes."

"Her name?"

"Amy Walker. Amy Thornbridge Walker."

"Oh, yes!" Mrs. Pidgeon's face suddenly lit with pleasure, not at Levine but at his reminding her of that particular child. Then the pleasure gave way just as suddenly to renewed bafflement. "It's about Amy? *She* came to you yesterday?"

"That's right."

"Well." She looked helplessly around the room, aching to find out more but unable to find a question that would get around Levine's reticence. Finally, she gave up, and asked him to wait while she went for Miss Haskell, the fifth grade teacher. Levine stood as she left the room, then sank back into the maroon leather chair, feeling bulky and awkward in this hushed heavy-draped office.

He waited five minutes before Mrs. Pidgeon returned, this time with Miss Haskell in tow. Miss Haskell, unexpectedly, was a comfortable fortyish woman in a sensible suit and flat shoes, not the thin tall bird he'd expected. He acknowledged Mrs. Pidgeon's introduction, hastily rising again, and Mrs. Pidgeon pointedly said, "Try not to be too long, Mr. Levine. You may use my office."

"Thank you."

She left, and Levine and Miss Haskell stood facing each other in the middle of the room. He motioned at a chair. "Would you sit down, please?"

"Thank you. Mrs. Pidgeon said you wanted to ask me about Amy Walker."

"Yes, I want to know what kind of child she is, anything you can tell me about her."

Miss Haskell smiled. "I can tell you she's a brilliant and well-brought-up child," she said. "That she's the one I picked to be student in charge while I came down to talk to you. That she's always at least a month ahead of the rest of the class in reading the assignments, and that she's the most practical child I've ever met."

Levine reached to his cigarette pocket, cut the motion short, awkwardly returned his hand to his side. "Her father died two weeks ago, didn't he?"

"That's right."

"How did they get along, do you know? Amy and her father."

"She worshipped him. He was her stepfather actually, having married her mother only about a year ago, I believe. Amy doesn't remember her real father. Mr. Walker was the only father she knew, and having been without one for so long—" Miss Haskell spread her hands. "He was important to her," she finished.

"She took his death hard?"

"She was out of school for a week, inconsolable. She spent the time at her grandmother's, I understand. The grandmother caters to her, of course. I believe her mother had a doctor in twice."

"Yes, her mother." Levine didn't know what to do with his hands. He clasped them in front of him. "How do Amy and her mother get along?"

"Normally, so far as I know. There's never been any sign

of discord between them that I've seen." She smiled again. "But my contact with Amy is limited to school hours, of course."

"You think there is discord?"

"No, not at all. I didn't mean to imply that. Just that I couldn't give you an expert answer to the question."

Levine nodded. "You're right. Is Amy a very imaginative child?"

"She's very self-sufficient in play, if that's what you mean."

"I was thinking about storytelling."

"Oh, a liar." She shook her head. "No, Amy isn't the tall-tale type. A very practical little girl, really. Very dependable judgment. As I say, she's the one I left in charge of the class."

"She wouldn't be likely to come to us with a wild story she'd made up all by herself."

"Not at all. If Amy told you about something, it's almost certainly the truth."

Levine sighed. "Thank you," he said. "Thank you very much."

Miss Haskell rose to her feet. "Could you tell me what this wild story was? I might be able to help."

"I'd rather not," he said. "Not until we're sure, one way or the other."

"If I can be of any assistance—"

"Thank you," he said again. "You've already helped."

Back at the station, Levine entered the squadroom and hung up his coat. Crawley looked over from his desk and said, "You have all the luck, Abe. You missed the whirlwind."

"Whirlwind?"

"Amy's mama was here. Dr. Sheffield called her about you checking up on her husband's death, and just before she came over here she got a call from somebody at Lathmore Elementary, saying there was a cop there asking questions about her daughter. She didn't like us casting aspersions on her family."

"Aspersions?"

"That's what she said." Crawley grinned. "You're little Sir Echo this morning, aren't you?"

"I need a cigarette. What did the Lieutenant say?"

"She didn't talk to him. She talked to me."

"No, when you told him about the little girl's report."

"Oh. He said to take two days on it, and then let him know how it looked."

"Fine. How about Thornbridge?"

"Accidental death. Inquest said so. No question in anybody's mind. He went swimming too soon after lunch, got a stomach cramp, and drowned. What's the word on the little girl?"

"Her teacher says she's reliable. Practical and realistic. If she tells us something, it's so."

Crawley grimaced. "That isn't what I wanted to hear, Abe."

"It didn't overjoy me, either." Levine sat down at his desk. "What did the mother have to say?"

"I had to spill it, Abe. About what her daughter reported."

"That's all right," he said. "Now we've got no choice. We've got to follow through. What was her reaction?"

"She didn't believe it."

Levine shrugged. "She had to, after she thought about it."

"Sure," said Crawley. "Then she was baffled. She didn't know why Amy would say such a thing."

"Was she home when her husband died?"

"She says no." Crawley flipped open a memo pad. "Somebody had to be with him all the time, but he didn't want a professional nurse. So when Amy came home from school that afternoon, the mother went to the supermarket. Her husband was alive when she left, and dead when she got back. Or so she says."

"She says Amy was the one who found him dead?"

"No. Amy was watching television. When the mother came home, she found him, and called the doctor."

"What about noises?"

"She didn't hear any, and doesn't have any idea what Amy means."

Levine sighed. "All right," he said. "We've got one timetable discrepancy. Amy says her mother was home and made a loud noise. The mother says she was out to the supermarket." His fingers strayed to his cigarette pocket, then went on to scratch his shoulder instead. "What did you think of the mother, Jack?"

"She's tough. She was mad, and she's used to having things her own way. I can't see her playing nursemaid. But she sure seemed baffled about why the kid would make such an accusation."

"I'll have to talk to Amy again," said Levine. "Once we've got both stories, we can see which one breaks down."

Crawley said, "I wonder if she'll try to shut the kid's mouth?"

"Let's not think about that yet. We've still got all day." He reached for the phone book and looked up the number of Lathmore Elementary.

Levine talked to the girl in Mrs. Pidgeon's office at eleven o'clock. At his request, they were left alone.

Amy was dressed as neatly as she had been yesterday, and seemed just as composed. Levine explained to her what had been done so far on the investigation, and that her mother had been told why the investigation was taking place. "I'm sorry, Amy," he said, "but we didn't have any choice. Your mother had to know."

Amy considered, solemn and formal. "I think it will be all right," she said. "She wouldn't dare try to hurt me now, with you investigating. It would be too obvious. My mother is very subtle, Mr. Levine."

Levine smiled, in spite of himself. "You have quite a vocabulary," he told her.

"I'm a very heavy reader," she explained. "Though it's difficult for me to get interesting books from the library. I'm too young, so I have to take books from the children's section." She smiled thinly. "I'll tell you a secret," she said. "I steal the ones I want to read, and then bring them back when I'm finished with them."

In a hurry, he thought, smiling, and remembered the baby next door. "I want to talk to you," he said, "about the day when your father died. Your mother said she went out to the store, and when she came back he was dead. What do you say?"

"Nonsense," she said, promptly. *"I* was the one who went

out to the store. The minute I came home from school, she
sent me out to the supermarket. But I came back too soon
for her."

"Why?"

"Just as I was coming down the hall from the elevator, I
heard a great clang sound from our apartment. Then it came
again as I was opening the door. I went through the living
room and saw my mother coming out of my stepfather's
room. She was smiling. But then she saw me and suddenly
looked terribly upset and told me something awful had happened, and she ran to the telephone to call Dr. Sheffield. She
acted terribly agitated, and carried on just as though she
really meant it. She fooled Dr. Sheffield completely."

"Why did you wait so long before coming to us?"

"I didn't know what to do." The solemn formality
cracked all at once, and she was only a child after all, uncertain in an adult world. "I didn't think anyone would believe me, and I was afraid if mother suspected what I knew,
she might try to do something to me. But Monday in Civics
Miss Haskell was talking about the duties of the different
parts of government, firemen and policemen and everybody,
and she said the duty of the police was to investigate crimes
and see the guilty were punished. So yesterday I came and
told you, because it didn't matter if you didn't believe me,
you'd have to do your duty and investigate anyway."

Levine sighed. "All right," he said. "We're doing it. But
we need more than just your word, you understand that,
don't you? We need proof of some kind."

She nodded, serious and formal again.

"What store did you go to that day?" he asked her.

"A supermarket. The big one on Seventh Avenue."

"Do you know any of the clerks there? Would they recognize you?"

"I don't think so. It's a great big supermarket. I don't
think they know any of their customers at all."

"Did you see anyone at all on your trip to the store or
back, who would remember that it was you who went to
the store and not your mother, and that it was that particular day?"

She considered, touching one finger to her lips as she

concentrated, and finally shook her head. "I don't think so. I don't know any of the people in the neighborhood. Most of the people I know are my parents' friends or kids from school, and they live all over, not just around here."

The New York complication. In a smaller town, people know their neighbors, have some idea of the comings and goings around them. But in New York, nextdoor neighbors remain strangers for years. At least that was true in the apartment house sections, though less true in the quieter outlying sections like the neighborhood in which Levine lived.

Levine got to his feet. "We'll see what we can do," he said. "This clang you told me about. Do you have any idea what your mother used to make the noise?"

"No, I don't. I'm sorry. It sounded like a gong or something. I don't know what it could possibly have been."

"A tablespoon against the bottom of a pot? Something like that?"

"Oh, no. Much louder than that."

"And she didn't have anything in her hands when she came out of the bedroom?"

"No, nothing."

"Well, we'll see what we can do," he repeated. "You can go back to class now."

"Thank you," she said. "Thank you for helping me."

He smiled. "It's my duty," he said. "As you pointed out."

"You'd do it anyway, Mr. Levine," she said. "You're a very good man. Like my stepfather."

Levine touched the palm of his hand to his chest, over his heart. "Yes," he said. "In more ways than one, maybe. Well, you go back to class. Or, wait. There's one thing I can do for you."

She waited as he took a pencil and a small piece of memo paper from Mrs. Pidgeon's desk, and wrote on it the precinct phone number and his home phone number, marking which each was. "If you think there's any danger of any kind," he told her, "any trouble at all, you call me. At the precinct until four o'clock, and then at home after that."

"Thank you," she said. She folded the paper and tucked it away in the pocket of her skirt.

At quarter to four, Levine and Crawley met again in the squadroom. When he'd come back in the morning from his talk with the little girl, Levine had found Crawley just back from having talked with Dr. Sheffield. It was Sheffield's opinion, Crawley had told him, that Amy was making the whole thing up, that her stepfather's death had been a severe shock and this was some sort of delayed reaction to it. Certainly he couldn't see any possibility that Mrs. Walker had actually murdered her husband, nor could he begin to guess at any motive for such an act.

Levine and Crawley had eaten lunch together in Wilton's, across the street from the station, and then had separated, both to try to find someone who had seen either Amy or her mother on the shopping trip the afternoon Mr. Walker had died. This, aside from the accusation of murder itself, was the only contradiction between their stories. Find proof that one was lying, and they'd have the full answer. So Levine had started at the market and Crawley at the apartment building, and they'd spent the entire afternoon up and down the neighborhood, asking their questions and getting only blank stares for answers.

Crawley was there already when Levine came slowly into the squadroom, worn from an entire afternoon on his feet, climaxed by the climb to the precinct's second floor. He looked at Crawley and shook his head. Crawley said, "Nothing? Same here. Not a damn thing."

Levine laboriously removed his overcoat and set it on the coatrack. "No one remembers," he said. "No one saw, no one knows anyone. It's a city of strangers we live in, Jack."

"It's been two weeks," said Crawley. "Their building has a doorman, but he can't remember that far back. He sees the same tenants go in and out every day, and he wouldn't be able to tell you for sure who went in or out yesterday, much less two weeks ago, he says."

Levine looked at the wall clock. "She's home from school by now," he said.

"I wonder what they're saying to each other. If we could listen in, we'd know a hell of a lot more than we do now."

Levine shook his head. "No. Whether she's guilty or innocent, they're both saying the exact same things. The death is two weeks old. If Mrs. Walker did commit murder, she's used to the idea by now that she's gotten away with it. She'll deny everything Amy says, and try to convince the girl she's wrong. The same things in the same words as she'd use if she were innocent."

"What if she kills the kid?" Crawley asked him.

"She won't. If Amy were to disappear, or have an accident, or be killed by an intruder, we'd know the truth at once. She can't take the chance. With her husband, all she had to do was fool a doctor who was inclined to believe her in the first place. Besides, the death was a strong possibility anyway. This time, she'd be killing a healthy ten year old, and she'd be trying to fool a couple of cops who wouldn't be inclined to believe her at all." Levine grinned. "The girl is probably safer now than she was before she ever came to us," he said. "Who knows what the mother might have been planning up till now?"

"All right, that's fine so far. But what do we do now?"

"Tomorrow, I want to take a look at the Walker apartment."

"Why not right now?"

"No. Let's give her a night to get rattled. Any evidence she hasn't removed in two weeks, she isn't likely to think of now." Levine shrugged. "I don't expect to find anything," he said. "I want to look at the place because I can't think of anything else to do. All we have is the unsupported word of a ten-year-old child. The body can't tell us anything, because there wasn't any murder weapon. Walker died of natural causes. Proving they were induced won't be the easiest job in the world."

"If only *somebody*," said Crawley angrily, "had seen that kid at the grocery store! That's the only chink in the wall, Abe, the only damn place we can get a grip."

"We can try again tomorrow," said Levine, "but I doubt we'll get anywhere." He looked up as the door opened, and Trent and Kasper came in, two of the men on the four to midnight shift. "Tomorrow," he repeated. "Maybe lightning will strike."

"Maybe," said Crawley.

Levine shrugged back into his overcoat and left the office for the day. When he got home, he broke his normal habit and went straight into the house, not staying on the porch to read his paper. He went out to the kitchen and sat there, drinking coffee, while he filled Peg in on what little progress they'd made on the case during the day. She asked questions, and he answered them, offered suggestions and he mulled them over and rejected them, and throughout the evening, every once in a while, one or the other of them would find some other comment to make, but neither of them got anywhere. The girl seemed to be reasonably safe, at least for a while, but that was the best that could be said.

The baby next door was crying when they went to bed together at eleven o'clock. The baby kept him awake for a while, and his thoughts on the Walker death revolved and revolved, going nowhere. Once or twice during the evening, he had absent-mindedly reached for a cigarette, but had barely noticed the motion. His concentration and concern for Amy Walker and her mother was strong enough now to make him forget his earlier preoccupation with the problem of giving up smoking. Now, lying awake in the dark, the thought of cigarettes didn't even enter his head. He went over and over what the mother had said, what the daughter had told him, and gradually he drifted off into deep, sound sleep.

He awoke in a cold sweat, suddenly knowing the truth. It was as though he'd dreamed it, or someone had whispered it in his ear, and now he knew for sure.

She would kill her tonight, and she would get away with it. He knew how she'd do it, and when, and there'd be no way to get her for it, no proof, nothing, no way at all.

He sat up, trembling, cold in the dark room, and reached out to the nightstand for his cigarettes. He pawed around on the nightstand, and suddenly remembered, and pounded the nightstand with his fist in frustration and rage. She'd get away with it!

If he could get there in time—He could stop her, if he got there in time. He pushed the covers out of the way and climbed from the bed. Peg murmured in her sleep and burrowed deeper into the pillow. He gathered his clothes and crept from the bedroom.

He turned the light on in the living room. The clock over the television set read ten till one. There might still be time, she might be waiting until she was completely asleep. Unless she was going to do it with pills, something to help sleep, to make sleep a permanent, everlasting sure thing.

He grabbed the phonebook and looked up the number of one of the private cab companies on Avenue L. He dialed, and told the dispatcher it was urgent, and the dispatcher said a car would be there in five minutes.

He dressed hurriedly, in the living room, then went out to the kitchen for pencil and paper, and left Peg a short note. "I had to go out for a while. Be back soon." In case she woke up. He left it on the nightstand.

A horn sounded briefly out front and he hurried to the front of the house, turning off lights. As he went trotting down the walk toward the cab, the baby next door cried out. He registered the sound, thought, *Baby next door,* and dismissed it from his mind. He had no time for extraneous thoughts, about babies or cigarettes or the rasp of his breathing from only this little exertion, running from the house. He gave the address, Prospect Park West, and sat back in the seat as the cab took off. It was a strange feeling, riding in a cab. He couldn't remember the last time he'd done it. It was a luxuriant feeling. To go so fast with such relaxing calm. If only it was fast enough.

It cost him four dollars, including the tip. If she was still alive, it was the bargain of the century. But as he hurried into the building and down the long narrow lobby to the elevators, the sound he'd heard as he'd left his home came back to him, he heard it again in memory, and all at once he realized it hadn't been the baby next door at all. It had been the telephone.

He pressed the elevator button desperately, and the elevator slid slowly down to him from the eleventh floor. It had been the ring of the telephone.

So she'd made her move already. He was too late. When he'd left the house, he'd been too late.

The elevator doors opened and he stepped in and pushed the button marked 4. He rode upward.

He could visualize that phone call. The little girl, hushed, terrified, whispering, beseeching. And Peg, half-awake, reading his note to her. And he was too late.

The door to apartment 4-A was ajar, the interior dark. He reached to his hip, but he'd been in too much of a hurry. The gun was at home, on the dresser.

He stepped across the threshold, cautiously, peering into the dark. Dim light spilled in from the hallway, showing him only this section of carpet near the door. The rest of the apartment was pitch black.

He felt the wall beside the door, found the lightswitch and clicked it on.

The light in the hall went out.

He tensed, the darkness now complete. A penny in the socket? And this was an old building, in which the tenants didn't pay directly for their own electricity, so the hall light was on the same line as the foyer of apartment A on every floor. They must have blown a fuse once, and she'd noticed that.

But why? What was she trying for?

The telephone call, as he was leaving the house. Somehow or other, she'd worked it out, and she knew that Levine was on his way here, that Levine knew the truth.

He backed away toward the doorway. He needed to get to the elevator, to get down and away from here. He'd call the precinct. They'd need flashlights, and numbers. This darkness was no place for him, alone.

A face rose toward him, luminous, staring, grotesque, limned in pale cold green, a staring devil face shining in green fire against the blackness. He cried out, instinctive panic filling his mouth with bile, and stumbled backwards away from the thing, bumping painfully into the doorpost. And the face disappeared.

He felt around him, his hands shaking, all sense of direction lost. He had to get out, he had to find the door. She was trying to kill him, she knew he knew and she was trying to kill him the same way she'd killed Walker. Trying to stop his heart.

A shriek jolted into his ears, loud, loud, incredibly loud, magnified far beyond the power of the human voice, a world-filling scream of hatred, grating him to the bone, and his flailing hands touched a wall, he leaned against it trembling. His mouth was open, straining for air, his chest was clogged, his heart beat fitfully, like the random motions of a wounded animal. The echoes of the shriek faded away, and then it sounded again, even louder, all around him, vibrating him like a fly on a pin.

He pushed away from the wall, blind and panic-stricken, wanting only to get away, to be away, out of this horror, and he stumbled into an armchair, lost his balance, fell heavily forward over the chair and rolled to the floor.

He lay there, gasping, unthinking, as brainlessly terrified as a rabbit in a trapper's snare. Pinwheels of light circled the corners of his stinging eyes, every straining breath was a searing fire in his throat. He lay on his back, encumbered and helpless in the heavy overcoat, arms and legs curled upward in feeble defense, and waited for the final blow.

But it didn't come. The silence lengthened, the blackness of the apartment remained unbroken, and gradually rationality came back to him and he could close his mouth, painfully swallow saliva, lower his arms and legs, and listen.

Nothing. No sound.

She'd heard him fall, that was it. And now she was waiting, to be sure he was dead. If she heard him move again, she'd hurl another thunderbolt, but for now she was simply waiting.

And the wait gave him his only chance. The face had only been phosphorescent paint on a balloon, pricked with a pin when he cried out. The shriek had come, most likely, from a tape recorder, played at full volume. That's all it was, a balloon and a tape recorder. Nothing that could kill him, nothing that could injure him, if only he kept in his mind what they were, and what she was trying to do.

My heart is weak, he thought, *but not that weak. Not as weak as Walker's, still recovering from his first attack. It could kill Walker, but it couldn't quite kill me.*

He lay there, recuperating, calming, coming back to himself. And then the flashlight flicked on, and the beam was aimed full upon him.

He raised his head, looked into the light. He could see nothing behind it. "No, Amy," he said. "It didn't work."

The light flicked off.

"Don't waste your time," he said into the darkness. "If it didn't work at first, when I wasn't ready for it, it won't work at all."

"Your mother is dead," he said, speaking softly, knowing she was listening, that so long as she listened she wouldn't move. He raised himself slowly to a sitting position. "You killed her, too. Your father and mother both. And when you called my home, to tell me that she'd killed herself, and my wife told you I'd already left, you knew then that I knew. And you had to kill me, too. I'd told you that my heart was weak, like your father's. So you'd kill me, and it would simply be another heart failure, brought on by the sight of your mother's corpse."

The silence was deep and complete, like a forest pool. Levine shifted, gaining his knees, moving cautiously and without sound.

"Do you want to know how I knew?" he asked her. "Monday in Civics Miss Haskell told you about the duties of the police. But Miss Haskell told me that you were always at least a month ahead in your studies. Two weeks before your stepfather died, you read that assignment in your schoolbook, and then and there you decided how to kill them both."

He reached out his hand, cautiously, touched the chair he'd tripped over, shifted his weight that way, and came slowly to his feet, still talking. "The only thing I don't understand," he said, "is why. You steal books from the library that they won't let you read. Was this the same thing to you? Is it all it was?"

From across the room, she spoke, for the first time. "You'll never understand, Mr. Levine," she said. That young voice, so cold and adult and emotionless, speaking out contemptuously to him in the dark.

And all at once he could *see* the way it had been with Walker. Somnolent in the bed, listening to the frail fluttering of the weary heart, as Levine often lay at night, listening and wondering. And suddenly that shriek, out of the midafternoon stillness, coming from nowhere and everywhere, driving in at him—

Levine shivered. "No," he said. "It's you who don't understand. To steal a book, to snuff out a life, to you they're both the same. You don't understand at all."

She spoke again, the same cold contempt still in her voice. "It was bad enough when it was only *her*. Don't do this, don't do that. But then she had to marry him, and there were two of them watching me all the time, saying no no no, that's all they ever said. The only time I could ever have some peace was when I was at my grandmother's."

"Is *that* why?" He could hear again the baby crying, the gigantic ego of the very young, the imperious demand that *they* be attended to. And in the place of terror, he now felt only rage. That this useless half-begun thing should kill, and kill—

"Do you know what's going to happen to you?" he asked her. "They won't execute you, you're too young. They'll judge you insane, and they'll lock you away. And there'll be guards and matrons there, to say don't do this and don't do that, a million million times more than you can imagine. And they'll keep you locked away in a little room, forever and ever, and they'll let you do *nothing* you want to do, *nothing.*"

He moved now, feeling his way around the chair, reaching out to touch the wall, working his way carefully toward the door. "There's nothing you can do to me now," he said. "Your bag of tricks won't work, and I won't drink the poison you fed your mother. And no one will believe the suicide confession you forged. I'm going to phone the precinct, and they'll come and get you, and you'll be locked away in that tiny room, forever and ever."

The flashlight hit the floor with a muffled thud, and then he heard her running, away from him, deeper into the apartment. He crossed the room with cautious haste, hands out before him, and felt around on the floor till his fingers blundered into the flashlight. He picked it up, clicked it on, and followed.

He found her in her mother's bedroom, standing on the windowsill. The window was open wide, and the December wind keened into the room. The dead woman lay reposed on the bed, the suicide note conspicuous on the nightstand. He shone the light full on the girl, and she warned him, "Stay away. Stay away from me."

He walked toward her. "They'll lock you away," he said. "In a tiny, tiny room."

"No, they won't!" And she was gone from the window.

Levine breathed, knowing what he had done, that he had made it end this way. She hadn't even understood death, and so it was possible for her to throw herself into it. The parents begin the child, and the child ends the parents. A white rage flamed in him at the thought.

He stepped to the window and looked down at the broken doll on the sidewalk far below. In another apartment, above his head, a baby wailed, creasing the night. *Make way, make way.*

He looked up. "We will," he whispered. "We will. But in our own time. Don't rush us."

AN AGENT NAMED RIDDLE

by H. A. DeRosso

The General, who was also known as Defender of the Republic, Father to the Poor, Provider to the Penniless—and many other self-imposed titles, was in an irritable mood this morning. His secretary feared she might be responsible for the General's frame of mind, for she was new at her job and had not been too expert the day before. Therefore, she sat very quietly and inconspicuously in a corner while the General carried on his business with his chief aide, Duarte.

"Yes, yes," the General was saying, clearly indicating that the disposal of this matter brought up by Duarte, should have been quite evident to him. "So Gallardo dared to criticize me in his paper. What should be done with him? Stupidness of a stupidity. Have him arrested. What else? And not for political reasons or for criticizing the government. We do not have political prisoners in our republic. We can not afford martyrs. Charge Gallardo with embezzlement or murder or something. What is next?"

Duarte's face had paled under its swarthiness. He knew what the consequences of displeasing the General might be. The General had been dictator of the island of San Leon for thirty years and was still going strong, while other dictators had risen and fallen during those years. The General ruled San Leon with an iron hand.

Duarte coughed nervously. "The matter, Excellency, of

finding an agent to infiltrate the rebels and report on Salas, and his connections with that *hijo de puta,* Archuleta."

"Ah, yes, Salas." The General's manner softened a little though his eyes remained cold. "You have such an agent?"

"Yes, Excellency. An American who goes by the name of Riddle. He is very expert in the business of a double agent and was sent to us with very high recommendations from our embassy on the mainland, for whom he has done some most valuable work."

"Riddle," the General said musingly, staring into the distance. "You are certain he understands his assignment? You are certain he is reliable?"

"As reliable as any double agent can be, Excellency."

"Yes. There is an element of risk involved."

"M at the embassy vouched for Riddle without reservations. Else I would not have hired him, Excellency."

"Very well. See that this Riddle starts on his job."

Duarte bowed and prepared to leave the room.

"And, Duarte," the General said, and as Duarte paused respectfully, "it will be your neck if anything goes wrong. Understand?"

The grayness returned to Duarte's face. He blinked and bowed again. "Yes, Excellency," he said in a strained voice and left the room.

The General laughed. The sound startled the girl and she looked with surprise at the General. She had been a clerk in a store until the General had been smitten by her beauty and had invited her to become his secretary. She had been too frightened and awed by the General's offer to dare to refuse.

"Poor Duarte," the General said, wiping tears from his eyes. "Such fear he has of me." He sobered quickly and scowled. "And rightly so. I did not jest when I spoke of his neck." He glanced at the girl. "Come, little one," he said with as much gentleness as he could ever summon. "I have a job for you, also."

Riddle had the feeling that he was being followed. It was an intuition born of a long familiarity with danger and many close calls. Survival in his business was all but impossible without the acquisition of a sixth sense. He could never quite describe the feeling. But the chill of death was in it and that was always enough to warn Riddle.

The mountain path he was following was walled with trees and brush on either side. As silently as some forest animal, Riddle faded into the trees and concealed himself. From his hiding-place he could observe, undetected, whoever should pass along the path. He turned his head once and, through a thinning of the forest, he saw the blue of the Caribbean far in the distance. Quite a difference from the countryside in southern Ohio, he thought, and then irritably put the remembrance from his mind. That was a part of his life he no longer cared to recall.

At first he thought it was a boy, but a second look told him it was a girl. He watched her move up the mountain path, rather vexed with the intuition that had given him a false alarm. But that happened now and then and he supposed it was nerves. A man in his business, no matter how well he schooled himself, could not help but get jittery once in awhile.

After waiting long enough to make sure that the girl was alone and was not being used as bait, he came out from hiding and proceeded up the path. A slight amusement touched him to think that now he was following her. He wondered if she possessed a sixth sense, too.

She did not. She had stopped to rest, sitting on a rock beside the path. Her back was to him, and she had no awareness of his approach until he could have almost reached out and touched her. And then it was the snapping of a twig underfoot that alerted her.

She jumped to her feet with a gasped shriek of alarm and whirled and started to bring up the rifle she was carrying. It was child's play for Riddle to reach out and shove the gun aside and then wrest it from the girl. She stood there, wide-eyed with fear, breasts rising and falling beneath the loose khaki shirt.

Riddle eyed her with approval. A good figure, he thought, despite the loose shirt and over-large trousers. And beneath the stains of sweat and soil on her face she should be quite pretty. Her blue-black hair was done up in a bun on the back of her head. He would have put her age at twenty or so.

Riddle drew himself up, for he was quite proud of his height and physique. Thirty-six years old, six foot two and not an ounce of suet on him. The tawny mustache gave him a dashing look, he was positive. There was a certain magnetism about him, he told himself, which accounted for all the conquests he'd made during the many years he'd knocked around the Latin American countries.

"What is such a young and pretty girl like you," he asked, "doing in these mountains?"

The girl stared at Riddle without answering. He offered her a cigarette, but she shook her head. Shrugging, he lit one for himself.

"Why were you following me?"

The girl's eyes widened again, but she did not speak.

"Lost your tongue, *querida*? I know you were following me."

"That is not so." Her voice was low and on the velvet side. "How could I have been following you when you just came behind me?"

Riddle smiled faintly. "I hid beside the path until you had passed me. Do you still deny it?"

The girl said nothing. Her eyes began to scan the ground.

Riddle hefted the rifle which he had taken from her. "Where did you get this, *querida*?"

The girl did not look up. "I found it."

Riddle laughed softly.

"I stole it then," she said with vehemence, and looked up with a glare of defiance in her dark eyes.

"Do you live hereabouts?"

"Who are you to be asking so many questions of me?"

"Perhaps I am with Salas," Riddle said softly.

Interest sharpened the girl's glance. "Are you?"

"This is on the edge of the territory controlled by Colonel Salas. Are you not aware of that?"

"Are you really with Salas?" The girl breathed the words.

"I said I was, did I not?"

"Will you take me to him?"

"Why?"

"I wish to help. I have heard of the movement against that tyrant in the capital. I wish to help against him. It is said that there are some women among those with Salas. If so, I want to join him. If not to fight, there are other things I can do. Cook, wash, care for the sick and wounded. Will you take me to Salas?"

Riddle grinned and stroked his mustache. "That I will—if I can find him. You see, *querida,* I am on my way to join him, also."

A happy look lit up her face and now there was no doubt that she was very pretty. "Then we can go on together. I felt so frightened and alone in these mountains. I am accustomed to the city. I have the rifle, but I am afraid I do not know how to use it." She gave a small, shaky laugh. "Do you know where to find Salas?"

"I do not," Riddle said, then chuckled. "But that is of no importance. We shall just keep walking until Salas finds us. After all, we are entering his territory." He put on his most charming expression. "I am called Riddle. And you?"
/ "Felicia."

He handed her back the rifle, allowing his hand to slide over hers as she took the weapon from him. She did not recoil. Rather, she smiled slightly at him. He smiled in return, then strode up the path, thinking that this promised to turn out much better than he had dreamed it would ...

It was late afternoon and they still had not seen anything of Salas and his men. They had stopped at an isolated farmhouse where they had eaten and rested. The farmer had pleaded ignorance to all of Riddle's questions, but Riddle sensed that the farmer was lying. Still, he could not blame the fellow for being concerned about surviving.

They moved on. The path dipped down into a broad valley, and the tops of the mountains began to hide the sinking sun so that long shadows filled the path with gloom. The girl was tiring. Riddle was carrying her rifle now as well as his own, but still the girl stumbled now and then with weariness.

"We will stop at the first house we come to," he told her, "and stay the night. There must be something soon. This valley looks like it should be inhabited, by at least a few farmers."

A small clearing soon bolstered his words, but the land lay fallow and abandoned and they moved on. The path turned sharply and the sound of voices ahead stopped Riddle and the girl abruptly. The voices were clipped and demanding, the tone that of military orders.

Riddle beckoned the girl to follow with a jerk of his head and faded soundlessly into the forest. She made too much noise and he had to caution her to be more careful. A tree branch struck her in the face and she gave a small cry of pain and Riddle angrily commanded her to stay where she was. He went on alone.

The voices guided him. The forest ended suddenly at the edge of another clearing and he could see the farmhouse there and the three lined up in front of it and several paces away from and facing them were five men dressed in the uniforms of the General's army. The three in front of the farmhouse wore the white shirts and white cotton trousers of the rebels of Colonel Salas. This patently was going to be an execution.

Swiftly, Riddle computed the odds. He was accustomed to taking chances: risk was a daily requirement in his profession. There was not much time to waste. One of the soldiers, a sergeant, detached himself from the others and took up a position to one side to give orders to the firing squad.

Riddle dropped the sergeant first, then, swiftly, before the others had begun to react, two more of the soldiers. The remaining two broke and ran, but the three who had been about to die pursued and caught them before they had reached the haven of the forest. One of the rebels used the rifle which he tore from a soldier's grasp to club his adversary to death. The other soldier managed to drop one of the rebels before the third was on him, ripping the gun out of the soldier's hands and then, while the soldier raised his arms and begged for mercy, shot him in the chest.

What had happened was a great stroke of luck, Riddle told himself afterward, but in his business a man had to be constantly on the alert to avail himself of any opportunity that might present itself. The success and failure of a mission, his very life, had often hung by a thread and he had managed to survive only through vigilance, foresight and swift and ruthless reaction to any danger.

The fact that he had killed three of the General's men, while in the pay of the General, did not bother Riddle at all. On the contrary, he found ironic amusement in the occurrence. He was always selling out one side to another and had become quite inured to this. Had he been troubled by the morals and ethics involved, he would have followed some other occupation.

The three rebels he had rescued from death led him, naturally, to Salas. The Colonel was a tall, lean man with a week's growth of black whiskers on his face. He had a piercing way of looking at a man, as if dissecting him. Riddle did not like this because he had too much to cover, too many dark deeds to enshroud. Therefore, he could hardly meet the direct, hard stare of Salas. It was a relief when Salas's eyes softened somewhat and he offered Riddle a cigarette.

They smoked together a few moments and Riddle thought of this as something like the old Indian custom of smoking the peacepipe. Anyway, he felt better. He was quite sure Salas would now accept him without doubts or suspicions. He couldn't have bargained for anything at all better than that.

"I see you brought a rifle and a pistol," Salas said. "That is good. Guns and ammunition are always in short supply with us. Remember this. Whenever you kill a government soldier, always retrieve whatever weapons and ammo he might have. The same goes for any one of us who should fall. Is that clear?"

"*Si, mi Coronel,*" Riddle said.

"You speak our language very well," Salas observed, "yet you are an American?"

"I have not been in the States in ten years."

The Colonel's eyes narrowed ever so slightly. "You have fought in other lands?"

Riddle smiled evasively. "I was in the United States Army.

Since then, I have fought wherever the cause of freedom called me."

Salas grunted. "I will not inquire into your politics. I demand only that you be loyal to our cause. There's no question about our needing experienced fighters."

"You will find me most experienced, *mi Coronel,* and loyal."

Salas grunted again. He glanced at the girl who had stood silently beside Riddle. "She is with you?"

"Yes," said Riddle.

"Very well. Find yourselves some quarters."

Things went well for Riddle during the next two weeks. He made what he considered reasonable progress. The connection between Salas and Feliz Archuleta, who was running the government on the neighboring island of Nueva Sevilla after overthrowing the dictator there, was nothing new. All of San Leon and the world itself were aware that there was no love lost between the General and Archuleta. Archuleta had vowed over the radio and television that the General would be the next tyrant to be overthrown. The movement that Salas was organizing was modeled after Archuleta's own and financed and supplied largely by Archuleta. Riddle did not concern himself too much with this facet of the movement since the General was well acquainted with it.

Instead, Riddle devoted his efforts to ferreting out and memorizing certain bits of information which he might carry back to the capital, a place to which he was most anxious to return. There were comings and goings at night, patrols, skirmishes with the government troops, air drops and disembarkations, all of which Riddle carefully noted and stored away in his memory. He was able to get about most of the territory held by the rebels and he computed the number of men Salas had and their deployment. He also learned the identity of two important businessmen of San Leon who, one night, paid Salas a long visit. All this information should prove most interesting to the General and might result in a bonus.

His progress with the girl, too, was better than he had

anticipated. She seemed to have fallen completely in love with him. She took to following him about wherever he went, so that it was all but impossible to get away from her for any appreciable length of time.

Her name was Felicia Ochoa, but he learned little else about her. She was possessed of a strange reticence when talking about herself that made Riddle wonder. The only reason she gave for deciding to join the rebels was that the General's secret police had captured her brother and tortured him to death because he had been suspected of revolutionary activities. That was enough to satisfy Riddle, for he considered his association with her a temporary one. He intended ditching her as soon as he could steal back to the capital.

Things were going very well indeed for Riddle; he was thinking that this was the easiest counter-espionage job in which he had ever engaged. When his world collapsed, it was entirely without warning or preparation.

He had returned from a patrol in which the rebels had ambushed and captured two truckloads of government military supplies and he was looking forward to the warmth and fervor of Felicia's embrace. While the patrol had been gone, several new recruits had arrived. One of them seemed startled when he saw Riddle and walked over to him to get a better look. Riddle did not recognize the fellow, a short, pudgy youth, but a strange inkling of doom iced his spine.

"Yes," the recruit said, "it's him. One of the General's spies. I recognize him now."

Riddle tried to brazen it out. Drawing himself up, he demanded angrily, "What manner of filth is this?"

"Yes," the recruit repeated, becoming excited as others crowded around. "I remember. He was employed by the San Leon embassy on the mainland. He betrayed us as we were trying to smuggle arms out of the country for Salas. He is a spy."

Riddle glanced about. The rebels had him ringed. An officer had drawn his pistol and had it pointed at Riddle. Still Riddle tried. "Are you going to listen to him, a man none of us know?" He singled out one of the men he had saved from death. "You, Perez. Do you doubt me? Do you not remember that day when the government patrol was about to shoot you? Would you be alive today if I had not intervened?"

Perez looked confused and ill at ease. The recruit began to shout "Spy! Traitor! Butcher! Would that God strikes me dead if he is not a spy! On the grave of my sainted mother, I swear that he is a spy!"

"Salas," Riddle cried. "Bring Salas here. Let him be the judge."

The men were all for killing Riddle there and then, but the officers held them back. Riddle was placed in a hut under heavy guard. The girl came to him, but only as far as the door. The guards would not allow her inside. She was pale and stared at Riddle with wide, frightened eyes.

He found that his fingers quavered as he lit a cigarette. "Get Salas for me," he said to the girl. "Hurry. He is out on inspection somewhere. Find him and bring him here to listen to me. Quickly."

He began to think the girl had failed him as time dragged on, but he realized it was his fear and anxiety that made the minutes seem to pass with interminable slowness. Perhaps she could not find Salas. Perhaps she had fled for her own safety. A lost, bitter taste filled Riddle's mouth.

He had about given up hope, when there was the sound of voices outside and then the guard stepped away from the door of the hut and the tall form of Salas stooped to enter. Salas stood with hands on hips, staring at Riddle who sat, bound, on the floor.

Salas said nothing. He just went on watching Riddle and something cold and nauseous formed in the pit of Riddle's stomach. *"Mi Coronel,"* he said, not at all ashamed to be begging now, "you must listen to me. True, I am in the employ of Duarte and the General, but that is not who I really work for. I am a double agent, for Nueva Sevilla and Archuleta. That is the truth. I swear it is."

Salas made no comment. Sweat began to trickle down Riddle's cheeks.

"I was hired by Archuleta to spy on San Leon. So I went to the mainland and did some good work for the San Leon embassy and they finally transferred me here to the island.

Then Duarte sent me here to report on the movement. I had to come, but I was only gathering enough harmless information so that I might transfer back to the capital and begin reporting to Archuleta again. Do you not see, *mi Coronel,* you and I are working for the same man. Feliz Archuleta."

Salas raised a hand and stroked the dark beard stubble on his chin.

"I do not expect you to believe me, *mi Coronel,*" Riddle went on. "But there is one sure way to discover if I am telling the truth. You are in radio contact with Nueva Sevilla. Call them. Ask them about me. Use my code name, 'Domingo.' You will find out then if I am lying."

Salas turned abruptly and left the hut. Riddle called after him, but the only reply was the retreating footsteps of the Colonel.

Riddle began to give way to despair. Night arrived, but not Salas. A lantern was placed in the hut so that the guards could better observe Riddle. He found himself thinking of his home back in Ohio and wondering why he had ever left it to roam these countries where there was no such thing as security or political stability. Furiously, he put the thoughts from him, for they were almost enough to make him weep.

He had completely given up hope, when the tall figure of Salas filled the doorway. Salas came forward and swiftly cut the ropes binding Riddle. Riddle began to recite his thanks, but Salas silenced him with a gesture.

The guards watched with obvious curiosity, but said nothing for Salas was the supreme commander. A jeep was waiting and Salas motioned Riddle into the vehicle. With startled surprise, Riddle noticed Felicia already sitting there. He climbed in beside the girl and Salas got behind the wheel and started the jeep.

Salas drove at high speed. He took the sharp mountain curves with frightening recklessness. The girl sat quietly beside Riddle and stared straight ahead. He took her hand once, but she withdrew it and sat there, strangely cool and distant.

"Where are we going?" Riddle asked Salas. "Can you not tell me at least that?"

"To an airstrip," Salas said. "A plane will come for you there."

"To take me to Archuleta? Is that where I am going?"

Salas grunted. He did not elaborate.

Neither Salas nor the girl spoke the rest of the way. After a few more attempts to engage them in conversation, Riddle gave up. The moon was high and bright in the Caribbean sky when they finally reached the airstrip. Riddle was surprised to find the landing field unguarded.

"There is no need," Salas explained. "This strip is rarely used. Most of my men do not even know of its existence."

Salas took some flares out of the jeep and, with Riddle's assistance, placed them and lit them on either side of the runway. Then Salas consulted his watch and announced that the plane should arrive shortly.

Riddle's heart was racing with excitement. He could not understand why that strange intuition of doom, that so rarely failed him, should be so strong in him now. There was nothing to worry about anymore. Soon the plane would land and he would climb aboard and in a couple of hours be safely in Nueva Sevilla and ready for further adventures. He had come through another close shave successfully.

A faint droning that grew louder announced the coming of the aircraft. Elatedly, he watched it circle the airstrip and then glide in for a perfect landing between the parallel rows of flares. With a panicked start, he recognized the plane as one belonging to the government of San Leon.

He turned on Salas and saw that Salas had drawn his revolver and was pointing it at him. Weakness overwhelmed Riddle, a feeling of hollowness. Salas was smiling faintly, but without humor.

Three men got out of the plane. Two of them carried submachine guns and stayed some distance away. The third man, an elderly, portly person dressed in a conservative business suit and holding an automatic pistol in his hand, walked up to them.

"You may put your gun away, Salas," the man said. "I will take over now."

"Si mi General," Salas said, and saluted.

The General smiled at the girl. "Ah, Felicia, my dear. I see you have carried out your assignment very well. You are still with the American. What is his name? Riddle?" Cold eyes speared Riddle. "You did not think that I would trust you, did you, Riddle? I trust no one. That is why I continue alive and in power unlike other rulers who come and go. I sent you to report on Salas because I did not trust him either and the girl to report on you. Is it true that you are really in the employ of that pig of an Archuleta?"

The walls of Riddle's throat were frozen, his tongue would not articulate, the words he wanted to say lay still-born in his brain.

"That is of no importance," the General said when Riddle did not speak. "You know too much so there is but one thing to do with you." With a gesture of his left hand he motioned the girl away from Riddle. Salas also started to go, but the General said very coldly and crisply, "Ah, no, Salas. You remain with Riddle."

Salas halted. He stood very tense and astonished. "But, *mi General,* have I not served you well? Have I not carried out every item that was assigned to me? Did I not inform you of Riddle's true employment? Did I not arrange all this?"

The General sighed. "That is true, Salas. It grieves me, but it could eventually mean my neck. I am not like those other rulers who have been fools and incompetents. I profit by their mistakes. It was very clever of me to send you to assume charge of the revolutionary movement. You have provided me with the names of all those liberals foolish enough to sponsor the movement. You have provided me with information concerning the strength and deployment of the rebel forces. My own army is ready to move. In twenty-four hours the movement will be crushed. You have done well, Salas. But it is what I intended you to do all the while. You see, it came to my attention before I detailed you to join the rebels that you had not always been for me. I had information that you had been dealing and conniving with certain parties who are not even for that pig Archuleta. To bring those parties into the open and establish their connection with you, I sent you here and then double-checked you with my own agents. Need I say more?"

"But those are all lies, *mi General*. I have always been loyal to you."

"Perhaps. But how can I be sure?" The General's voice turned sad. "Look at it this way, Salas. You are a definite threat to me. Since you took charge of the movement you have become very popular in San Leon. I have realized for a long time that you were a potential rival." The General shook his head. "I can not risk that, Salas. I am sorry. I grieve."

The General backed away slowly, keeping his pistol aimed at Salas and Riddle. When he was out of the line of fire, the General shouted at the two with the submachine guns.

"Tomas! Pedro!"

The echoes of the shots were still ringing in the girl's ears. She had turned her back on the sight. Tears of fright and horror wanted to stream out of her eyes, but she forced them back. She dared not let her emotions be known.

The General motioned Tomas and Pedro into the plane and then put his hand on the girl's arm to help her up the ramp. "You did very well, little one," the General said in a pleased voice. "I shall see that you are provided with many pretty things when we are back in the capital. You will find me most generous."

The girl was thinking: Just as he killed Salas, he might someday kill me. After all, I am the only one who knows the truth about Salas. Tomas and Pedro did not hear, because they were too far away and the motors drowned out the words. Like the General said, it is the matter of one's neck. I am young and wish to live. I have much fear of the General and, being only a girl, I do not know what I can do. But I promise myself, if the opportunity arises, I shall try to see to it that he dies . . .

HOMICIDE EN ROUTE

by C. B. Gilford

In Boston, Lieutenant Dave Lefkowitz of Homicide made a long-distance, person-to-person call to New York. "I want Jordan Bennett," he said. "He's an attorney. He's got an office somewhere in town there, but I don't know the number. Make it quick, will you? It's urgent."

He left the phone instrument cradled against his ear as he turned toward his underling, Sergeant Ross. "I want to let Bennett know about this first thing," he said. "Remember I told you about Bennett? I met him in New York when he was defending in the Giardello case. He's a nice guy, Bennett is."

Lefkowitz slouched confidently back in his chair, an unaccustomed grin on his jowly face. He waited.

In the New York central office, the call from Boston was relayed to Laura Shields. She was a pretty blonde girl, almost beautiful. But she had never let the fact that she was good-looking interfere with her job. She was an efficient operator. So when the request from Boston came through, she started to look up Jordan Bennett's phone number promptly and methodically. Her forefinger raced down the page.

In San Francisco, Lieutenant (j.g.) William Wheeland, United States Naval Reserve, made a long-distance, person-to-person call to New York. "I want Miss Laura Shields," he said. "I could give you her home phone number, but she should be at work right now. She's a long-distance operator. And say, put it through quick, will you, sweetheart? This is a matter of life."

He was in a public phonebooth, without anyone to talk to. So he just sat there, whistling and drumming his fingers against the glass door. His face was ruggedly handsome, and he was grinning too.

In the New York central office, the call from San Francisco was relayed to Dottie Myers. Dottie was a plain girl in her thirties who had never married. Now her expressionless face lighted with sudden excitement. She was sitting perhaps fifteen feet away from Laura Shields.

"Laura," she shouted, "there's a call for you from Frisco!"

Laura Shields had just found Jordan Bennett's phone number. But the magic word "Frisco" changed her from an efficient long-distance operator to a suddenly lovesick female. Nevertheless, she did have enough presence of mind to say into her mouthpiece, "Boston operator, will you hold the line please?"

Then with her whole body trembling, she shouted back to Dottie Myers, "Dottie, switch it over here to me!"

It was a matter only of seconds while the San Francisco operator verified her party. But it seemed infinitely longer to Laura Shields. Finally, however, the voice of Lieutenant (j.g.) William Wheeland was speaking to her across a whole continent.

"Laura, is that you?"

"This is me, Bill."

"My ship just tied up here."

"Oh, that's wonderful."

"Do you still love me?"

"Yes . . . yes . . . of course. Do you love me?"

"You bet I do."

"Well, say it."

"I love you. And I want to marry you now instead of next December."

"Oh, Bill . . ."

"Well, what about it? Will you marry me this week? Will you?"

A long pause, while Laura Shield's whole future hung in the balance. "Oh, yes, Bill, yes."

"Will you come out here and marry me?"

"Yes . . . yes . . . when?"

"I've got it all figured out. I've got three or four days' duty aboard ship. I know how you are about flying. But that'll give you time to come out on a train. Then after that I'll have a couple of weeks. Honey, Frisco is a great place for a honeymoon. How does it sound to you?"

"It sounds wonderful, Bill."

"Then you'll come?"

"Oh, yes."

"I'll make a reservation for you at the Mark and meet you there. Okay?"

"Okay."

"Can you start today?"

"Yes. I'm sure I can arrange things here at the office."

"Then I'll see you at the Mark, let's say Saturday."

"All right, Saturday."

"I love you."

"I love you, Bill."

"I'd better buzz off now. See you Saturday. 'Bye."

"Bye . . ."

Laura Shields was trembling even more when the conversation was finished. She had to see about getting off. And she had two hours more of duty, but she knew somehow that she could never stumble through it.

"Peg," she said to Peggy Thomas, the thin girl right next to her, "will you take over for me? There's a call from Boston on my line."

In Boston, Lieutenant Dave Lefkowitz was impatient. He had been listening to the Boston operator repeat the request for the phone number of Jordan Bennett, Attorney. He turned again to Sergeant Ross.

"I don't know what's the matter with them girls today," he said. "They can't seem to remember anything . . ."

In his New York office, Jordan Bennett stood staring at the open suitcase before him. Bennett was young, not yet thirty, of medium height but not heavily built, with a good-looking face and brown, slightly waving hair. The suitcase he was staring at was already packed. Right on top of the pile of shirts lay a gun, a .38 automatic.

He stood there that way for almost a minute, then glanced quickly at his wristwatch. Decisively and determinedly, he closed the suitcase, snapped the latches, picked it up by the handle, and went out through the door. The door locked behind him.

When he had gone perhaps three steps down the hall, he heard his phone ringing. He stopped. The phone rang twice again. Jordan Bennett consulted his wristwatch. Once more he made a decision. He walked on down the corridor toward the elevator. Behind him, his phone continued to ring.

Laura Shields just managed to get on board the train as it left Grand Central. She purchased her ticket from the conductor, who also contrived to find her a roomette. Sitting alone, finally, she still could not catch her breath, still could not quite control the trembling excitement that tingled out to her fingertips and clear down to her toes.

She was going to get married. She had no trousseau, the ceremony would be brief and in some strange place; there wouldn't be any friends or relatives there, no reception, probably not even any flowers. None of it would be the way she had so often dreamed of it.

But it would be all right, she told herself, because Bill would be there, and Bill was the man she wanted to marry. And Bill was in the Navy, and in the Navy you can't control where you're going to be or when you're going to be there.

She hadn't had time to buy a book or any magazines, so she sat and stared out of the window as the train plunged westward. But even that pastime was quickly denied her. Within half an hour after departure, it began to grow dark.

She waited till the porter had issued the last call before she went back to the diner. Even then it was only for something to do. She wasn't in the least hungry.

And it was there in the diner that she first noticed the two men. She wasn't really being observant, because her mind was far away, far down the track ahead of her in Frisco where she'd meet Bill. It was really the strange way the men acted or rather the strange way the first man acted which must have finally penetrated to her consciousness and she became aware of it.

In the beginning she imagined that he kept glancing straight at her. He was sitting two tables away and facing her. He was eating, but obviously not interested in his food. She felt more and more uncomfortable as the thing went on. Till she realized that he wasn't really looking at her at all, but instead was looking past her, over her shoulder. She couldn't help being curious at what or whom he found so fascinating. But when she finally managed to turn around to see, she discovered that the target of all those glances was only another man. And that this second man was going through the same routine. He'd look up from his plate, toward the first man, then would turn aside and stare almost guiltily out of the window. Neither of them seemed in the least aware of her presence between them.

The whole business puzzled her, gave her something to think about, a respite from her impatient longing for Frisco and Bill Wheeland. But after it was over she forgot about it until she encountered those same two men in the lounge car about two hours later. They were seated at opposite ends of the car, one engrossed in a magazine, the other in a newspaper crossword puzzle. But they looked up every few minutes, as if each was checking whether the other was still there.

She left them there finally, engrossed in their strange, mutually absorbing game, and went to bed. But lying sleepless in the dark of her roomette, Laura Shields found that the two men intruded into her thoughts, at times almost displacing Bill Wheeland.

She finally slept, however, out of sheer nervous exhaustion. When she awoke, the train was passing through Indiana. She dressed and left the confinement of the roomette. It was in the corridor that she saw the men for the third time.

She herself was walking toward the rear of the train

when suddenly one of them, the slighter of the pair, appeared at the end of the corridor and came walking toward her. He scarcely noticed her, but brushed by in the narrow space and disappeared into the next car forward. Then a moment later the second man came at her, walking very fast. He shouldered past with a murmured apology and disappeared in the wake of the first.

At breakfast, she could hardly get them out of her mind. The two men obviously knew each other, yet they were not traveling together. Now one of them seemed to be trying to run away and the second was pursuing. From being only curious, she now proceeded to get worried. Possibly one of them, the pursuer maybe, was a criminal of some kind. Or it could just as easily be the other way around. She wondered if she ought to report the matter to the conductor.

But she didn't. It was none of her business, she decided, and she might be ludicrously misinterpreting the whole thing anyway. The train huffed into Chicago, and she amused herself with watching the passengers getting off and on, the switching of cars, the other trains sliding in and out. She didn't see the two men anywhere. Perhaps, she thought —or even hoped—that they'd disembarked here in Chicago.

And later, when the train bore westward across the plains, she didn't see them either. She had an uneventful lunch, and afterwards retreated to her roomette again. The excitement of everything, the suddenness of Bill's call, the suddenness of her departure, the nearness of marriage and a new life—this was all beginning to tell on her. She was acquiring a headache and she wanted a nap.

She did nap, off and on. But at five she was dreadfully awake again, and the headache was more insistent. She had aspirin in her purse, but she felt she might use a drink too. For the headache and maybe to get into training for all that wedding champagne. And perhaps find someone to talk to. The hours were dragging along much too slowly. She could almost agree now with what Bill always said, that flying was the best way to travel. She freshened her makeup, and left the narrow confinement of the roomette, seeking a change, surcease, a small drink, the sound of voices, distraction.

In the club car, she walked quickly down the path between the little tables, trying to scan the potential companions without making it seem she was just hunting for someone to leech onto. Then two things happened at once. She saw one of the men, the slighter of them, the one who'd been running away. The sight of him startled her somehow, because maybe she'd already dismissed him as caught, robbed, apprehended, handcuffed, or even murdered. Or at least he'd gotten off at Chicago. Secondly, and at precisely the same moment, the train lurched into a curve. She should have been wearing her flats, but instead she was on spike heels. She lost her footing completely, fell, and almost ended up in the man's lap.

She undoubtedly would have if the man hadn't been just as anxious to prevent that mishap as she was. He rose out of his seat, grabbed both her arms, and steadied her till the train leveled out again. The only casualty was his drink, which turned over and emptied itself on the table, while the glass rolled violently from edge to edge without ever actually falling off.

But the man was very nice about it. "Are you all right?" he asked her.

"I'm all right," she said, "but I spilled your drink . . ."

"Never mind that. But are you sure you're all right? You look pale."

She had to admit—though not to him—that she did feel unsteady. And if she was pale, probably it had been the sudden sight of him.

"Sit down here if you like."

She didn't know why she accepted the invitation. The man was only being kind, wasn't insistent about it. And to the rest of the people in the car it probably looked like a pickup, arranged by her, of course. But she did feel that unsteadiness, and she wanted to get out of the aisle and the limelight as quickly as possible.

The man helped her into the chair which he'd been occupying, then went around the table and took the other chair. The waiter arrived and wiped up the spilled liquid. She found herself saying yes, she'd like a drink, bourbon and soda. Her host ordered his with plain water.

"It's always so hard," he said, "to walk in trains. Sailors probably manage it better than anybody."

That was her cue to tell him about Bill just to dispel any notion he may have had that she *had* tried to fall into his lap deliberately. She also said it loud enough for a few nearby tables to hear, just in case anybody else had had similar suspicions.

"Yes," he told her, "I noticed your ring."

That remark relieved her a bit. He couldn't have thought she'd aimed for his lap.

Over the drinks, they exchanged names. His was Jordan Bennett and his destination was Los Angeles.

"Going home?" she asked him.

"No," he said noncommittally. "Business trip."

She remembered then who he was, and about the other man. She leaned back in her chair and tried surreptitiously to see if that other man were anywhere in the car. She couldn't locate him and somehow it made her feel better.

"Are you married?" she asked him.

"Haven't been that lucky," he said.

She wondered what Bill would think of her sitting here drinking with a strange, unmarried man. It would be better if he were married. No, perhaps it wouldn't either. The ethical aspect was confusing.

So she insisted on paying for both their drinks, his to replace the one she had spilled for him. But this little argument led almost inevitably to his suddenly insisting that she have dinner with him. She rather amazed herself by ending up doing just that.

Jordan Bennett was a nice man, but he was unobtrusive about it. He had good manners, so good that one didn't notice them. And he was easy to talk to, a patient listener, yet always ready with something to say if the conversation lagged. He was handsome, but not excessively so. His brown hair had a wave or two in it; his face was a bit thin; he was wearing good clothes; and he put on horn-rimmed glasses when he read the menu.

"You didn't wear those when you were doing that crossword puzzle," she said without thinking.

He showed momentary perplexity, then seemed to know

to what she was referring. "You mean this morning in the lounge car?" he asked her.

She blushed, but she had no explanation to offer except the truth. "Yes," she said.

"I'm flattered."

He'd been so pleasant that suddenly she decided to plunge deeper. "I may as well confess," she told him. "I watched you and that other fellow both."

"That other fellow?" he repeated evasively.

"You know very well whom I mean, Mr. Bennett. He's maybe an inch taller, and a bit heavier than you. He has plainer features than you, kind of a grim jaw, brown hair cut rather short . . ."

"My, you are observant."

"I didn't have anything else to do."

"What else did you notice, Miss Shields?"

"You both acted very oddly toward each other, I thought."

His eyes twinkled, but his overall mood was somber. "Yes, I guess it must look rather odd," he said.

"You two do know each other then?"

"Oh, yes indeed. We know each other quite well."

"Then why do you sit in different parts of the train and not speak to each other, and yet keep an eye on each other, and then chase each other up and down the train?"

"How do you mean?"

"Well, I saw him following you. I not only saw it, as a matter of fact, you practically knocked me over. I didn't know what was happening, but it certainly looked like he was chasing you."

Jordan Bennett had gray eyes that she could see now were very troubled. His light, bantering manner had been only a mask. "Miss Shields, it's rather a complicated point as to which one of us is chasing the other," he said.

"I don't know whether you're just trying to lead me on," she answered, "or whether you're hinting I should stop asking questions about things which don't concern me. But I'll be good. I'll stop."

Quite suddenly then his manner changed. He stared across the table at her intently, probingly. His gray eyes studied her face for a long moment. "No, I don't want you to stop," he said. "In fact, I think I want to tell you all about it."

But actually he waited till the meal was finished and they had walked back to the lounge car. They found two chairs together and sat down. He offered her a cigarette, which she refused. He lit one for himself and began.

"I'm a lawyer, but I don't suppose you've heard the name. Jordan Bennett, Attorney-at-Law?"

"I don't think so . . ."

"It's hardly likely that you would have. I haven't been in the racket terribly long. So the name isn't as famous as I had hoped it would be some day.

"Had hoped?"

"Yes, past tense, Laura. I've abandoned the law. And believe it or not, it wasn't because I lost my first big case. In fact, I won it."

"And you're quitting because you won a big case?"

"That's right, I won it. And now I sincerely wish I hadn't."

"Tell me . . ."

"I want to tell you, Laura. I have the most intense desire to tell someone, someone who's intelligent and who might possibly be sympathetic. That's why I'm choosing you to burden with my troubles. Anyway, I suppose you're familiar with the practice of the courts to appoint a lawyer—usually a beginner—to defend a criminal if the latter had no lawyer?"

"I've heard of it," she said.

"Well, I was appointed to defend a man who was accused of being a maniac and a murderer . . ."

He paused as he ground his cigarette into an ashtray. Laura merely watched him.

"We'll call this man Paul, if you don't mind," he continued. "If I told you his full name, you might recognize it because you might remember the case. Murders of this kind usually get a big play in the papers. Well, the thing was quite simple. Paul denied any knowledge of the crime, and his apparently spotless record was a point in his favor. The things against him were the fact that he was picked up near the scene of the crime just a few minutes after it had happened, plus the fact that he had no alibi. The girl had been strangled, so there was no weapon, no fingerprints, nothing of that sort. Just circumstantial evidence. Do you follow me?"

"I think so."

"There was one more thing against Paul. An intangible thing, but still very potent. I'm referring to the emotional reaction this kind of crime usually stirs up in people. In this particular case, everyone was so incensed that it was quite a job to impanel the jury. Too many prejudiced people. It would have been much easier to gather a lynch mob."

He lit another cigarette, drew deeper puffs, so that the tip glowed more intensely.

"I talked to Paul several times, and each time he told me exactly the same story, without it seeming made up or rehearsed. He was a quiet fellow, came of a good family, had a decent office job. Also—which was much in his favor—he had a girl friend, to whom he had been almost, but not quite engaged. On the night of the crime he'd had a date with this girl, but they had a quarrel and parted angrily. He was driving around in his car, just driving, sort of cooling off before he went home. Unfortunately he was driving in the same neighborhood where this girl, who was a complete stranger to him, was strangled and murdered. But Paul claimed that he had not committed the crime, that he had never even left the car. But his story had a built-in problem, don't you see?"

Laura had been listening avidly. "Yes, he was in an emotional state," she said now.

"Exactly. But it didn't prove, of course, that he had committed the murder. At least it didn't prove it to me. I believed Paul. So I based my defense on that belief, and on his character. He had no history of mental aberration. A psychiatrist examined him and found no marked abnormality. I simply pointed out to the jury that a sane man of Paul's character and background could not reasonably be accused of the crime unless there was more than circumstantial evidence. So the trial, you see, was never a test of fact, but a test between two emotions, sympathy for a nice young man and hatred for the sort of crime in which he was involved?"

"And you won?" Laura asked.

"The sympathy won, yes. Paul was acquitted. Of course, a man who's been accused of a thing like that, even if he is acquitted, can never resume his old life completely. There is always a certain stigma. There will always be some people who will persist in suspecting him. But I had won the legal contest."

"You should have been happy about that," Laura said.

Jordan Bennett's second cigarette had burned down to a short stub and he snuffed it out. Then he was silent for a moment, staring out at the lights of a town streaking by the train windows.

"I was for awhile," he answered finally. "But as I said, Paul had trouble resuming his former life. Partly out of a desire to help him, and partly because I found him an attractive companion, I became his friend. We saw a great deal of each other. I shouldn't have done that. A lawyer ought to conclude his case, accept the verdict, and forget about it. He shouldn't become his client's keeper for the rest of his life. The trouble is, you get to know a man better as his friend than as his lawyer. I got to know Paul too well."

When Jordan Bennett fell silent again, Laura urged him on. "What did you find out about him?"

"Several things. First of all, he was definitely subject to violent emotional outbursts. Not very frequent, but certainly violent. And here's the point of the whole thing. When he became emotional this way, he was capable of doing things that he didn't remember afterwards. Like this instance. I was with him at his home one evening when he called up this girl friend of his. I happened to know that she'd been cool toward him since the trial, and I'd hinted to him that he ought to forget about her. But he seemed to prefer to torture himself. He phoned her this evening, and she gave him the brush-off. He was shaking with emotion by the end of the conversation, and when he hung up he went straight over to a table where there was a framed picture of the girl. He took the picture and smashed it on the floor, breaking the glass, of course. Then he suggested we go out to a bar and have a drink. I went out with him, and we had several drinks. When we returned, I went into his house with him, because I wanted to see him safely in bed. He saw the broken picture still lying on the floor, and said it must have fallen off the table. I told him it hadn't, that he'd deliberately broken it. He kept on insisting that he hadn't. I finally gave up arguing with him and left. But you get the point, don't you, Laura?"

"He really didn't remember breaking the picture," Laura said.

"Yes, that was my interpretation at least. Well, you can imagine the conclusion I finally came to after several incidents of this sort. Paul could well have strangled and killed that girl without remembering having done it. In other words, I had secured the acquittal and freedom of a homicidal maniac. And worst of all, if he had killed someone once, he could quite possibly do it again."

Laura was conscious of a chill tingling through her body. She shivered under its impact.

"The question was what to do about it," Jordan Bennett continued. "I consulted the psychiatrist who had examined Paul before the trial, and that gentleman wasn't very helpful. He'd look into it, he said, if I could lure Paul into becoming his patient. Which I tried to do, in a roundabout way, incidentally, and failed. He also pointed out that this kind of thing, recurring temporary amnesia, was hard to pin down and would need long observation. I tried to think of a legal method of getting Paul committed to an institution for that observation, but couldn't manage anything. It always boiled down to the fact that I was the sole witness, and the authorities would have to take my word for everything. To make a long story short, there was no legal way of solving the problem. And it was my problem. I was completely responsible. And the only solution would have to be an illegal one."

Again Jordan Bennett lapsed into silence. Laura had begun to wish she hadn't asked so many questions, that he hadn't told her this story. Now she had an unwanted responsibility, to listen, to sympathize, maybe even to help.

"I tried the next best thing first though," he finally resumed. "I urged Paul to give himself up voluntarily, preferably to the state authorities, and to submit to a long period of observation. Surely, I pointed out to him, he himself wouldn't want to be wandering around in his dangerous condition, a potential, homicidal threat to every human being within his reach. Well, I pretty much knew I'd fail with that approach, and I did. Paul told me I must be the crazy one. We had quite a bitter argument. Finally, I said to him I would give him a little time to think it over. If he didn't decide to give himself up, I'd have to do something drastic. I was responsible for him. Rather than have him kill someone else, I'd kill him first."

Laura closed her eyes. The chill was permeating her whole body. She could guess the ending of the story now.

"I let him have a couple of days to think," Jordan said, "but I kept an eye on him all the time. He tried to escape by getting on this train. I followed him. And here we are."

"And, of course, that other man is ... Paul?" Laura said.

"Yes. Perhaps you'll understand now why we're acting so oddly toward each other."

Impulsively, Laura put her hand on Jordan's arm. "But you haven't been trying to kill him?" she asked fearfully. Then a worse, more horrible thought hit her. "Where is he now? You haven't killed him already?"

Jordan put his hand on top of hers. "Thanks for the sympathy," he said. "That was what I was looking for. But don't worry, I haven't killed him. He's in his compartment, I'm sure, and I know where that is. This train won't make a stop till midnight, so he can't get off. No, I'm still watching and waiting. But if he hasn't decided to surrender himself by the time we get to California, then ..."

Laura Shields had been left alone at eleven o'clock. Jordan Bennett had told her good night and had gone. Although he didn't say so precisely, she knew that he wanted to be ready for the midnight stop. At eleven-thirty, she went back to her roomette. But since she wasn't sleepy, she didn't get undressed. She took off only her shoes, and then she sat in the darkness waiting.

The train was well on time. It pulled into the station at

five of twelve and stayed about fifteen minutes. Laura scanned the platform outside her window without seeing either Jordan Bennett or Paul. When the train finally slid out of the station, she didn't know whether to feel relieved or more apprehensive.

So she still didn't sleep. She tried to think of Bill, tried to form his face in her mind, to conjure the feeling of his kiss. These were imaginings which she'd always been able to summon up so easily. But now somehow they were difficult. Jordan Bennett was clearer in her mind than Bill was.

When a knock came at her closed door—it must have been about one o'clock—she opened it immediately, thoughtlessly. Probably it was Jordan Bennett, she felt, whom she'd see out in the corridor. But in that confident surmise she was mistaken. It was the man Jordan Bennett had called Paul.

She got a single impression of him in that first moment, rather than of a mass of details. Yet it was the details that added up to the impression. First of all his suit was rumpled. Either he had been sleeping in it or—this thought chilled her—he had been fighting. His tie was askew also, and there was a film of sweat on his face.

And she did not know exactly how to read the man's face. Basically it was composed of good, honest features. The close-cropped brown hair gave him a boyish look, as did the smoothness of his skin and the lightness of his beard. His jaw was strong, his mouth clean-cut. Only his brown eyes seemed at all strange. They were bloodshot, perhaps unnaturally bright.

Still, there was nothing in particular about him to make her afraid. She was really going on Jordan Bennett's word. Perhaps this man had killed a girl. At least he'd been tried for murder. Perhaps he was insane and could kill someone again. She wouldn't have been afraid of him if she hadn't heard about him from Jordan Bennett.

But she was afraid. She had slid her compartment door open wide, and now she tried to slide it back again. In this she succeeded only partially. The door encountered an obstacle just a few inches before it closed shut, and though she continued pushing on it, it could close no farther. Then she knew the reason. The man had put his foot in the way of the door.

She still could have screamed or pressed the button of the porter's bell. But some instinct prevented her. Whether he would have allowed her to do either of those things, she did not know.

"You're Laura Shields, aren't you?" he asked.

"Yes," she admitted.

"I'm Paul Demaray," he said. "But I know you've seen me, and I know Bennett has told you about me."

She stared up at him without knowing how to answer or what to do next, and she also wondered how he'd found out her name. The name Paul Demaray struck only the most faintly familiar chord. She must have read about him, but there were so many . . .

"The lounge car is closed," he was saying. "May I come into your compartment?"

"Why?" That scream was close to her lips now.

"I want to talk to you," he said. "Bennett seems to have had a sympathetic ear for his lies. I'm hoping I might find one for the truth."

If he had deliberately calculated the very thing to say to cause her to let him enter peaceably, he could scarcely have chosen better. Jordan Bennett's story had fascinated her, yet she had known it had been composed more of supposition than of fact. Now the hint that there could also be the element of lies as opposed to truth in his account, gave it all another, a new, an even more fascinating dimension.

She had little choice in the matter, but at least it allowed her to be less fearful for herself when she said to him, "Come in, Mr. Demaray."

She sat down. When he came in and closed the door behind him, she accepted his explanation. "I don't want anybody listening to us." When he sat beside her, so close that their shoulders touched, she accepted that too as being inevitable in a space as tiny as the roomette.

"Now what all did Bennett say?" he asked her.

She repeated the story Jordan Bennett had told her, as accurately as she could remember it. He listened quietly, calmly.

"The bare facts are there," he said finally, "but Bennett and I interpret several things a bit differently. May I explain what I mean?"

Ten minutes of sitting there close to him had soothed her fears somewhat, and she really did want to know. "Tell me, Mr. Demaray," she said.

"Well, first of all there's the trial. I guess what he did was the best thing to do from a legal, courtroom standpoint, and I'm grateful that it got me acquitted. But I always disagreed with Bennett on the method of proving my innocence. You see, he merely matched circumstantial evidence with circumstantial evidence. The prosecution said I was in the neighborhood. I was emotionally upset, and so forth. Bennett replied with the psychiatrist's evidence that I was sane, with my personal history of good family, job, all that stuff. But I don't think either side proved anything. Where's the logic? If I got angry with *one* girl, why should I kill another girl? Don't you see, Miss Shields? It doesn't make sense, even if I'd been certified insane. If I'd killed *my* girl, the girl I'd had a date with, all right, that makes sense—to kill the person who has done something against you. I can see myself doing that. I can imagine myself killing a girl who has insulted me. That is, if I'm capable of killing anybody at all. Now this is the logic that Bennett still doesn't see. That's why he's able to imagine now that I actually did commit that murder."

Laura Shields had listened with rapt attention, her eyes never leaving Paul Demaray's face. The face wasn't as handsome as Jordan Bennett's. And Paul's words weren't as slick and polished. But they impressed her.

"You didn't commit that murder, did you?" she asked.

"No, I didn't," he said simply.

They looked at each other for a moment. She felt close to him somehow, not just physically close.

"Then there's the business of that picture," he went on. "Bennett claims I broke the picture, then didn't remember breaking it. Well, the fact is that I did remember doing it. But I told a ridiculous lie, and then when I told the truth,

Bennett wouldn't believe me. And it's a pretty important thing, because it's what gave Bennett this whole cock-eyed idea of his, that he'd better do sometthing to stop me from killing more people. You see, Miss Shields, here's something again that Bennett's legal mind just can't understand. He can't understand that I could have lied because I didn't want him to know how hurt I was, and how childishly I'd tried to hurt back. I was ashamed of being so childish. Do you see?"

"I don't know," she began honestly.

"Well, here was a girl who was just about ready to marry me before the trial. I was acquitted. In other words, a jury of twelve people said I was innocent. So why didn't she believe them? I'd been accused, yes, but I'd been proven innocent. Why was she afraid of me just because I'd been accused of doing something horrible? Oh, I know what you're going to answer, Miss Shields. That lots of innocent people have to suffer that way. That they can never escape being suspected of the thing they'd been cleared of. Well, it was bad enough for other people to act that way. But my girl! Nobody knows how much that hurt. Maybe I could have killed her right then, because like I said before, she was the one who hurt me. But all I had there to hurt back was her picture. It was silly, breaking that picture. So I was ashamed. And I was half-drunk. And I lied. But Bennett keeps on believing the lie. And it's ridiculous. Of course I remembered breaking the picture. Why should I forget that and remember everything else? Why should I? It's perfectly ridiculous."

As he had talked, Laura Shields had felt the excitement growing in her. Somehow, she knew, she had been fated to meet these two men here on this train, because she alone had the power to reconcile them. They had confided in her. So they must trust her. And she could help them.

"Oh, Paul!" she said, and she laid a hand on his arm as she'd done with Jordan Bennett. "It isn't that Bennett is illogical. It's just that he has a different kind of logic from yours. You both make sense. Do you realize that I listened to both of you, and I believed both of you? Now you've got to understand each other. I want to get you together and make you understand. You're both too nice to have this happen. Jordan mustn't try to kill you. It would ruin his life. And you mustn't die. Because you're innocent, and because you're good . . ."

He stared down at her. His face had softened, relaxed. "Thanks, Laura," he said.

"It's what I actually think," she answered.

He stopped staring at her then, leaned his head back against the cushion and shut his eyes. When he spoke it was so softly that she could scarcely hear his words above the clack-clack of the train wheels.

"You're a godsend to me, Laura. To find one person who doesn't hate me or suspect me or isn't afraid of me. To find one person who really *accepts* my innocence and therefore treats me like everybody treated me before all this happened. I don't feel so much like a monster anymore. I feel human again. And maybe, like you say, you can even settle things between Bennett and me. But what else can you do for me, Laura? I have a whole life to rebuild, Laura. How much help can you give me in that?"

"I'll do whatever I possibly can, Paul," she said.

"You know," he went on, "it's so much more important to have a woman tell me something like that. A man can be impersonal about another man. To a man, all other men are just sort of things. So a man could tell me that he accepts me back into the human race and it doesn't mean too much. But a woman always takes the personal view. A matter of sex really, I guess. But if a woman accepts me, it means acceptance on that personal basis. It means that she could stand my touch without shuddering. It means she could stand my making love to her without her thinking she was being embraced by something unclean, some loathsome reptile. She might not accept me as her lover, but at least she'd accept me as a man . . ."

He had opened his eyes and he was looking at her again now. His look was as soft and placid as his tone. "You're as beautiful as you are kind, Laura," he said.

She laughed. "You've got your mind off yourself now," she told him.

"Laura," he went on, "a man gets tired of dealing forever with hard things like murder and trials and logic. It's good just to look at something soft and beautiful. Do you know something else, Laura? I had this girl friend, you know. Well, she used to let me kiss her. Before the trial, that is. But after the trial, even though I saw her quite a few times, she never let me kiss her anymore."

"She was cruel and unjust."

"So I haven't kissed a woman for more than a year."

"You'll find someone again, Paul. Someone new . . ."

"May I kiss you, Laura?"

She wasn't afraid of him. She understood him perfectly. "I'm engaged," she said.

"Yes, I know. Bennett told me. And I see the ring."

"As a matter of fact, I'm going to be married Saturday."

"Yes, I know that too."

"So I shouldn't go around kissing other men, do you think?"

He stirred a little in his seat, turning his shoulders so that he more nearly faced her. "As an act of charity, Laura. A little emotional therapy for a sick man."

She considered. She felt a little like she'd felt when she sat in the lounge car with Jordan Bennett. Slightly confused. Slightly guilty.

"All right," she said finally.

He leaned forward, and his mouth came down on hers. She closed her eyes and remained motionless. It was a gentle kiss, but his lips lingered for a long time. Finally, without really meaning to, she moved back, breaking off the kiss abruptly.

"What's the matter?" he asked. His face stayed close to hers, and his eyes seemed brighter than before.

"Nothing's the matter," she said, "but I'm still engaged."

"Did you like my kissing you?"

"Well . . ."

"Did you like it?"

"I'm not supposed to like it, am I? I'm engaged."

"Laura, for pity's sake, will you stop telling me you're engaged? Did you like it?"

"I'm not supposed to."

"Will you stop it! Answer my simple question. Did you like it?"

She hesitated, uncertain now. "I suppose so . . ."

"Just yes or no, Laura. Yes or no?"

"All right then. Yes . . ."

His right hand came to her shoulder, reached around her, drew her to him. He kissed her again, but this time not so gently. His mouth was hot, and she could feel the sweat on his face. She struggled, somehow managed to get both her hands on his chest, and finally succeeded in pushing him back.

"Stop it, Paul," she told him harshly. "You have no right to do that."

"You said you liked it."

"I liked it once, but I didn't want you to keep it up."

"Why not? Is there something wrong with me?"

"It isn't that. But I told you I'm engaged."

"Engaged! Don't say it again! Because it's not the real reason!"

"Paul, it is the real reason."

"You say you believe me, that I'm innocent, that I'm acceptable to you as a man. But you only say it. You don't act it."

"What do you expect me to do!"

She was angry now, and she fought him, pounding her fists against him, then digging her nails into his face. Her anger and the pain awoke him to greater violence. He stood up, pushing her down on the seat with his greater weight. Then his fingers went for her throat.

"You hypocrite!" he hissed at her. "You damned hypocrite!"

It didn't last long. Finally, there was only the sound of Paul Demaray's labored breathing, but it in itself was almost as loud as the muted roar of the train wheels. He stood up straight, swaying to the rhythm of the train's movement.

"But I didn't kill Shirley Giardello," he said aloud. "She didn't do anything to me. I didn't even know her . . ."

In Arizona, Jordan Bennett discovered the dead body of a girl. But he didn't tell anybody. He didn't raise the alarm. Because he didn't want anybody interfering with him before he could do what he had to do. He walked forward three cars and pushed open the door of a compartment that wasn't locked.

Paul Demaray was sitting there on the seat, his elbows on his knees, his face buried in the palms of his hands. He didn't move when Bennett entered and slid the door softly closed behind him.

"I waited too long," Bennett said, his voice shaking. "I wanted to give you the chance to do it yourself. But you did something else, didn't you?"

Demaray didn't raise his head, but talked in muffled tones through his hands. "What did I do, Bennett?" he asked.

"You know damned well what I'm talking about."

"No, I don't . . . no, I don't." He raised his head suddenly, and showed Bennett his scarred face. "Look at me. What happened to me?"

Bennett was biting his lower lip savagely. "You know what happened," he muttered. "She did that to you."

"She? Who are you talking about, Jordan?"

Jordan Bennett laughed. It was a hard bitter laugh, the sound of iron grinding against stone, lubricated by tears. "I know what you're trying to pull. Say you don't remember. Go on, say it."

"I don't remember. Honestly, Jordan. I know something awful happened. I know I did something. But I don't know what it was."

"Shut up! To think I once believed such a thing was possible. That you could commit murder and not remember. But it was worse than that, infinitely worse. You did it all right. But you remembered too! You're an incredibly horrible specimen, cruel and selfish. You get hurt a little and you strike out without caring. You don't care who you hit, just so you hit somebody. Just to satisfy your vengeful pride."

"You don't understand, Jordan . . ."

"No, thank God I don't understand you."

Jordan Bennett closed the door behind him. Then he pressed the trigger. And he kept on shooting till the gun was empty.

In the city of Boston, Lieutenant Dave Lefkowitz initiated a long-distance phone call. "Jordan Bennett," he said. "He's an attorney. Make it person-to-person. I want you to locate him . . ."

In San Francisco, Lieutenant (j.g.) William Wheeland called New York. "Laura Shields," he said, his voice a little husky and unsteady. So that there wouldn't be any mistake, he spelled the name.

In the New York central office, Dottie Myers said, "I'll look up Jordan Bennett's number . . ."

But that was when Peggy Thomas shouted above the low chatter of voices. "Hey, girls!"

The din quieted gradually. "I've got another call from that Navy lieutenant in Frisco," Peggy went on. "He's asking for Laura again. I guess she didn't get there yet."

"Gee, this is Saturday," Dottie Myers said. "This is the day she was going to get married." Remembering then, she spoke into her mouthpiece. "Hold the line please . . ."

In Boston, Lieutenant Dave Lefkowitz growled his displeasure. "What's the matter with them operators?" he asked Sergeant Ross. "Three days now I've been asking 'em to get Bennett for me. I want to give him the good news that I got the hophead here who admits he killed Shirley Giardello. But the world could come to an end while I'm holding the line here . . ."

THE LISTENING CONE

by Ed Lacy

When he'd come to in the hospital, after his heart attack, the docs had told Bucky to "go home and rest" but he could hardly tell them he didn't have a home. He'd had many rooms, and there were a few ex-wives around someplace, but no home. Bucky still had $785 from his last stick-up, and he rented a cheap room in this quiet part of the city and rested, as the doctors had told him. Like any dying animal, Bucky wanted the protection of an unknown neighborhood, where the many punks and goons he'd belted and muscled over the years wouldn't know he was flat on his wide back, defenseless.

Over the weeks, sprawled on the narrow bed, Bucky wondered what he was going to do. He could stay with the holdups and strongarm stuff, but the thought of his ticker suddenly stopping in the middle of a getaway spoiled the type of bullyboy confidence he needed. Often he fingered his hard and bulky body and wondered why, after fifty years of carrying him through all kinds of dangers, it was failing him now. At such times he refused to believe he was sick; but whenever he went down the hall to the bathroom, one fast step and the quick tension in his chest sharply reminded Bucky of reality.

Mostly he slept, read a lot, and didn't think too much about the future. The room was ten bucks a week, and for another eleven dollars weekly the elderly landlady was delighted to bring him two light meals a day, the newspapers and magazines she'd finished reading. Indeed, she was pleased at having such a nice, quiet roomer. Money wasn't an immediate problem; his roll would easily last six months at this rate. But after that, what? Bucky was used to quick money, drinks, fast women and faster action.

During the afternoons he'd sit by the one window, gazing at the phone booth on the corner, the modest apartment houses across the street. The street meant people, and people translated into suckers and money, if only Bucky could think up an angle, something a guy with a bad heart could get going. It was a big problem, having to use his head now instead of his muscles.

In one of the magazines there was an ad for a listening device, using the same principle employed in larger models for tracing missiles. The ad claimed the device could pick up conversations hundreds of feet away. Bucky made a slow and careful trip to the mailbox, sent a letter with twenty bucks for the described gadget.

When the large package arrived, Bucky set it up on the one table in his room. He had no idea of the electronics involved, but he followed the directions carefully—a large metal cone was set on a small tripod and there were stethoscope earphones. Pointing the device at two housewives talking on the sidewalk across the street, Bucky heard:

". . . and I told the cashier never mind what's marked on the cans, your ad said three for a dollar and . . ."

He pointed the listening cone toward three little girls jumping rope. ". . . I,J,K,L,M . . . You missed on M. So your boyfriend is . . . Marvin! There! Fat Marvin is your boyfriend!"

For the first time since he "fell out" in a bar, Bucky forgot about his heart as he practiced the rest of the afternoon with the listening device. By 4 P.M. he was bushed and went to sleep.

His landlady awoke him at 6 P.M. with his bland supper. Then, for a half hour, Bucky impatiently listened to his radio. When it was dark outside and the windows across the street full of lights, Bucky put on his robe, turned off his own light and set the listening device near the window.

He plugged in the delicate earphones and aimed the listening cone at the lighted windows. Although he rarely saw anybody at the open windows, he clearly overheard conversations.

". . . off the TV! I told you to finish your homework *first*. I don't want to say it again, but . . ."

"Well, darling, you should have seen her face—you know that dopey look she gets—when I bid and made a small slam. She like to fell right through the table."

". . . can't afford it. What's more, I'm tired. Can't we just stay home for one night, take it easy?"

"The choice is yours, pardner; either you give me a fresh horse, a six-shooter and the gold, or I'll knife your squaw. I've killed from Dodge City to Buffalo Hills, so one more killin' ain't going to change things for me, no-how . . . Look, ma, no cavities! Yes, this bright little girl knows that by using . . ."

Going from window to window, Bucky heard teenage conversations, bits of radio and TV shows, banal gossip, and petty family battles. Then he patiently started covering the windows of the next apartment house.

At a dimly lit third floor window, Bucky at first thought he was listening to another TV drama.

". . . found the money! All right, Beth, now you know. So what about it?"

"That's all you can say, what about it? Frank, are you crazy? $20,000! Do you think that won't be missed at the bank? You'll be jailed!"

"Maybe, but I hope not. I have a foolproof system. Beth, if you hadn't been so nosey, you never would have known about this."

"Exactly what are you going to do with all that money, Frank?"

"Nothing, for now. I've been taking a thousand a month, making withdrawals from old savings accounts which haven't been touched in years. When I have $50,000, I'm going away. If you wish to come with me, fine. If not . . ."

"Go with you? Where, Frank, to jail?"

"Beth, I never meant for you to know how I got the

money. I was going to tell you I'd won the sweepstakes. Baby, listen to me: do you know what's been wrong with us? The petty routine of working, eating, sleeping has become a rut, dulled the happiness we once had. With both of us working, we haven't any real life together. I don't plan to end up a retired teller, or be a manager of some branch bank when I'm sixty-five."

"But, Frank, this is stealing!"

"Legally, yes. But I saved them hundreds of thousands when the bank was held up, took a bullet in my belly, and what did I get for it? A letter of . . ."

"They gave you two months' sick leave, paid your hospital bills."

"That sure was big of them! Beth, there's no point in arguing. I want ten years of seeing Europe, giving myself a chance to paint. I'd like you to come along, but if not, I'll go it alone."

"Frank, Frank, will you talk sense? Please, put the money back before it's too late!"

"Honey, I can't put it back, it would be like signing a confession. What's more, I don't want to. Can't you understand that I'm desperate for this chance at happiness? I'm not going to let my youth slip by. I'm sorry, but my mind is made up.

"Oh Frank, please, please, give it back, explain . . ."

"That's impossible. There's no turning back, so stop the whine. I'm going out for a walk."

Bucky heard a door slamming, then heavy silence. Peering from his window, he saw a tall man leave the apartment house minutes later, but in the dim light he couldn't see much of the man. He heard the sounds of Beth weeping, then those of a phone being dialed.

"Eddie? Beth. Yes, I told him I knew. No, he flatly refuses to give it back. He says it's impossible. Oh, Eddie, I don't know what to do now. I . . . of course I still want to leave him but he's in such a mess. The fool!"

There was a faint silence. Bucky couldn't hear what was being said on the other end of the wire. Then, "Sure, I'll be firm. But it's such a nightmare. Yes, all right. Good night, dearest."

This was followed by more weeping, then the sounds of dishes being washed. Removing the earphones, Bucky turned on his light and made a rough sketch of the apartment windows, marking "their" third floor with an X.

Snapping off the light again, Bucky aimed the listening cone at a lighted window two floors above "them" and heard:

". . . she says. Well, you know me, I gave her a piece of my mind. So she called over the manager and I told him how long I'd had a charge account in the store, that I'd paid cash and had been shortchanged a quarter. So he bows all over himself and says, 'Mary, give Mrs. Parks 25¢. It's just one of those things, Mrs. Parks. You can see the position of our cashier'."

Bucky put the listening device on the table and switched on his light. On his drawing of the apartment windows he wrote MRS. PARKS across the window. Then he took one of his pills and slept soundly, ready for his next move.

At 6 A.M. he was at his window again, the cone pointed toward "their" window. In the gray dawn he heard nothing until 6:45, when radio music suddenly came on. Minutes later Beth said, "Frank, get up."

Sounds of water running mixed in with radio music and news. At 7:10 Beth called out, "Frank, your coffee's getting cold. How many eggs?"

"None, thank you. Only toast."

"Frank, you haven't been eating lately. Can't you see the strain this money has put you under? I beg you to . . ."

"Beth, stop it. I don't want the money mentioned again, ever! I mean that. All you have to think about is if you want to go with me when I'm ready to take off."

"But that will be two years or more. What if the bank finds out?"

"That's a calculated risk I'm taking. If I'm caught, I'll go to jail alone. Forget you ever saw the money in the shoe-box in the closet, and you'll be in the clear. Okay? Beth, don't start the tears flowing. Pass the sugar, please."

Bucky heard them leave the apartment, but so many young couples were leaving for work he couldn't decide which was Frank and Beth. Not that it mattered.

Returning to bed, Bucky dozed for two hours until his landlady knocked with his breakfast. Seeing the odd-looking cone on the table, she said, "So that's what came in the big box yesterday. What is it?"

"A fancy aerial for my radio. Supposed to get California when I hook it up. Seems a nice day, I think I'll get some sun."

"Yes. Well, don't overdo it."

Resting until 11 A.M., Bucky dressed slowly and then, walking with studied care, he crossed the street and stepped into the lobby of the apartment house. The names beside the bells had Parks in apartment 5G. The name beside 3G was Edwards.

Walking slowly, Bucky reached the corner phone booth and asked information for the phone number of Frank Edwards at the address across the street. Then Bucky returned to his room, bushed but happy. He was operating.

At 5:30 P.M. his listening cone was aimed at the Edwards' window. Bucky made a note of the time when the door opened at 5:45. Some twenty minutes later he heard the door opening again and Beth calling, "Frank?"

"I'm in the bedroom, working."

"I'll start supper."

Bucky kept the cone aimed at the Edwards' window for the next few hours, stopping only for his own supper. He heard parts of various TV shows, and once Frank called out, "Hon, turn the TV down a little. I can't concentrate on my studying here."

Bucky remained in bed until after breakfast, thinking through the details of the shakedown. It was perfect, no possible connections; he didn't know what Frank Edwards looked like, and Edwards had never seen nor even heard of Bucky. Frank hadn't seen the cone either, and never would. Perfect, not the smallest link.

Resting all day, Bucky decided against using the hall phone of the rooming house. At 5:15 P.M. he walked slowly to the corner phonebooth and dialed Frank Edwards' number. There wasn't any answer. Bucky kept dialing every few minutes. Finally a man's voice asked, "Yes?"

"How are you, Frankie?"

"I'm okay. Who's this?"

"A buddy. Listen, I . . ."

"Who is this?"

"Frankie, cut the small talk and listen carefully. You wouldn't want the bank to know about that twenty grand you've taken, would you?"

There was a second of shocked silence, then Edwards asked, "Who are you?"

"Never mind who I am. Frankie, don't try leaving town or anything, or I'll have to blow the whistle at the bank. It will only cost you five grand to . . ."

"I don't know what you're talking about!" Frank snapped, hanging up.

Bucky waited a moment, dialed again. When Edwards answered, Bucky growled, "The price has gone up, I want $6,000. Don't ever hang up on me again or it'll cost you. Look, I know all about the money in the closet, in the shoe-box. I'll call you again, Frankie." Hanging up, Bucky waited a moment, left the phonebooth to join the many people passing on their way home from work.

On reaching his room, panting a little, Bucky set up his listening device and heard Beth say, "Don't be an idiot, Frank! Of course I didn't tell anybody about the money. I'm scared even to think about it. What makes you ask such a question?"

"Nothing. Be sure you don't tell anybody. You may not believe this but, in my own way, I'm doing this for us."

"I wish to heaven you'd never started."

"Okay, let's not talk about it, Beth."

Bucky undressed slowly and rested. After supper he read the papers and went to sleep. The following afternoon he was in the phonebooth at 5:45. Frank answered on the first ring. Bucky said, "Frankie, don't take it out on Beth, she didn't tell me."

"W-who are you?" Edwards' voice shook with rage.

"Frankie, I'm a guy who knows you have twenty grand and are lifting a thousand a month from the bank, going to Europe someday. It's worth six grand to protect that dream, isn't it, painter?"

There was silence on the other end. Glancing at his wristwatch, Bucky said, "Don't be rude, Frankie, or it will cost you another grand."

"What do you want?"

"Like I told you yesterday, six thousand to keep me quiet. I have my own dreams, see. I'm not a hog, not asking much. I won't tap you again."

"How can I be sure of that?"

Bucky chuckled. "You can't, buddy. But take my word, the honor among thieves jazz. Are we in business, buddy?"

"Yes. When . . . oh . . . will I see you?"

"I'll tell you when, and where to leave the dough. Good night, Frankie."

Back in his room, Bucky stood to one side of the window, saw a tall young man with red hair staring out of the Edwards' window at the passing people below. Chuckling, Bucky undressed and waited for his supper. Later, in the darkness of his room, he pulled the table over to the window, the effort starting the pain in his barrel chest. He set up the listening cone so that no part of it was on his windowsill. Aiming at the Edwards' window, he heard Beth ask, "Why so moody tonight, Frank?"

"Nothing. I'm . . . a little tired."

"This Saturday is Mama's birthday, how about us spending the weekend with my folks? You need a change."

"Beth, why don't you go? It will give me a chance to catch up on my hobby, my work here. I'll get plenty of rest, too."

"You see what that money is doing? You're afraid to leave the house! I'm jumpy as a cat, myself."

"Come on, that's nonsense. Look, Beth, you know what will happen if I go along, the usual bickering. It will only spoil your mother's birthday. Hon, take the Friday train and return Sunday afternoon."

"Well, they are expecting me. Frank, do you want to watch Danny Kaye?"

"Sure, honey, turn it on. We haven't watched TV together for a while."

Phoning the next afternoon, Bucky told Frank, "Hello, this is your pal."

"Some pal!"

"But I am. Here's a tip, Frankie. Don't dye your red hair when you finally scram to Europe. If the bulls are looking for you, that's exactly what they'll expect you to do."

"Thanks! When do we meet, get this over with?"

"Don't worry, Frankie, I'll tell you when."

"Make it this weekend."

"Frankie, don't give me orders. I know Beth will be away, seeing her folks. Oh, here's another tip: Beth's two-timing you. There's a guy called Eddie who . . ."

"Eddie is her . . . Why you miserable snoop!"

"Such language. I ought to- raise the ante. I'll call you soon, have my money ready," Bucky said, glancing at his watch as he hung up.

That night Frank Edwards stayed in his window, studying the dark street below. Bucky sat up in bed and slowly smoked *one* cigarette. Once, when he had a job working over a guy for a loan shark, the shark had arranged for the victim to walk by the public phone booths outside the main library. Bucky had been sitting in a phone booth inside the office building lobby across the street from the library, with a view of the street and the booths. When the mark passed, the loan shark had merely called from his booth to the one Bucky was in, fingering the slob.

Bucky decided he could use the same layout for this. He'd tell Frank to put the $6,000 in an ordinary paper bag and wait. Bucky would then taxi down to the library, call Frank from there, telling him to be waiting outside the end booth in an hour. Bucky would then sit in the lobby booth on the other side of the street. He'd ring the end booth, Frankie would answer and be told to place the bag under the seat and take off. All the time Bucky would be watching the scene. If things were okay, he'd simply stroll across the street, pick up the money, take a couple of cabs back to his room.

Bucky was sure it wouldn't be too tiring. And if Frankie played it stupid, tried anything, Bucky would stay away from the booth, make new arrangements a few days later. Time was on his side.

The following night Bucky didn't phone. He sat in his dark room, the listening device aimed at the Edwards' window. He heard only the sounds of a few TV shows, although once Beth asked, "Frank, what are you so restless about? You stare and stare at the phone."

On Friday Bucky called at 5:45 P.M. There wasn't any answer. At 6:20 Frank finally answered. Bucky asked, "Seeing Beth off?"

"Yes, damn you!"

"Frankie, I'm ready to take my share. I'll call you later, with instructions. But don't try to be clever, it won't work. One phony move, and I'll call the bank Monday."

"Okay, I'll do as you say. When will you phone?"

Bucky grinned. Frank must think he was dealing with an amateur.

"Give me some idea when? I need time to get the money ready."

"How long does it take to stuff six grand into a paper bag? I'll call you tonight, tomorrow, or Sunday. Stay home, pal." Bucky hung up, waited for a few people to pass the booth and joined them.

In his room, Bucky felt restless. Taking an extra heart pill, he decided to make the pick-up that night. He'd phone Frank at 7:30, tell him to wait for another call, then take a cab to the library and phone from there. The office building lobby didn't close until 9:00 and the whole deal should be finished before then, without much strain on Bucky's heart.

It was dark at 7:10 when Bucky closed the door of the corner booth, and the light came on automatically as he dialed Frank. Edwards answered on the first ring. Bucky said, "This is *der tag,* old buddy. D Day—D standing for dollars. You got the money ready, in a plain paper bag?"

"Yes. Look, hold it for a moment."

"Sure, take your time," Bucky said, glancing at his watch, thinking: The dope is trying to find out if I'm calling from a public booth, waiting to hear the operator ask for more money. As though that will do him any good.

Waiting thirty seconds, Bucky hung up. After another four minutes, wanting a smoke badly, he dialed again, heard a busy signal: Edwards' receiver was still off the cradle.

Puzzled, Bucky turned in the cramped booth to look

over at the apartment house, then up at Frank's window. It was dark, but the dim light from a lamp post gave a faint shine to a kind of large ring in the window, something metallic . . . round . . . like a *listening cone!*

Bucky saw Frank Edwards' red head coming out of the apartment entrance, on the run. Frantically, Bucky pushed the booth door open, started racing down the street. He staggered after a dozen steps, pitching face down on the sidewalk.

Looking up from his notebook at the small crowd around the corpse, the patrolman asked, "Now, who saw this man have the heart attack?"

"He's really dead?" Frank Edwards asked.

"He'll never be any deader. Did you see it all?"

"Well, officer, yes, I suppose so," Frank said slowly. "I live across the street, and was on my way to the store for . . . a can of beer. I saw this big man leave the booth. He seemed to be running or walking fast. I really didn't notice him until he fell. That's all."

"Did you know him? Ever see him before?" the cop asked.

Frank shook his head. "No, sir. No, I never saw him before in my life." There was true amazement in Frank's bewildered voice.

COP KILLER

by James Holding

Kangaroo Kelly was a happy man.

And why not? He had youth. He had a pretty wife named Nora. He had a neat little duplex on Seventh Street half paid for. He had a job he liked. And he even had more than his share of black Irish good looks.

Except, of course, for his unfortunate tendency toward steatopygia.

This malformation had earned him, as you can easily imagine, a wide variety of nicknames during his lifetime, of which 'Kangaroo' was by all odds the least offensive.

Yet Kangaroo Kelly had learned to ignore with lordly indifference all his colleagues' labored attempts at humor on this subject and was therefore, as stated, a truly happy man.

His job contributed as much to his happiness as any of the other nice things he had going for him. For Kelly was lucky enough to have secured the job he'd always wanted, ever since he was a grade school shaver hanging around Young's Dairy Store with his pals on Friday afternoons after school, sucking on an ice cream cone, or a coke, and watching with something approaching awe the majestic passage of Clancy, the neighborhood patrolman, as he walked his beat.

To Kangaroo, Clancy had been an impressive symbol of law and order, a completely admirable man with an enviable way of life. And Kelly had frequently confided to his companions then that when he got big enough, what he'd like to be was a cop like Clancy. *If* he got big enough. For in those days, aside from his behind, he was kind of puny.

He got big enough, all right. And not just his rear section, either. He got big all over. He went two-twenty now on the gym scales, most of it muscle. And for four years, he had been Patrolman Kangaroo Kelly of the Juniata Police Department, happily walking a solo night beat on Juniata's South Side, and enthusiastically trying to keep assaults, muggings and purse-snatchings somewhere within reasonable bounds in his own tiny quadrant of the toughest section in the city.

He gave the job his best efforts, too, because he was deeply conscious of his responsibilities and exceptionally proud of the law enforcement traditions he was expected to uphold. He didn't laugh at danger; on the other hand, he didn't believe in fearing it, either. For he not only had great faith in his own ability to take care of himself while discharging his job; he also believed implicitly in the infallibility of the police force when it came to avenging one of its own in the event of injury or death inflicted by a criminal.

Pacing the streets of the South Side in the dark, dangerous, dragging hours before dawn, Kelly would often feed himself cheerfully this little morale booster: "Any of these mugs rub me out, even by accident, they're dead, too. And they know it. For there's six hundred cops in this town who'll get them for it if it takes a hundred years. I'm a cop. And you don't kill cops. Unless you want a fast ticket to hell yourself."

Occasionally, swinging his nightstick jauntily and walking with his tireless pigeon-toed stride down the streets of his beat, Kangaroo Kelly would run into Binksy Caputo. Binksy had been in high school with Kelly, a member of his class. They hadn't been friends, exactly. But they hadn't been enemies, either. A kind of rough *laissez-faire* had existed between them and still did. Binksy, it was true, had always laughed at Kangaroo's ambition to join the police force.

"What are ya, a sucker?" he used to say. "A big dumb sucker? The dough is on the other side, Big Tail. Why be a cop and starve when you can be a crook and get rich?" And he'd sneered good-naturedly at Kelly's earnest attempts to explain how he felt about the police.

After he left school, Binksy followed his own advice. Only he didn't get rich. Far from it. He was a petty thief, a mugger, a pickpocket, who had been sent to the County Workhouse twice for short terms, once as a result of Kangaroo Kelly's testimony. Binksy lived from hand to mouth when he was home in a tenement on Flora Street.

Meeting Kangaroo by accident at the mouth of an alley, or on Express Street behind the brewery, or in the doorway of one of the South Side's two hundred dingy bars, Binksy would greet him in his taunting voice, "Hi, sucker! Still keeping us bad guys in line?"

And Kelly might reply, "Yep, Binks. Not doing too bad, either. Tripped up Spokane Jones the other night and you won't be seeing him again for one-to-three."

And Binksy would laugh: "Won't you ever learn, Big Tail? One guy! Out of this jungle! You send one guy to the sneezer and you're the greatest thing in crime prevention the world ever saw."

"Nuts," Kelly would say. "Keep your nose clean, Binks, or I'll show *you* the inside again, old Buddy."

"Face it, Big Tail," Caputo would grin, "You can't win. There's too many of us and not enough of you."

Kelly would pace slowly and solemnly away, very dignified. "Any cop is worth twenty of your kind, Binks," he'd throw over his shoulder. "So there's enough of us. Don't worry."

But there weren't. Because the muggings and the purse-snatchings and the assaults in Kangaroo Kelly's territory gradually increased to the point where a single patrolman, no matter how dedicated, simply couldn't control it.

That's when they assigned Kangaroo Kelly a partner. He wasn't too pleased about it at first, since he'd always been a solo operator and liked the feeling of personal, individual responsibility that carried with it. But he knew very well that he needed help. So he agreed with every evidence of pleasure when Pete was assigned to him.

Pete's full name was a long German mouthful ending in Augsburg or something of the sort, but right from the beginning, Kangaroo Kelly and all the other patrolmen at South Side Station started to call him plain Pete, and he seemed to like that all right. The day they told Kangaroo about his new partner, the Sergeant took him aside and explained to him that Pete was new on the force, he was young and green, but he'd passed the training with flying colors.

"You'll have to do most of the thinking for the both of you for awhile," the Sergeant said, looking across to where Pete was standing quietly, watching them but beyond earshot. "Teach Pete your way of doing things, Kangaroo. It shouldn't take long for you to get used to him and for him to get used to you so you can work together smooth. One thing I do know about Pete: Lieutenant Randall at the Police Training School says he'll be a tiger on the job; he won't be scared of any man, beast or devil, even on the stinking South Side. You ought to make a good team."

Kangaroo looked over at Pete, took in his broad shoulders, his relaxed stance, his quick brown eyes and the generally intelligent look of him, enhanced, no doubt, by the touch of premature gray in his dark hair, and nodded slowly.

"Looks like he'd make a good partner, Sarge," he said. "Where's he living?"

The Sergeant grinned, a little embarrassed. "He ain't found a place yet," he said. "You got room for him at your house?"

"My God," Kangaroo said, aghast. "Nora won't go for that!"

"Who knows?" said the Sergeant. "Take him home and introduce him to Nora and see how it is. She may take to him."

"Well," said Kelly doubtfully, "I'll try it."

"He'll pay board," the Sergeant reminded him cannily. "You and Nora could use a little extra mazoo, I imagine?"

"That we could," Kelly said. He went over to Pete. "How's

about coming out and meeting my wife?" he suggested. "She'll want to know my new partner."

He took Pete home and introduced him to Nora. Naturally, Kangaroo didn't say anything at first about the Sergeant's idea that Pete might live with them temporarily until he got a place of his own. But Pete was so polite and ingratiating in his manners to Nora, he shook hands so seriously and his eyes were so obviously full of admiration for Nora's looks and ways, that Nora went as soft as caramel pudding to her husband's new partner, and actually brought up the subject of where he was going to live herself. That was Kangaroo's cue, of course.

And once it was decided and agreed on, Pete—with his amiable, unassuming manner and his unique ability to appear almost as withdrawn and unobtrusive as though he weren't there at all—fitted in fine at the Kelly's house from the start. Much to the surprise of Nora and Kangaroo, neither their freedom nor their sense of man-and-wife privacy suffered much from Pete's presence. It's true that Nora commented once that Pete ate an awful lot, and another time that he was so big that she almost hated to have him sit on her delicate period sofa. But Kangaroo pointed out that Pete was built big and needed big meals just as he did, and that after all, he *was* paying board, for Pete's sake! Whereupon they both grinned at this inadvertent joke and Nora agreed that Pete really was a darling and she was glad to have him in the house. They both quickly grew fond of him and began to include him in their limited social life, as well as in Kangaroo's grim nightwork.

Kangaroo soon found that Pete was an excellent partner. True to Lieutenant Randall's advance billing, Pete was a tiger on the job. He feared nothing, although he tried to be prudent in exposing himself to danger, at Kangaroo's urging. Between them, Pete and Kangaroo in their first month on the beat together began to make some sizeable dents in the record of petty crimes committed in their territory. Six months after they began walking the beat together, they had won the undoubted respect of all the hoodlums who operated there, and had even injected a pinch of wholesome fear into the criminal broth of the neighborhood.

Pete was the quietest fellow that Kangaroo Kelly, inclined to garrulity himself, had ever known. Pete walked beside him mile after mile every night, smelling out illegal activities with a fine sensitive perception, but very seldom making any attempt to communicate directly and at length with his partner. Perhaps words weren't needed, Kangaroo thought. For he realized that the communication between them was intuitive and instantaneous in emergency, that their sense of responsibility equally shared, of danger mutually faced, was drawing them more closely together as partners and friends with every night that passed.

Actually, only two things seemed important to Pete, as far as Kangaroo could tell. One was the job. You couldn't have any doubt of Pete's interest in that when you watched him, big-muscled and quiet, light and quick on his feet despite his size, prowling the dark streets of the South Side with his eyes open and seeking, his head tilted a little forward in constant alertness, and a small anticipatory grin on his face.

The other thing Pete valued, Kangaroo thought with a half-embarrassed shyness, was himself. There was no doubt that Pete admired and liked Kangaroo, felt comfortable and contented when working with him, and was perfectly willing to let Kangaroo boss the team and to defer to his orders when orders were necessary.

Even Binksy Caputo was impressed with Pete, although he wouldn't openly admit it. Kelly introduced Pete to Binksy on their first meeting with the remark, "This is a guy we got to keep an eye on, Pete. Binksy Caputo. A bad character. Been inside twice."

And Binksy laughed arrogantly, but with a threat of something beside arrogance in his voice, and said, "You got a partner, Big Tail. Well, what do you know? God knows you needed one, buddy!" He slanted his eyes at Pete, but Pete just stood there after his nod at the introduction, seeming slightly amused, and said nothing. He bulked big in the rosy light of a bar sign overhead. His calmness and apparent indifference, along with Binksy's pseudo-friendship for Kangaroo Kelly, made Binsky bold. He said insolently, "He's big, ain't he, Kangaroo? But big ain't smart. You're proof of that, Big Tail. And he looks even dumber than you!"

Now Pete wasn't amused any more. He made an annoyed sound in his throat and reached for Binksy, but Kangaroo laughed and pulled him back with a hand on his shoulder. "Let him alone, Pete," he said. "He's scared of us and trying not to show it, that's all. He's always had a big mouth. Telling me there aren't enough of us cops to handle the bad guys. Now he's not so sure, since I got a partner."

They left it at that. But as they walked away down Flora Street, Binksy couldn't resist calling after them jeeringly, "Two dumb cops are twice as dumb as one dumb cop, Big Tail! Don't forget that!"

Pete wanted to go back and knock a little respect for the law into Binksy, but Kangaroo just grinned tolerantly and shook his head. He called back to Binksy: "Don't you ever let us catch you out of line, Binks, or you'll think the roof fell on you."

Which was a considerable understatement, if anything. Because the next time they saw Binksy Caputo, he had definitely stepped out of line. And more than the roof fell on him.

About three months later, Kangaroo and Pete were walking down Express Street behind the brewery at three-twenty of a balmy summer morning, a little late on their rounds because of a purse-snatching incident earlier that had held them up for awhile. Express Street, silent and deserted at this hour, littered with a week's accumulation of torn paper, discarded beer cans and worse, went right past the door of a glass-fronted annex at the rear of the brewery where the brewery's important officials and clerical staff had their offices.

As Kangaroo and Pete reached the top of the brewery block, a hundred yards away from the entrance to this office annex, they saw by the flickering illumination of a streetlight a furtive figure emerge from a half-opened window of the place, drop to the ground against the wall, and then make off down Express Street ahead of them.

They didn't know then that it was Binksy they'd seen. But they knew from the mode of egress he'd used that he wasn't merely a brewery employee working late in the office.

Their reaction was instantaneous. Kangaroo said in a tight voice, "Let's get him, Pete!" And he began to run toward the fleeing man, fumbling with his holster.

Pete took off after the fugitive as though he were jet-propelled. He was faster than Kangaroo, whose overgrown derrière didn't help his running any. He soon left his partner yards behind.

The fugitive, now lost to view momentarily in the shadow of the brewery's shipping shed which bordered the street here, heard behind him the thud of Pete's hurrying feet on the pavement, flung one startled glance over his shoulder, and exchanged his leisurely pace for as fast a one as he could muster.

But Pete was faster than he was, too. He closed the gap between them rapidly. And suddenly, just under a street-light at the corner of the main brewery building, the prowler realized he couldn't escape and turned at bay, his back against the wall of the brewery, his arms raised shoulder high in an involuntary gesture of defense.

Kangaroo, coming as fast as his bulk permitted down the street, saw then that the man they were chasing was Binksy. "Hold it!" he bellowed. "Hold it!"

Pete's momentum was more than he could master instantly, however. And besides, the wonderful exhilaration of doing his beloved job boldly and well was upon him. He had thrown himself bodily at Binksy, grabbing for his arms, before Kangaroo's shout could halt him.

Pete and Binksy went to the ground together in a furious scuffle that lasted only a few seconds. Binksy was yelling at the top of his voice in pain and fury. Kangaroo was coming up on the run, his gun out now. "Hold him, Pete, hold him!" he panted, short of breath. "That's the stuff, Pete! I'm here."

At that moment, the muffled sound of a shot echoed on the stale air of Express Street.

Pete relaxed his hold on Binksy. He rolled slowly over on his side, groaning deep in his throat as though he were very tired. Then he lay perfectly still on the dirty pavement except for a small twitch in his legs.

Slowly Binksy rose to his feet and backed against the brick wall of the brewery. His eyes glinted wildly in the harsh glare of the streetlight.

Kangaroo saw then that Binksy had a gun in his hand and that there were bloodstains on the arm of his sport shirt.

But Pete, his partner, was Kangaroo's first concern. He stood looking down at Pete's sprawled body, shocked, dazed, unbelieving for a moment. Struggling to accept the grim fact that his partner was suddenly dead, killed in the line of duty (there was no doubt at all in his mind that Pete *was* dead. Those limply scattered limbs and the big hole in Pete's chest were all he needed), callously shot down by a worthless punk over what was probably an unimportant piece of petty thievery. Kangaroo entirely forgot his own safety. He didn't even look at Binksy, who still clutched the gun in his hand and held it aimed shakily at Kangaroo's belly.

Up to that moment, Kangaroo had always been a happy man. But now, staring down at Pete, he felt his sense of happiness desert him for the first time. His uncomplicated delight in life and living drained out of him as though it were running out of a hole in him somewhere, like the one in Pete's chest. And he felt a vicious riptide of rage and resentment rushing in to take its place.

He raised his eyes to Binksy, crouched bloody and disheveled twenty feet away against the wall. "You're in bad trouble, Binks," he said in a harsh whisper. His breath was still sawing in and out from his run. "You killed a cop."

Binksy didn't change the aim of his gun or blink his eye, but he looked at Kangaroo with a very funny expression. "It was an accident," he said. "I didn't even have my gun out. But he jumped me and I panicked. I had to do *something,* you can see that, can't you?"

"You didn't have to kill him," Kangaroo said softly. "Look at him, Binks. Dead. A good cop. Worth twenty of you."

Binksy licked his lips and a sudden stab of mortal fear

knifed through him as he saw how stiff and jaw-tight Kangaroo Kelly was holding his face.

"Listen, Big Tail," he said, his words tumbling over each other. "I tell you I didn't mean to do it. It was accidental. I'll drop my gun and you can take me in on a breaking and entering charge. Okay?"

Slowly Kangaroo shook his head. "That ain't enough, Binks. Not for you. You ever hear what happens to you when you kill a cop?"

"Yeah, a *human* cop, for God's sakes!" Binksy said hoarsely. "But not a damn canine cop like Pete, there!" He swallowed. "Just a lousy police dog!"

Kangaroo didn't seem to hear him. "Pete was a great partner," he said, "and a damn good cop. You killed him Binks."

"I killed a dog. Not a cop."

"You killed a cop," said Kangaroo. "So you're dead yourself. You know that, don't you?"

For a second or two, Binksy Caputo didn't say anything. He was watching Kangaroo's eyes and they told him nothing. Then he switched his gaze from Kangaroo's eyes to his gun hand, still hanging limp at his side, the big service revolver held almost negligently in lax fingers.

And suddenly, without a single doubt, Binksy knew it was true. He knew that Kangaroo Kelly was going to kill him . . . to exact his life in return for the life of the German shepherd dog that Kangaroo called his partner.

In a third of a second, Binksy's mind assessed the situation: here he stood, a known criminal with a record, with a gun in his hand, caught redhanded in another illegal act. He'd already murdered Kangaroo's dog. Any court in the world would certainly believe that Kangaroo was merely doing his duty if he shot Binksy down out of hand. Kangaroo Kelly would be exonerated. He'd be commended by his department, probably promoted.

And Binksy Caputo would be nothing but dead.

So Binksy made a fast, bitter decision. He steadied his gun on the lower segment of Kangaroo's belly and pulled the trigger.

A split second ahead of him, Kangaroo moved. He saw

Binksy's hand steady the gun and his finger whiten with pressure on the trigger. He didn't have time to get his own gun up to shoot first.

So he just turned his back on Binksy's flaming gun.

The slug took him high up in his right buttock. The great soft cushion of mirth-provoking flesh he carried there absorbed the bullet, slowed it down, stopped it, the way a bank of fresh soft snow will absorb a thrown snowball.

He felt no pain at all. Not yet. But as he swung his revolver up across his turning body and squeezed off one careful shot at Binksy, he was thinking wryly that finally, after all these years, he'd found a reason for being glad that people called him 'Kangaroo', 'Big Tail' and all those other offensive names.

Seeing Binksy, the cop killer, fall to the street with a police bullet in his brain, Kangaroo Kelly stooped down and patted his dead partner's shoulder, and knew that someday he'd begin to feel happy again.

THE DEATH OF AUTUMN

by Hal Ellson

The letter lay on the desk. Miss Fairfax didn't open it, didn't have to. The bad news inside had long been expected. The bank was readying to take the house, but Miss Fairfax was of another mind about that. It was her house and would remain hers. Not that she had the cash, but there were the jewels; her beautiful precious heirlooms would save the house.

From an intricately carved chest she took the jewels, admired them, then carefully placed them in a little black bag and closed it—fifty-thousand dollars in jewelry. "Now let them try to take my house," she whispered, and looked out the window.

Leaves swirled and thrashed below on the lawn, a bird skipped across the hedges, and now a single leaf fell from an almost naked tree. A brown and faded leaf, touched with the death of autumn, but Miss Fairfax failed to see it. She was listening to the big clock, counting its strokes. Finally they stopped.

Time to leave. Sighing, she rose and moved quietly to the door. She closed it behind her, descended the stairs.

Below, the hall was shadowed and filled with the odor of musk. She paused before the coatrack, slipped on a simple black coat, long black gloves, set a tiny wisp of a hat on her head and observed herself in the mirror.

Like a dark pool, the shadowed glass gave back the startling image of a younger self. Long, long ago when the ivy, which now covered every inch of the house, had barely scaled the first-floor window ledges, she'd looked like this.

Oh, dear, how beautiful I was, the old woman thought, and the mirror apparition vanished. Quickly she turned away and entered a room off the great hall. In her absence, silence accumulated, threatening, weighed. Miss Fairfax stood listening in the room off the hall and at last heard the big clock. It stood at attention, its bland face lost in shadow, but time—softly and cruelly the heavy pendulum marked the relentless passage of each second.

Miss Fairfax bestirred herself, entered the hall again, gripping the black leather bag. Gently she set it down when she stepped out to the porch. She locked the door and went down the steps. Whirlpools of leaves swirled on the lawn.

A taxi waited at the curb. The driver met her at the gate and reached for the bag.

"Never mind, young man," she said curtly and did not give it up. Her two thin hands gripped it tightly as she moved toward the taxi.

The driver sprang forward, opened the door, closed it behind her, climbed behind the wheel and drove to the railway station. Once more he opened the door, helped the old woman alight, but didn't dare touch the bag which she gripped so tightly. Must be a million bucks in it, he muttered to himself after accepting his fee and a tip.

A minute later a train huffed into the station. Refusing to relinquish the bag to the conductor, Miss Fairfax climbed aboard, found a seat and placed the bag on her lap, gripping it tightly. This, of course, attracted her fellow passengers; they smiled in amusement, but there was one who didn't. A young man had boarded the train behind Miss Fairfax and he, too, was aware of the little black bag. As the train moved out of the station he left his seat and sat down beside Miss Fairfax.

The old woman turned, and the young man smiled. He was well-dressed, clean-cut. Miss Fairfax returned his smile, then, by way of conversation, mentioned the pleasantness of the weather, the lack of rain.

"There's nothing like autumn. You can't beat it," the young man replied.

"A beautiful season," Miss Fairfax went on. "A little sad, but then it wouldn't be autumn if it weren't."

The young man nodded agreement and the train moved on through the countryside. Dusk fell, gathering the shimmering landscape into its sombre cloak. Dark clumps of trees and blue hills fled past. The train rocked gently now. Up ahead the engine wailed softly.

A lulling sound, and Miss Fairfax began to nod; her small waxen hands relaxed their grip on the bag, but not for long. Suddenly she became alert. "Goodness, I almost fell asleep," she exclaimed. "But that was refreshing. Isn't it strange how a moment seems so long and helps so much when you close your eyes?"

The young man arched his brows. "If you're tired, why not sleep a bit?" he suggested.

"Oh, no. We were talking and it was rude of me to close my eyes."

"Not at all. In fact, I didn't notice."

A white lie; Miss Fairfax smiled, looked out the window. Night had fallen; lights flashed briefly and the dark devoured them. She turned back to the young man, her voice rising: "Are you going far? I'm getting off at Rockport. Do you know the town?"

"My station."

"Ah, then, you do know it?"

"Yes, I've old friends there."

"Really? Then perhaps you know the Hamiltons?"

"No, but my friends have often mentioned them. Lovely people."

"They are old, old friends of mine."

"You're visiting with them?"

"Well, no." Miss Fairfax' hands tightened on the bag. "I've some business to tend to," she said, and the thread of conversation broke.

"Rockport!" the conductor called out, moving up the aisle.

As the engine hissed to a stop, passengers arose and the

young man turned to Miss Fairfax. "May I help you with your bag?"

The old woman hesitated a moment, then handed it over with a "Thank you, you're a gentleman." Then, somehow it happened. Too small and frail to make her way against the younger passengers who were anxious to get off the train, she was left behind and the last of all to dismount from the high steps. Now she looked around for the helpful young man and saw no sign of him. Bewildered, she watched the others moving away, the crowd thinning out, and suddenly her hand flew to her mouth.

Her scream startled those who were still on the platform. A man moved toward her, then another. The first took her arm and gently asked what was wrong. She was weeping now and her reply made no sense at all. The man waited patiently, tried again. By this time she had got control of herself. "My jewels. Fifty-thousand dollars worth. Oh, my!" she cried. "They're gone. I let that young man carry my bag and he ran off with it."

So he had; a matter for the police. Five minutes later Rockport's chief of police entered the railway waiting room and questioned Miss Fairfax. No, she wasn't acquainted with the young man who'd stolen her bag, nor could she describe him in particular. He was young, fair, and had a very nice smile. That was all the frustrated chief could get from her.

He shook his head. "We'll do our best, Miss Fairfax, but we haven't so much information to go on."

"Yes, I know. I know."

"All that jewelry. You shouldn't have been carrying it about. That was foolish. Why—"

"Oh, but I had to. I was going to sell it all. You see, the bank wants to take my house."

The police chief shook his head and patted her hand. "I'm sorry about that. We'll catch the thief and give him what he deserves."

Words, mere words; the jewels were gone, the house lost. Miss Fairfax shook her head. "He was such a nice-looking young man," she said and began to weep again.

The police chief patted her hand once more. "Train for

Bellville's arriving. Better go home. We'll be in touch."

Miss Fairfax nodded and arose. The train thundered into the station. The chief took the old woman's arm, led her out to the platform and helped her aboard the train.

Leaves rustled on the lawn, stirred by the night wind. The big house stood dark and silent. Miss Fairfax mounted the steps, let herself in, closed the door. The big clock in the hall was ticking away, delivering its fatal message. "Doom. Doom. Doom," it relentlessly intoned.

The old woman removed hat, coat, gloves, stepped into the livingroom, reached for the light switch and stopped her hand. A tall table lamp sprang to life. Dark, rich furniture glowed in the room. In the chair next to the lamp the handsome young man who had relieved Miss Fairfax of her bag nodded and grinned at her.

"Goodness, you're here already, Roger," she said.

"A fast car's quicker than a train," Roger replied. "How did it go at Rockport?"

"Oh, marvelous. Everything went off just as we planned. The chief of police was so sympathetic. He put me on the train and promised to do his best to catch you."

"And never will," Roger laughed.

"Not with the description I gave him," the old woman said. "Oh, it was so easy, so very, very easy."

"Naturally. A poor innocent old woman like you, anyone would be taken in."

"And everyone was. It was just like acting in a play and so exciting." The old woman smiled triumphantly, then crossed the room and picked up the little black bag from the table where her nephew had placed it. "All my beautiful jewelry," she exclaimed. "Now I can keep it, and the insurance . . ."

"Fifty thousand dollars," said Roger. "A lot of money."

"More than enough to pay off the bank, but the insurance people, do you think they'll be suspicious?"

"They always are, but there won't be any difficulty with them," Roger said easily. "They'll pay through the nose and like it."

"Yes, yes, they'll pay." The old woman smiled and opened the bag. One by one she laid out her jewels. "Oh, my. Oh, my, how beautiful they are!" she exclaimed.

"Very," Roger said quietly. "But, personally, I prefer sports cars."

"Yes, I know, and to each his own. But look at this." The old woman held up a magnificent brooch.

"Sports cars and cold cash," Roger went on, his voice oddly impersonal now.

"You have your sports car," the old woman reminded him. "As for the cash, that'll come, but you'll have to wait. I've a few years in me yet, you know."

"A few years?" Roger shook his head. "I can't wait that long. After all, stealing your heirlooms and collecting the insurance was my idea, dear Auntie. If not for me . . ."

"Yes, if not for you and your cars and your gambling debts, I wouldn't have done what I did," the old woman snapped. "Ah, you're greedy and ungrateful."

"Greedy," Roger admitted. "And sly," he added with a grin. "Now I wonder how I acquired those characteristics?"

The old woman placed the brooch in the bag, the other pieces followed. Then she turned to her nephew and said, "How much do you want?"

"I won't be greedy. Half the insurance money will do."

"And the rest when I die, not to mention my jewels and the house. Hmph! Well, at least I hope you can wait till the claim is paid."

"I'll try to be patient," Roger grinned.

She left him to put away her heirlooms, mumbling angrily to herself, "Greedy and sly, greedy and sly."

A half-hour later she called him to the kitchen where she had put out a cold supper. She herself didn't eat. Tea sufficed her. "Still angry?" asked Roger with a grin. "Come on, Auntie, the liverwurst is tasty tonight."

"I've no appetite," she answered and watched him hungrily consume his sandwich. *Greedy and sly; much too greedy, and not sly enough,* she thought, and turned her head.

The big clock in the hall was scoring the time. "Doom! Doom! Doom!" it chanted in faultless rhythm. The old woman smiled to herself and listened to the unhurried notes, while her nephew heard nothing, for he was too busy eating a liverwurst sandwich laced with a relish of sweet pepper—and poison.

OF MEN AND VENGEANCE

by Donald Honig

A man could forget, he could forget almost anything, but no day could be safe from what this man had experienced as a boy, from the sudden vivid brightening of the old remembering. As he strove to forget, so the child he had been had striven to remember, to retain, as if in an effort of self-flagellation. David was twenty-five now; the memory had been ticking remorselessly within him for nearly eleven years.

The boy had remembered because the hurt had been inflicted against him, and the hurt, rising and ebbing with time, had remained stubborn and vindictive, and a constant agitation to the man, panting for revenge.

He had been fourteen and, as much as fourteen could be, in love. His love had been a schoolboy idyll, the courtship conducted shyly and wistfully. The little girl, Estelle, had been very pretty, with long yellow hair and a bright, demure face. David, of course, had not wanted any of his friends to know where his affections were falling, so he planned secret meetings with her, mostly in her backyard where they sat and played games on the lawn or climbed high into the pear tree (often she would hide from him up there), or sat on the embankment behind her yard and watched the freight trains go by. He was in love that summer, he would never forget it, it had been a dream woven of sun and grass.

Grim remembering and panting revenge concerned that dark cloud-massing afternoon toward the end of the summer, when he had agreed to meet her in the backyard. (Her parents would be away that afternoon, she had told him, so if the rain did come they would be able to sit in the house and play her phonograph). So, undaunted by the massing black rainclouds that were threatening to inundate Capstone at any moment, he had run from his house to hers, running through the sidestreets under the leafy elms and oaks that were swishing massively in the strong rushing wind. There was a faroff drum of thunder as he ran into the alleyway leading into her backyard. He called her name.

Even before he saw her, he saw the man crashing through the scrub trees and knotted intricate bramble behind the house, which stood on the crest above the freight tracks. He caught the man's face in profile—it was a dark swarthy face he had seen about the neighborhood—and instantly the word, the name, *Keller!,* flashed, almost involuntarily across his mind simultaneously with the lightning which split the black clouds with a white stabbing. The thunder crashed overhead now and a few drops of rain struck swiftly with loud splats. The man disappeared over the embankment, a fleeting falling figure, as David yelled, "Stop!" He saw her then, lying on the grass, and for a moment it all seemed like a joke—her head was turned toward him and her eyes were fixed upon him and it was all very tense and unreal and he was about to utter her name when the lightning flashed again and made her eyes gleam like sequins and the thunder broke with a booming fall. She did not move as the rain struck her in noisy, blinding sheets. From below, in low grumbling, he heard the passage of a freight train.

He ran home, terrified. When he burst into the house, soaking wet, his parents mistook his tears for rain. He ran upstairs and sat shivering in his room, trying to remember what he had seen, trying to see it again so he could believe it. He went to the telephone and called the police, holding the receiver in both hands against his ear, listening to the buzzing which was broken off by a voice.

"Hello?"

"Hello," he said. "I want to tell . . . about Estelle Sampson. A man killed her this afternoon . . ." The words frightened him. He pushed the phone down on the cradle and ran back into his room.

He said nothing further to anyone. He was afraid that he would be implicated. (His youthful imagination, conjured up all manner of persecution for himself, particularly when it became apparent that Keller had got away.) When—because he had been her friend—the police came to his house to talk to him, he said he had not gone to Estelle's house because of the imminent thunderstorm, that he had started out for there but the rain had intervened and he had gone back home. And he denied having made the phone call. They believed him and the little girl's murder went unsolved. The broken brush behind the house, where someone had recently run, was the only clue. Also, the Sampson house had been ransacked, and the police surmised that the little girl had surprised the intruder as he was leaving and for it paid with her life.

As he walked mournfully and cautiously in the streets during the next few weeks (and not without the beginnings, like a dark foreboding, of guilt and complicity) it became apparent to David that Keller, who before had seemed present everywhere, had gone.

His love became like a little tomb in his mind, a tiny inscribed stone, enduring before his eyes like a true stone endures before the trees. It became like something beatified and asleep inside of him.

For awhile there was great excitement in the neighborhood. His classmates (school had begun soon after) chattered incessantly about the murder, but David remained aloof from all the talk. Then it all gradually faded and people began to forget. But in David's mind it remained cruelly vivid. He could not stop thinking of what had happened. It seemed to him that it had ruined his life. It hung among his thoughts like a black cloak, creeping into his sleep, threatening to become an eternal and integral part of his existence. And a sense of guilt haunted him, lengthening across his soul like an infinite shadow. As he grew older he realized that he had willfully suppressed his own better judgment at the time of the murder, when he had not told the police what he had seen.

He remained in Capstone, living with his parents. After high school he took a job in one of the factories in town, working on a machine, first as a helper then as cutter. Because there was little variance of duties for him and he stood all day in one place, he found he had little to think about except the past, and, more specifically, the one thing that had so thoroughly dominated his past. He became mired in the job. After work he went straight home. His weekends became part of his routine, monotonous and unvarying. Because his moods were so singularly depressing, he was constantly seeking solitude in which to contemplate them.

He seldom went out with girls. Never again did he feel with a girl that complete rapport he had felt with Estelle. He seemed unable to foment new love, and so his heart continued to dwell upon and nurture the old. Gradually he let it evolve into the dimensions of stark tragedy. (At times he even preferred this kind of solitude and isolation to the companionship of the few friends he had.) Because his home was so close to that of the dead girl's and because he was continually encountering her family on the street, there was little chance of the incident fading from his mind. Over and over, that day with all its attendant darkness and thunder and fear would be rekindled in his mind. As year fell upon year his feeling of guilt worsened, became more complicated, finally demanding of him the resolve: *If ever the chance is given me, I will kill him.*

It might have gone on like that forever, this bitter stabbing from the past, had he not seen Keller again. David had been walking down Grant Avenue, shuffling aimlessly through the afternoon shoppers (and, ironically, he had been thinking about the little girl that morning, having passed her father and mother on the street) when, passing Pete's Capstone Restaurant, he glanced in through the window and saw the dark stony face that he had not forgotten and would never forget, that had been blasted into his brain eleven years ago. He stopped dead and gazed at Keller as intently and as uninhibitedly as though Keller were not look-

ing back at him from the booth. It was incredible, like
something that had materialized from the darkest nightmare, sitting there before him in mute and stony confronta-
tion. As they stared at each other, Keller's head lifted, just a
trifle, a light coming into his eyes, enough to make David,
hurrying away now with a cold, flustered and shocked feeling, think, *He knows I know. He knows that I was the one.*

That evening David sought out his friend Roy who had
recently graduated from the police academy. He found Roy
sitting alone at a table in Marshall's Bar. He joined him at
the table, pulling his chair far in, sitting close against the
table.

"Roy, do you remember Estelle Sampson?" he asked.

"That sounds like somebody we went to school with," Roy
said.

"It is—or was. She was the little girl who was murdered.
It's quite awhile back, more than ten years now."

Roy nodded. "Oh, yes," he said. "I remember that. She
was found strangled or something. And I don't think they
ever found out who did it, did they?"

"That's it. That's the one. Well I need some legal advice."

"Don't tell me you're going to make a confession at this
late date," Roy said with a laugh, picking up his drink.

"Yes, it is a confession of sorts," David said thoughtfully.
"I know who did it, Roy. I've always known."

Roy sipped his drink and put the glass back down, his
eyes fastening curiously upon David's face. "You do?"

"I saw the man."

"When?"

"At the time, and then—after all this time—again, today. He's back in Capstone. Do you remember a man named
Keller? He was always sort of a hanger-on who floated
around town. I think he was even an ex-convict."

"I remember him. He was sort of a shady fellow. Yes,
he's back in town. I've seen him."

"Why did he come back? What do you think made him
come back?"

"Now slow down," Roy said, lighting a cigarette, frowning at the smoke for a moment. "Let's go about this in an orderly manner."

David told him the story of that dark rainy day, of finding Estelle lying dead in the yard and of seeing Keller fleeing through the trees and disappearing over the hill, of running back home and, except for his anonymous phone call, never saying a word to anyone.

"And now he's back," David said, his voice intense, puzzled. "Why? For what?"

"If all you say is true," Roy said, "you'd still have a hard time going about proving it. Are you that positive he's the same man you saw running through the trees on an overcast day ten years ago? That's the first thing you'd be asked you know. Are you that sure?"

"Do you think I could ever forget?"

"Still, I don't think you could make it stick," Roy said.

"But something has to be done," David whispered intensely. "He's a murderer. He killed that little girl. You don't remember her like I do. She was the most beautiful little thing . . ."

Roy expelled smoke across at him. "It would never stick. You'd be letting yourself in for something unpleasant, something that you wouldn't be able to finish."

"All right, then; then let me tell you something. It might be too late for the law. But that man remains a murderer. He's still a murderer. I don't care if this is fifty years later. Nothing can change that. Maybe I couldn't make it stick, but remember this—*I* know what he did. And I'm just as guilty for not speaking up at the time. Don't you think that's been haunting me all my life?"

"Don't do anything foolish, Dave. As far as the law is concerned he's done nothing wrong. You would be held responsible for anything you did to him."

"But you don't understand. He's back now. He might disappear again tomorrow and never come back. This might be my last chance."

"You're that sure he's the man?"

"Of course. I saw him running through the trees."

"Then how would you explain his running away like that when he's got only one leg?"

"One leg?" David asked, incredulous.

It was true. He saw Keller the next day, going up the avenue on crutches, his right leg gone below the knee.

For the next week or so he kept seeing the man on crutches. Keller seemed to be on the avenue every minute of the day, either standing somewhere or else moving along in smooth, effortless hops. David would watch him; Keller would stare back at him, their eyes locking, staring moodily at each other.

Why has he come back? David kept asking himself, the question haunting and recurrent and unanswerable. Why, after all this time would he risk coming back? The man certainly knew that someone had seen him, had shouted at him that day. Was he that contemptuous or that confident or that indifferent?

The more David saw him, the more the need to avenge the little girl and assuage his own burning conscience surged within him. If the police were powerless to dispense justice at this late date, then he would do it himself. Keller could disappear again, overnight, and then it would be too late.

Familiarizing himself with Keller's habits, he learned that the one-legged man drank beer nightly in Jim Carson's tavern down near Mount Branch cemetery, sitting alone at a corner table. At midnight Keller would leave, walking slowly down the avenue, far down to where he had moved into an abandoned shack near Newtown Creek.

David waited in the shadows that night, trembling with the action he had resolved. Once he realized that he was going through with it, his heart almost burst with excitement, almost as though he could not believe it. All the sorrow and guilt from all the years had risen like the ghosts of his outraged innocence, chanting the death song in his heart. And now that excitement was inside of him in a frenzy that was nearly uncontrollable.

He drew back into an alleyway as the door of Carson's opened and Keller appeared there, coming out, twisting on his crutches to shut the door behind him. Then the swarthy man—thinner now than he had been when David had seen him crashing through the brush behind Estelle's house those many years ago—began walking, his one leg and his crutches skipping him rhythmically forward, his arms moving like rowing. David let him reach three blocks ahead and then separated himself from the shadows and began following, standing his coat collar up against the chill night, walking close to the buildings, his eyes fast upon the slow-moving, patiently hopping man ahead.

They passed the cemetery and went through the business district, passing the houses and the stores, moving into Capstone's dark industrial end, coming to the warehouses and brickyards and the dark haunted factories (many of which had shut down after the war). They crossed the freight tracks, passing a pair of abandoned box cars that rose like mountains in the mist that was coming stealthily in, a cold wet breath clouding the night; it made David move to a block behind. He could hear the steady, inexorable tap of Keller's crutches. *He knows I'm following,* he thought. *He must know.*

Keller crossed the street, swinging himself carefully over the glistening cobblestones, going through the mist like a phantom, like the last of a maimed and crumbled race. He went through an empty lot, carrying himself into the weeds. David crossed and followed into the lot, softly, listening for the sound of the crutches on the soft, damp earth. But he heard nothing. Keller was gone. David stood still, squinting in the mist that was folding and unfolding around him in a slow, tantalizing mass. The creek was just ahead. He could see the faint outline of the drawbridge, could hear, from far down the dark malodorous water, the lonely owl-cry of a barge. He moved slowly toward the creek, his hand moving the weeds aside like a wand.

"Yes?" The voice came coldly out of the mist, followed by the man himself, coming forward on his crutches that seemed almost alive the way they supported him.

David stared at him, feeling terror and anger, and it was like a long-threatening specter had suddenly been incarnated before him.

"You've followed me a long way," Keller said.

"Longer than you think," David said, lifting his hands from his coat pockets.

"Why?"

"You know why."

Keller studied him for a moment, carefully, leaning his full weight forward on the crutches. "You must have been a young boy at that time," he said.

"But I've never forgotten."

"Nor have I."

"You came back here. Why?"

"Why shouldn't I have come back if I chose? What has an innocent man to be afraid of?"

"Innocent?"

"Does that surprise you?"

"I saw you there."

"You saw me running. That was what you saw. Do you remember that?"

David stared at the whiteness that was Keller's face, beginning to feel an uneasiness, something that he wanted to believe but did not know if he would be quite able to.

"That little girl was dead when I got there," Keller said, his voice strangely cold now, bitter. "She must have fallen from the tree. I never touched her. I was in the house—I was guilty of that—and I heard a thud in the yard. When I came out I saw her. Then you yelled. So I ran."

"You must have run far."

"It looked very bad. Even you believed that I had done it, didn't you?"

"Then all these years . . ." David said. "I thank God now that I never told." It was incredible. He felt it in his heart, then all through his body—the recession and the melting of the heat and the vengeance, feeling it expiring in his veins. Suddenly, after all these years, he could forget. He shook his head in disbelief as for the first time in ten years there was no tension in his body.

"So you think it's over?" Keller said.

David looked at him, at the face in front of him in the mist that was gazing with a heaviness, almost a deadness.

"So you think it's as simple as that?" Keller said. "You asked me why I came back. I came back to find the man whom I knew would seek me out. I knew that if you were still here you would come to me."

"You hoped I would come to you?"

"Oh, yes, I hoped very much. I came back to make amends with you. You shouted that day. You made me run. You made me go through the trees and over the hill. You made me panic and lose my footing and go rolling all the way down to the tracks where the train was passing. I caught the train all right, but it caught me too. I had no choice but to hold on, even though part of me was being mangled."

David looked down, at the stump of Keller's leg.

"But I . . ." David never finished. There was the sudden lifting and arcing of a crutch that came smashing against the side of his head. He toppled back, felt himself suddenly spilling over the embankment, rolling halfway down. He could hear the sluggish dark water lapping below, and then, in his stunned, blackening consciousness, heard a furious scratching as the now crazed Keller appeared above him, grotesque and terrifying in the mist, hopping on a single crutch, falling forward with a fury and urgency as though he had fallen a thousand miles, flinging the crutch like a spear as he fell, the crutch hitting the soft damp earth next to David's head and sliding down into the creek. Keller fell on top of him and they rolled down into the creek, thrashing the black water as they struggled and went under, Keller's strong prehensile fingers closing around David's throat.

David felt the waters rising all around him, Keller upon him like a great and swarming fish, pressing him down. He felt the water crushing in his lungs. His arms were around Keller's neck. They locked inextricably in the depths below the healing, slow-passing water that moved on as dark and as eternal as forgetting.

The circles vanished from the water, and into the dark, like some strange and lonely relic, the crutch swam alone with the laggard tide toward the East River.

JUST CURIOUS

by James H. Schmitz

Roy Litton's apartment was on the eighteenth floor of the Torrell Arms. It was a pleasant place which cost him thirty-two thousand dollars a year. The livingroom had a wide veranda which served in season as a sundeck. Far below was a great park. Beyond the park, drawn back to a respectful distance from the Torrell Arms, was the rest of the city.

"May I inquire," Roy Litton said to his visitor, "from whom you learned about me?"

The visitor's name was Jean Merriam. She was a slender, expensive brunette, about twenty-seven. She took a card from her handbag and slid it across the table to Litton. "Will that serve as an introduction?" she asked.

Litton studied the words scribbled on the card and smiled. "Yes," he said, "that's quite satisfactory. I know the lady's handwriting well. In what way can I help you?"

"I represent an organization," Jean said, "which does discreet investigative work."

"You're detectives?"

She shrugged, smiled. "We don't refer to ourselves as detectives, but that's the general idea. Conceivably your talents could be very useful to us. I'm here to find out whether you're willing to put them at our disposal from time to time. If you are, I have a test assignment for you. You don't mind, do you?"

Litton rubbed his chin. "You've been told what my standard fee is?"

Jean Merriam opened the handbag again, took out a check and gave it to him. Litton read it carefully, nodded. "Yes," he said, and laid the check on the table beside him. "Ten thousand dollars. You're in the habit of paying such sums out of your personal account?"

"The sum was put in my account yesterday for this purpose."

"Then what do you, or your organization, want me to do?"

"I've been given a description of how you operate, Mr. Litton, but we don't know how accurate the description is. Before we retain you, I'd like you to tell me exactly what you do."

Litton smiled. "I'm willing to tell you as much as I know."

She nodded. "Very well. I'll decide on the basis of what you say whether or not your services might be worth ten thousand dollars to the organization. Once I offer you the assignment and you accept it, we're committed. The check will be yours when the assignment is completed."

"Who will judge when it has been completed?"

"You will," said Jean. "Naturally there will be no further assignments if we're not satisfied with the results of this one. As I said, this is a test. We're gambling. If you're as good as I've been assured you are, the gamble should pay off. Fair enough?"

Litton nodded. "Fair enough, Miss Merriam." He leaned back in his chair. "Well, then—I sometimes call myself a 'sensor' because the word describes my experiences better than any other word I can think of. I'm not specifically a mind reader. I can't predict the future. I don't have second sight. But under certain conditions I turn into a long-range sensing device with a limited application. I have no theoretical explanation for it. I can only say what happens.

"I work through contact objects; that is, material items which have had a direct and extensive physical connection with the persons I investigate. A frequently worn garment is the obvious example. Eyeglasses would be excellent. I once was able to use an automobile which the subject had driven daily for about ten months. Through some object I seem to become, for a time which varies between approximately three and five minutes, the person in question." Litton smiled. "Naturally I remain here physically, but my awareness is elsewhere.

"Let me emphasize that during this contact period I *am* —or seem to be—the other person. I am not conscious of Roy Litton or of what Roy Litton is doing. I have never heard of him and know nothing of his sensing ability. I am the other person, aware only of what he is aware of, doing what he is doing, thinking what he is thinking. If, meanwhile, you were to speak to the body sitting here, touch it, even cause it severe pain—which has been done experimentally—I wouldn't know it. When the time is up, the contact fades and I'm back. Then I know who I am and can recall my experience and report on it. Essentially, that's the process."

Jean Merriam asked, "To what extent do you control the process?"

"I can initiate it or not initiate it. I'm never drawn out of myself unless I intend to be drawn out of myself. That's the extent of my control. Once it begins, the process continues by itself and concludes itself. I have no way of affecting its course."

Jean said reflectively, "I don't wish to alarm you, Mr. Litton. But mightn't you be running the risk of remaining permanently lost in somebody else's personality . . . unable to return to your own?"

Litton laughed. "No. I know definitely that can't happen, though I don't know why. The process simply can't maintain itself for much more than five minutes. On the other hand, it's rarely terminated in less than three."

"You say that during the time of contact you think what the other person thinks and are aware of what he's aware of?"

"That's correct."

"Only that? If we employed you to investigate someone in this manner, we usually would need quite specific information. Wouldn't we have to be extremely fortunate if the person happened to think of that particular matter in the short time you shared his mind?"

"No," said Litton. "Conscious thoughts quite normally have thousands of ramifications and shadings the thinker doesn't know about. When the contact dissolves, I retain his impressions and it is primarily these ramifications and shadings I then investigate. It is something like developing a vast number of photographic prints. Usually the information my clients want can be found in those impressions in sufficient detail."

"What if it can't be found?"

"Then I make a second contact. On only one occasion, so far, have I been obliged to make three separate contacts with a subject to satisfy the client's requirements. There is no fee for additional contacts."

Jean Merriam considered a moment. "Very well," she said. She brought a small box from the handbag, opened it and took out a ring which she handed to Litton. "The person in whom the organization is interested," she said, "was wearing this ring until four weeks ago. Since then it's been in a safe. The safe was opened yesterday and the ring taken from it and placed in this box. Would you consider it a suitable contact object?"

Litton held the ring in his palm an instant before replying. "Eminently suitable!" he said then.

"You can tell by touching such objects?"

"As a rule. If I get no impression, it's a waste of time to proceed. If I get a negative impression, I refuse to proceed."

"A negative impression?"

Litton shrugged. "A feeling of something that repels me. I can't describe it more definitely."

"Does it mean that the personality connected with the object is a repellent one?"

"Not necessarily. I've merged with some quite definitely repellent personalities in the course of this work. That doesn't disturb me. The feeling I speak of is a different one."

"It frightens you?"

"Perhaps." He smiled. "However, in this case there is no such feeling. Have you decided to offer me the assignment?" he asked her.

"Yes, I have," Jean Merriam said. "Now then, I've been told nothing about the person connected with the ring. Since very few men could get it on, and very few children would wear a ring of such value, I assume the owner is a woman—but I don't know even that. The reason I've been told nothing is to make sure I'll give you no clues, inadvertently or otherwise." She smiled. "Even if you were a mindreader, you see, you could get no significant information from me. We want to be certain of the authenticity of your talent."

"I understand," Litton said. "But you must know what kind of information your organization wants to gain from the contact?"

Jean nodded. "Yes, of course. We want you to identify the subject by name and tell us where she can be found. The description of the locality should be specific. We also want to learn as much as we can about the subject's background, her present activities and interests, and any people with whom she is closely involved. The more details you can give us about such people, the better. In general, that's it. Does it seem like too difficult an assignment?"

"Not at all," Litton said. "In fact, I'm surprised you want no more. Is that kind of information really worth ten thousand dollars to you?"

"I've been told," Jean said, "that if we get it within the next twenty-four hours, it will be worth a great deal more than ten thousand dollars."

"I see." Litton settled comfortably in the chair, placed his clasped hands around the ring on the table, enclosing it. "Then, if you like, Miss Merriam, I'll now make the contact."

"No special preparations?" she inquired, watching him.

"Not in this case." Litton nodded toward a heavily curtained alcove in the wall on his left. "That's what I call my withdrawal room. When I feel there's reason to expect difficulties in making a contact, I go in there. Observers can be disturbing under such circumstances. Otherwise, no preparations are necessary."

"What kind of difficulties could you encounter?" Jean asked.

"Mainly, the pull of personalities other than the one I want. A contact object may be valid, but contaminated by associations with other people. Then it's a matter of defining and following the strongest attraction, which is almost always that of the proper owner and our subject. Incidentally, it would be advantageous if you were prepared to record my report."

Jean tapped the handbag. "I'm recording our entire conversation, Mr. Litton."

He didn't seem surprised. "Very many of my clients do," he remarked. "Very well, then, let's begin . . ."

"How long did it take him to dream up this stuff?" Nick Garland asked.

"Four minutes and thirty-two seconds," Jean Merriam said.

Garland shook his head incredulously. He took the transcript she'd made of her recorded visit to Roy Litton's apartment from the desk and leafed through it again. Jean watched him, her face expressionless. Garland was a big gray-haired bear of a man, coldly irritable at present—potentially dangerous.

He laid the papers down, drummed his fingers on the desk. "I still don't want to believe it," he said, "but I guess I'll have to. He hangs on to Caryl Chase's ring for a few minutes, then he can tell you enough about her to fill five typed, single-spaced pages . . . That's what happened?"

Jean nodded. "Yes, that's what happened. He kept pouring out details about the woman as if he'd known her intimately half her life. He didn't hesitate about anything. My impression was that he wasn't guessing about anything. He seemed to know."

Garland grunted. "Max thinks he knew." He looked up at the man standing to the left of the desk. "Fill Jean in, Max. How accurate is Litton?"

Max Jewett said, "On every point we can check out, he's completely accurate."

"What are the points you can check out?" Jean asked.

"The ring belongs to Caryl Chase. She's thirty-two. She's Phil Chase's wife, currently estranged. She's registered at the Hotel Arve, Geneva, Switzerland, having an uneasy off-and-on affair with one William Haskell, British ski nut. He's jealous, and they fight a lot. Caryl suspects Phil has detectives looking for her, which he does. Her daughter Ellie is hidden away with friends of Caryl's parents in London. Litton's right about the ring. Caryl got it from her grandmother on her twenty-first birthday and wore it since. When she ran out on Phil last month, she took it off and left it in her room safe. Litton's statement, that leaving it was a symbolic break with her past life, makes sense." Jewett shrugged. "That's about it. Her psychoanalyst might be able to check out some of the rest of what you got on tape. We don't have that kind of information."

Garland growled, "We don't need it. We got enough for now."

Jean exchanged a glance with Jewett. "You feel Litton's genuine, Mr. Garland?"

"He's genuine. Only Max and I knew we were going to test him on Caryl. If he couldn't do what he says he does, you wouldn't have got the tape. There's no other way he could know those things about her." Garland's face twisted into a sour grimace. "I thought Max had lost his marbles when he told me it looked like Phleger had got his information from some kind of swami. But that's how it happened. Frank Phleger got Litton to tap my mind something like two or three months ago. He'd need that much time to get set to make his first move."

"How much have you lost?" Jean asked.

He grunted. "Four, five million. I can't say definitely yet. That's not what bothers me." His mouth clamped shut, a pinched angry line. His eyes shifted bleakly down to the desk, grew remote, lost focus.

Jean Merriam watched him silently. Inside that big skull was stored information which seemed sometimes equal to the intelligence files of a central bank. Nick Garland's brain was a strategic computer, a legal library. He was a multimillionaire, a brutal genius, a solitary and cunning king beast in the financial jungle—a jungle he allowed to become barely aware he existed. Behind his secretiveness he remained an unassailable shadow. In the six years Jean had been working for him she'd never before seen him suffer a setback; but if they were right about Litton, this was more than a setback. Garland's mind had been opened, his plans analyzed, his strengths and weaknesses assessed by another solitary king beast—a lesser one, but one who knew exactly how to make the greatest possible use of the information thus gained— and who had begun to do it. So Jean waited and wondered.

"Jean," Garland said at last. His gaze hadn't shifted from the desk.

"Yes?"

"Did Litton buy your story about representing something like a detective agency?"

"He didn't seem to question it," Jean said. "My impression was that he doesn't particularly care who employs him, or for what purpose."

"He'll look into anyone's mind for a price?" It was said like a bitter curse.

"Yes . . . his price. What are you going to do?"

Garland's shoulders shifted irritably. "Max is trying to get a line on Phleger."

Jean glanced questioningly at Jewett. Jewett told her, "Nobody seems to have any idea where Frank Phleger's been for the past three weeks. We assume he dropped out of sight to avoid possible repercussions. The indications are that we're getting rather close to him."

"I see," Jean said uncomfortably. The king beasts avoided rough play as a matter of policy, usually avoided conflict among themselves, but when they met in a duel there were no rules.

"Give that part of it three days," Garland's voice said. She looked around, found him watching her with a trace of what might be irony, back at any rate from whatever brooding trance he'd been sunk in. "Jean, call Litton sometime tomorrow."

"All right."

"Tell him the boss of your detective organization wants an appointment with him. Ten o'clock, three days from now."

She nodded, said carefully, "Litton could become extremely valuable to you, Mr. Garland."

"He could," Garland agreed. "Anyway, I want to watch the swami perform. We'll give him another assignment."

"Am I to accompany you?"

"You'll be there, Jean. So will Max."

"I keep having the most curiously definitive impression," Roy Litton observed, "that I've met you before."

"You have," Garland said amiably.

Litton frowned, shook his head. "It's odd I should have forgotten the occasion!"

"The name's Nick Garland," Garland told him.

Still frowning, Litton stared at him across the table. Then abruptly his face paled. Jean Merriam, watching from behind her employer, saw Litton's eyes shift to her, from her to Max Jewett, and return at last, hesitantly, to Garland's face. Garland nodded wryly.

"I was what you call one of your subjects, Mr. Litton," he said. "I can't give you the exact date, but it should have been between two and three months ago. You remember now?"

Litton shook his head. "No. After such an interval it would be impossible to be definite about it, in any case. I keep no notes and the details of a contact very quickly grow blurred to me." His voice was guarded; he kept his eyes on Garland's. "Still, you seemed familiar to me at once as a person. And your name seems familiar. It's quite possible that you have been, in fact, a contact subject."

"I was," Garland said. "We know that. That's why we're here."

Litton cleared his throat. "Then the story Miss Merriam told me at her first visit wasn't true."

"Not entirely," Garland admitted. "She wasn't representing a detective outfit. She represented me. Otherwise, she told the truth. She was sent here to find out whether you could do what we'd heard you could do. We learned that you could. Mr. Litton, you've cost me a great deal of money. But I'm not too concerned about that now, because, with your assistance, I'll make it back. And I'll make a great deal more besides. You begin to get the picture?"

Relief and wariness mingled for an instant in Litton's expression. "Yes, I believe I do."

"You'll get paid your regular fees, of course," Garland told him. "The fact is, Mr. Litton, you don't charge enough. What you offer is worth more than ten thousand a shot. What you gave Frank Phleger was worth enormously more."

"Frank Phleger?" Litton said.

"The client who paid you to poke around in my mind. No doubt he wouldn't have used his real name. It doesn't matter. Let's get on to your first real assignment for me. Regular terms. This one isn't a test. It's to bring up information I don't have and couldn't get otherwise. All right?"

Litton nodded, smiled. "You have a suitable contact object?"

"We brought something that should do," Garland said. "Max, give Mr. Litton the belt."

Jean Merriam looked back toward Jewett. Garland hadn't told her what Litton's assignment was to be, had given her no specific instructions, but she'd already turned on the recorder in her handbag. Jewett was taking a large plastic envelope from the briefcase he'd laid beside his chair. He came over to the table, put the envelope before Litton and returned to his place.

"Can you tell me specifically what you want to know concerning this subject?" Litton asked.

"To start with," Garland said, "just give us whatever you can get. I'm interested in general information."

Litton nodded, opened the plastic envelope and took out a man's leather belt with a broad silver buckle. Almost immediately an expression of distaste showed in his face. He put the belt on the table, looked over at Garland.

"Mr. Garland," he said, "Miss Merriam may have told you that on occasion I'm offered a contact object I can't use. Unfortunately, this belt is such an object."

"What do you mean?" Garland asked. "Why can't you use it?"

"I don't know. It may be something about the belt itself, and it may be the person connected with it." Litton brushed the belt with his fingers. "I simply have a very unpleasant feeling about this object. It repels me." He smiled apologetically. "I'm afraid I must refuse to work with it."

"Well, now," Garland said, "I don't like to hear that.

You've cost me a lot, you know. I'm willing to overlook it, but I do expect you to be cooperative in return."

Litton glanced at him, swallowed uneasily. "I understand—and I assure you you'll find me cooperative. If you'll give me some other assignment, I assure you—"

"No," Garland said. "No, right now I want information about this particular person, not somebody else. It's too bad if you don't much like to work with the belt, but that's your problem. We went to a lot of trouble to get the belt for you. Let me state this quite clearly, Mr. Litton. You owe me the information, and I think you'd better get it now."

His voice remained even, but the menace in the words was undisguised. The king beast was stepping out from cover; and Jean's palms were suddenly wet. She saw Litton's face whiten.

"I suppose I do owe it to you," Litton said after a moment. He hesitated again. "But this isn't going to be easy."

Garland snorted. "You're getting ten thousand dollars for a few minutes' work!"

"That isn't it. I . . ." Litton shook his head helplessly, got to his feet. He indicated the curtained alcove at the side of the room. "I'll go in there. At best, this will be a difficult contact to attempt. I can't be additionally distracted by knowing that three people are staring at me."

"You'll get the information?" Garland asked.

Litton looked at him, said sullenly, "I always get the information." He picked up the belt, went to the alcove and disappeared through the curtains.

Garland turned toward Jean Merriam. "Start timing him," he said.

She nodded, checked her watch. The room went silent, and immediately Jean felt a heavy oppression settle on her. It was almost as if the air had begun to darken around them. Frightened, she thought, *Nick hates that freak . . . Has he decided to kill him?*

She pushed the question away and narrowed her attention to the almost inaudible ticking of the tiny expensive watch. After a while she realized that Garland was looking at her again. She met his eyes, whispered, "Three minutes and ten seconds." He nodded.

There was a sound from within the alcove. It was not particularly loud, but in the stillness it was startling enough to send a new gush of fright through Jean. She told herself some minor piece of furniture, a chair, a small side table, had fallen over, been knocked over on the carpeting. She was trying to think of some reason why Litton should have knocked over a chair in there when the curtains before the alcove were pushed apart. Litton moved slowly out into the room.

He stopped a few feet from the alcove. He appeared dazed, half-stunned, like a man who'd been slugged hard in the head and wasn't sure what had happened. His mouth worked silently, his lips writhing in slow, stiff contortions as if trying to shape words that couldn't be pronounced. Abruptly he started forward. Jean thought for a moment he was returning to the table, but he went past it, pace quickening, on past Garland and herself without glancing at either of them. By then he was almost running, swaying from side to side in long staggering steps, and she realized he was hurrying toward the French doors which stood open on the wide veranda overlooking the park. Neither Garland nor Jewett moved from their chairs, and Jean, unable to speak, twisted around to look after Litton as they were doing. She saw him run across the veranda, strike the hip-high railing without checking, and go on over.

The limousine moved away from the Torrell Arms through the sunlit park, Jewett at the wheel, Garland and Jean Merriam in the back seat. There was no siren wail behind them, no indication of disturbance, nothing to suggest that anyone else was aware that a few minutes ago a man had dropped into the neatly trimmed park shrubbery from the eighteenth floor of the great apartment hotel.

"You could have made use of him," Jean said. "He could have been of more value to you than anyone else in the world. But you intended to kill him from the start, didn't you?"

Garland didn't reply for a moment. Then he said, "I could have made use of him, sure. So could anyone else with ten thousand dollars to spare, or some way to put pressure on him. I don't need somebody like Litton to stay on top. And I don't like the rules changed. When Phleger found Litton, he started changing them. It could happen again. Litton had to be taken out."

"Max could have handled that," Jean said. Her hands had begun to tremble again; she twisted them tightly together around the strap of the handbag. "What did you do to get Litton to kill himself?"

Garland shook his head. "I didn't intend him to kill himself. Max was to take care of him afterward."

"You did something to him."

Garland drew a long sighing breath. "I was just curious," he said. "There's something I wonder about now and then. I thought Litton might be able to tell me, so I gave him the assignment."

"What assignment? He became someone else for three minutes. What happened to him?"

Garland's head turned slowly toward her. She noticed for the first time that his face was almost colorless. "That was Frank Phleger's belt," he said. "Max's boys caught up with him last night. Phleger's been dead for the last eight hours."

BEYOND THE WALL

by Nedra Tyre

Poor dear, Ellen Williams thought, as she looked with pity at her new acquaintance on the high, narrow hospital bed. Because of all the dressings and splints and casts, Margaret Collins seemed to have more than the usual number of arms and legs.

For a moment Ellen had an attack of stagefright; she was supposed to entertain the injured woman. Margaret Collins' cousin, Anne Fitzgerald, had urged Ellen to talk about her travels. "For years I've wanted you two to meet and now is a good time. Margaret has been so active that recovering from her injuries is terribly hard on her. Be an angel and go to see her. May I tell her you'll drop by for a long visit on Tuesday afternoon? Incidentally, Ellen, she's awfully fond of mystery and intrigue. She's a psychologist and keenly interested in peculiar behavior and crime. So if you've run into any of that on your trips do tell her about it."

Figuratively speaking, Ellen Williams feared she had a limp bouquet of faded wildflowers to offer Mrs. Collins instead of the exotic blossoms of intrigue and mystery Anne Fitzgerald had suggested. Conducted tours, which were all that Ellen had ever taken, didn't lend themselves to mysterious happenings or attract exciting, provocative people. They catered to no-nonsense, middle-aged persons eager for their money's worth.

Anyway, here Ellen was, eager to do her best to divert the woman who had broken almost everything but her neck in an automobile accident.

"How nice of you to come," Mrs. Collins said, smiling at her slight, uncommonly pretty, plainly dressed, middle-aged visitor. "I'm eager to hear about your travels. I've always wanted to travel. Now I'm afraid I never will. But then if I'd really wanted to I'd have managed to travel long before this, wouldn't I? Don't we arrange to do the things that we want most to do?"

Mrs. Collins was a psychologist and must know what she was talking about. Even so, Ellen had to object. "I'm not so sure," she said. "To tell you the truth, I've had traveling thrust upon me. I'd never budge from Lexington if my sons didn't insist that I travel. They don't believe me when I say I'd much rather stay at home. Now then, is there any particular place you'd like to hear about?"

"No. Anything will be nice."

Mrs. Collins' face wore the glowing expectancy of a child reaching out for a Christmas present. A sense of inadequacy made Ellen squirm in her chair. She was afraid that she would be a great disappointment to Mrs. Collins. All the same, she must do as well as she could, and her brain riffled through her travels.

Now that she put her mind to it, there was something unusual about the tour she took to Berlin in August 1961, a few days after The Wall went up. It was an exciting time, no question about it. The peace of the world was in jeopardy then.

Ellen Williams cleared her throat. "I'm ashamed to say I'm not politically minded," she said. An apology was no way to begin. Well, she would have to tell it as it came to her. "I skip editorials and political columns, so I hadn't the slightest notion that a crisis was imminent when I took a tour to Germany in August 1961. I arrived in England a few days before the tour began and took some day trips around London.

"I was at Woburn Abbey when an Australian woman started talking with me about the grave situation that had arisen on Sunday when East Berlin had been sealed off. I told her I was supposed to begin a bus tour the next day that would arrive in West Berlin on Friday. She said she was positive the tour would be canceled, that no reliable agency would take a group to West Berlin at such a critical time.

"But when I got to my hotel late that afternoon my mailbox was empty—there was no notice from the agency about any cancellation. So I had a light supper, took a bath, set my alarm and got up at six. I packed, had some tea, checked out of the hotel, hailed a taxi and went to Victoria Coach Station. I had allowed more than ample time. We were supposed to assemble at seven-thirty and I was the first one there.

"A young man hurried over to me. He said he was Alex, the courier for Tour 612. He asked for my name and checked it against a list on a clipboard. He said many people had become uneasy and canceled the tour; of the thirty-six persons who had booked it, all but eighteen had withdrawn."

Margaret Collins said, "You know, I don't blame them. I'd have been too much of a coward to go through with it. I like excitement, but at secondhand, to read or hear about."

"No one there that morning seemed apprehensive. They were looking forward to the tour. Incidentally, it turned out that everyone but me was a British subject. I was the only person from the United States. A large, exuberant woman named Louise Willoughby, who had a brother-in-law on the *Times,* said he had predicted war in a fortnight because of The Wall, and he had called her a fool for persisting in going to Berlin. 'I booked this tour in January,' she said, 'and I intend to take it.' That was the attitude of everyone—to carry out what had been planned.

"Well, we got on a bus and headed for Dover. There we queued up and had our passports checked and boarded a steamer. The Channel crossing was miserable—so many passengers were terribly seasick. Luckily no one in our group was seriously bothered, though Mr. Mauldin, from the Midlands, looked queasy the first hour.

"We disembarked at Ostend. There was no bus waiting for us, and Alex, our guide, was obviously concerned. He tried not to show his misgivings. He said he would go find out about the bus, and meantime, as we had a long drive ahead, he suggested that we have some refreshments before we set out. We explored the waterfront a bit and pushed our way inside a small, very crowded pastry shop and ordered coffee and cake.

"After we had eaten and left the shop, Alex wasn't in sight. Nor was there a bus anywhere with our tour name and number on it. We were muttering and mildly complaining when Alex rushed up to say that our driver had quit when he had learned we were going to West Berlin. He had understood that he was to drive only in West Germany; he had a wife and three little boys and had refused to take any unnecessary risk.

"Luckily a competent, more venturesome driver had been located and was then hurrying home for his clothes and toothbrush and would be back in a few minutes.

"Mr. Mauldin, the man from the Midlands, said that he didn't blame the defaulting driver a bit, and if he had nippers at home he wouldn't be heading for West Berlin and trouble either."

"Nippers," Mrs. Collins' tongue savored the word. "That's English slang for young boys, isn't it?" Somehow she manipulated her casts and splints and dressings so that she leaned more attentively toward Ellen Williams.

Mrs. Collins' responsiveness put Ellen on her mettle. How ought she to continue? How was she to introduce the mystery? Because there was something mysterious. It couldn't have been her imagination, and yet it might have been—except for the last night. Even then it might have been the champagne. Yet what did the champagne have to do with it?

She mustn't let her mind canter ahead. She must hold it in check; present the bits properly and in sequence. What she must do now was to get on with the tour.

"After all that delay we were quite late in leaving Ostend and it had begun to rain. Robert, our new driver, a Belgian, whipped us through the rain as if he wanted to deliver us to our fate, whatever it was. We rushed through Bruges and Ghent to Antwerp, our first overnight stop.

"When we crawled out of the bus we were all very tired and almost starving. In the dining room the waiters were impatient and scowled over our lateness. The food they served was cold. My small room was shabby. There wasn't any hot water. When I climbed into bed I wondered, as I so often do when I travel, what I was doing in a strange country and why I had left home, and I promised myself that I was not going to take another trip as long as I lived."

That was enough about her own feelings. It was time that Ellen mentioned Mrs. Brown. She was telling things as they had happened, and she hadn't been aware of Mrs. Brown until the second day.

"The rain hadn't let up at all by morning, but we were all cheerful enough and Robert soon got us to Holland. We drove through Breda and Tilburg and then stopped at Hertogenbosch for coffee.

"I can't remember the name of the town where we had lunch. Anyway, the restaurant had set aside for us a long table with places for twelve and some smaller tables. I plopped down at the large table and then I noticed a woman sitting alone. She was wearing dark glasses and a hat with a rather wide brim. I thought how unpleasant it was for her to be alone, so I rose and went over. I asked if I might join her, thinking she would welcome me. She gave a slight nod. I told her my name and said I was from the United States. She didn't answer. Then I said something about our having had more than our share of rain. By then we had been served soup. She finished hers hurriedly and got up and left. I thought she must have been taken ill suddenly. Then I realized that she didn't want to sit with me. I felt snubbed and embarrassed by her behavior."

Mrs. Collins, the perfect audience, nodded in agreement. "I should think you would have felt like that," she said. "There you were on a pleasure tour and someone had behaved in a very rude and abrupt way."

"As soon as lunch was over we got back on the bus. Mrs. Brown had been sitting directly behind me, and when she got on I had already sat down. She walked by and I glanced up in case she looked in my direction or stopped to make some explanation of why she had left the table. She looked straight ahead. She completely ignored me."

"Was she rude to the others?"

"Well, you see the others weren't traveling alone as I was, so maybe they didn't notice. I never did mention Mrs. Brown to anyone and no one mentioned her to me." Perhaps that was where she had made a mistake. She should have discussed Mrs. Brown with the others, but—Ellen Williams wasn't a gossip. Yet what actually could she have told? Impolite behavior cropped up everywhere—tours and tourists were not immune.

"Do go on, Mrs. Williams."

"Again we were late in arriving at our overnight stop. By then we had crossed over into West Germany and were at Minden. Alex asked us to go directly to dinner and said he'd give us our room numbers and keys after we had eaten. Our long ride had made us hungry and we enjoyed the food. The meal was a heavy one, typically German—soup, meat, potatoes.

"When we had finished, Alex was waiting in the lobby with the keys. I was the last one and Alex was apologetic when he finally turned to me. He said no single room was available, that in fact only one room remained and Mrs. Brown and I would have to share it. There was a convention or a fair or something, and there were no more accommodations anywhere in Minden. I looked around for Mrs. Brown, but she wasn't in the lobby. Alex said he had already explained the situation to her. I told him that sharing was quite all right and I understood that it was no fault of his. He thanked me for my attitude.

"Naturally I felt uneasy about Mrs. Brown. She had already snubbed me twice. It was perfectly obvious that she wanted to have nothing to do with me and I had no intention of thrusting myself upon her. I knew that my bag would be put in the room and I decided not to go up until bedtime. Mrs. Brown could have the room to herself until then.

"I sat in the lobby and wrote postcards. Then two of the group, very nice elderly sisters from Scotland, asked me to take a walk with them. We browsed at all the shop windows and even though it was quite late we found a place open with fruit for sale. It was so tempting that we all bought some. By then we had begun to yawn and realized that we ought to go to bed.

"When I entered the room I was surprised to find it empty. I thought Mrs. Brown would already have gone to bed. I undressed and ate some fruit. It was luscious but I couldn't eat it all.

"Well, Mrs. Brown could snub me again if she liked, but I wanted her to have the fruit that was left. I set two peaches and some grapes on a paper napkin and put them on the small bedside table for her. Then I took off my shoes and set them outside the door to be polished. After that I put on my nightgown. I turned out the light and pulled up the cover—one of those great feather comforts that literally smother you. I was sorry that I was an anathema to Mrs. Brown—I pictured her sitting up in the lobby all night rather than share a room with me. Then I fell asleep.

"A shrill ringing woke me.

"I climbed out of bed to answer the telephone. A man with a charming, quite heavy accent greeted me in English and said breakfast would be ready in half an hour. I looked at the bed next to mine. Mrs. Brown was in it, her face hidden by the covers. She had crept into the room sometime during the night without disturbing me.

"I was sure she had been aroused by the bell and I said, 'Good morning. That was our call to get up. Breakfast is at seven-thirty.'

"Mrs. Brown moved slightly. She said nothing.

"I felt gauche and out of place, which was stupid, wasn't it? The room was as much mine as hers. Anyway I hurried to dress. I intended to get out as quickly as I could. I hadn't unpacked the night before and I had only to shove my nightgown in my case. Then I set the case outside for the porter to pick up.

"When I grabbed my pocketbook I noticed there were two peach seeds and some grape stems on the table next to Mrs. Brown's bed. She might not speak to me but she at least had eaten the fruit. Somehow that made me even more upset.

"I was dressed except for my shoes. They were waiting newly polished for me in the hall. In my stockingfeet, I left the room. Two pairs of pumps, almost identical, were placed near the door. I put mine on and started toward the stairway.

"Suddenly I was in great pain. My feet were killing me. Traveling must have made my feet swell. I couldn't walk another step. I looked down and realized that in my confusion and anger I had put on Mrs. Brown's shoes instead of my own. Both pairs were black calf with sensible heels—the great difference was that Mrs. Brown's were much smaller than mine.

"I changed into my own shoes and went downstairs.

"At breakfast everyone was excited. This was the day we were to drive from Helmstedt through the narrow corridor across East Germany into West Berlin. Alex told us he had telephoned late the night before to his representative in West Berlin. In spite of the tension, there didn't appear to be any immediate danger. Hopefully our tour would proceed as scheduled.

"As I talked with Alex and some of the other tourists about the adventures the day's run might bring, I had almost forgotten about Mrs. Brown. I hadn't seen her at breakfast. I was aware of her again when she walked down the aisle of the bus, but I purposely looked out of the window when she passed by and sat behind me. I became angry all over again at the memory of her rudeness.

"Rain dogged us for a time but when we reached Helmstedt and our first East German checkpoint the sun shone wanly. A great pole swept down to bar us from the autobahn. Propaganda posters with photographs of Ulbricht were plastered around and about. Lining the highway on each side of us were tall barbed wire fences.

"After we had sat waiting for half an hour, two men boarded the bus and checked our passports. Alex and Robert got off with their credentials and entered a wooden hut. Their clearance was more involved than ours. At last we were allowed to progress a short distance to another barrier; after an additional check there, we were permitted to proceed. All along the road at short intervals we saw watchtowers from which soldiers and guns leaned out like gargoyles jutting from a gothic cathedral.

"The road was clogged with traffic and we often had to slow down. Occasionally we met busloads of tourists headed toward West Germany. They waved or gave us the thumbs-up sign. American and British army trucks swept past; some were on their way east, some west. The high barbed wire along the road fenced off vast fields under cultivation; men and women farm laborers were leaning close to the ground, working hard, a few yards beyond us; they didn't raise their heads to watch us go by. Hops grew on the barbed wire in places and hid its ugliness.

"The distance from Helmstedt to West Berlin is about a hundred and ten miles. It seemed measureless. At last we submitted to a final Communist clearance and soon afterward we saw a sign welcoming us into the American sector of West Berlin.

"Our destination was just ahead. Some of the tourists got up and took hand luggage from the overhead racks. Others put on their coats. I wanted to tidy up for our arrival. I reached in my pocketbook for my lipstick and compact. When I opened the compact I must have held it rather high; the mirror captured the face of Mrs. Brown in the seat behind me.

"I've never seen such despair on a countenance. Hers was the face of a mother holding a dead child. It was the face of a person having her last lucid moment before she descends into madness, or of someone headed for the gallows. It was so appalling that I forgot about my makeup. I snapped the compact shut to blot out that vision of utter misery. I felt like an intruder. I had stumbled on something not meant for me, and I was angry at myself for having been angry at Mrs. Brown.

"I was so stunned by Mrs. Brown's desolation that I had not been paying attention to what we were passing. To distract myself I glanced out of the bus window. My first impression of West Berlin was that it seemed brand new; every building might have been finished that instant for our benefit.

"Our hotel also looked spanking new and was very attractive. The large lobby was pleasantly furnished; the restaurant directly off the lobby was light and inviting.

"As soon as I had unpacked I went out for a walk. The hotel was in the middle of town. The zoo was nearby and very tempting. I'm crazy about zoos. I paid my entrance fee and wandered around. There was no atmosphere of crisis. Parents and children were enjoying themselves, the animals and the sunny afternoon. The open air restaurant was filled with people. A band played waltzes. A little train rushed by jammed with waving, joyously screeching children.

"After a while I left the zoo to saunter along the street. Just across the way was Kurfurstendamm, the heart of the shopping district. I walked into KaDeWe, a big department store, and bought some gifts for my daughters-in-law. The shoppers looked like shoppers everywhere, and so did the salesclerks. There was no feeling of alarm or apprehension, no hysteria. It seemed simply a nice afternoon in August in a carefree city.

"I had dinner early and ate alone. I saw none of my group in the restaurant. I had almost forgotten my concern over Mrs. Brown. Perhaps I had exaggerated her unhappiness. All the same, I was deeply sorry for her.

"The next morning after breakfast Alex and Robert took us on a sightseeing tour of West Berlin. We saw the Funkturm and the Le Corbusier Apartments. We drove through the Tiergarten past Congress Hall and out to Charlottenburg Castle. We stopped at Spandau Prison and Templehof Airport and the Town Hall and Free University.

"When Robert put us out at the hotel, Alex asked us to hurry with our lunch as we were scheduled to go into East Berlin at one-thirty.

"We marched immediately into the dining room, but once we were served we couldn't eat; our excitement was too high. Mrs. Willoughby—she was the one, you'll remember, whose brother-in-law worked for the London *Times*—said it was all touch-and-go. She said, 'We must keep our wits about us while we're in East Berlin. Last night I went out to dinner with some British newspaper people and some

Berliners. They all warned that the situation is explosive. Anything can set it off.'

"At that the sisters from Scotland said they weren't going. Mr. Mauldin tried to persuade them to change their minds. Their objections to his plea were so strong that they won him over, and he said on second thought he wasn't going— it would be senseless to take such a great risk. There were other defections. For a while it looked as if Alex and Robert would be taking an empty bus into East Berlin.

"But our jitters subsided; our spirit of adventure soared again; by one-fifteen we had assembled in the lobby.

"A little later Alex counted us as he always did to be sure no one was ever left behind. Then he frowned. Someone was missing. We were seventeen instead of eighteen. Mrs. Brown was the absent one. We all looked at our watches. There was still five minutes to spare. We waited. On the dot Mrs. Brown joined us. Then Alex led us around the corner where Robert and the bus were waiting. Alex announced over the loudspeaker that when we entered East Berlin a guide would meet us. He said we were absolutely forbidden to discuss The Wall with the guide and under no circumstances were we to talk about politics.

"In moments we had approached the Friedrichstrasse checkpoint. Two East Germans entered and asked for our passports. Other uniformed men banged around outside opening the luggage compartments. One man crawled beneath the bus to search there. After a while we were given permission to drive across into East Berlin. The bus might have become afraid; it lurched, then stalled, and finally bumped past the last barricade.

"Just beyond the barricade a slight young man wearing a raincoat hailed us. Alex opened the bus door and spoke some German. The man entered the bus and Alex introduced him as Hans, our East Berlin guide.

"Hans' smile was pleasant; his English was perfect; he said without any hint of irony that he hoped we would enjoy our visit.

"A light rain began to fall as we drove through the bleak, empty streets. After the sparkling newness of West Berlin,

East Berlin was drab indeed. Everything looked gray—the streets, the buildings, the great open spaces, the clouds. Rubble from the bombings was everywhere. A feeling of tragedy was as heavy as the rain clouds.

"There wasn't any traffic. The dingy houses and blocks of flats seemed without tenants. At last we saw someone—a solitary man stood in a doorway, but he paid no attention to us. Farther on a woman glanced down from the balcony of an apartment house, but her eyes didn't register our existence.

"All the time Hans was commenting on East Berlin, giving figures about population, area, industries, rents, wages, the standard of living. We crossed Unter den Linden, we saw the State Opera House and the State Library and Humboldt University. We passed Hitler's bunker. Somewhere or other we stopped at a kiosk and got postcards.

"Then we drove to Treptow Park. We stopped there, got out of the bus and followed Hans along a path to the Soviet War Memorial.

"The rain increased, splashed loudly as we strained to hear Hans' statistics about the number of Russian soldiers buried there and the height and material of the Memorial. Suddenly the rain was like a cloudburst. It routed us. We ran the long distance back to the bus. We were drenched and bedraggled as we jostled each other to climb inside. Mrs. Brown was just ahead of me as we entered the bus and my footsteps followed in the puddles left by her soaked shoes.

"Hans' composure didn't falter; he said we were quite lucky as our tour was over except for our visit to the Pergamon Museum. We'd be sheltered there, so it wouldn't matter whether or not it rained.

"The rain didn't slacken at all. It shrouded the bus windows, erasing East Berlin from our view. After a while the bus stopped and Hans said we had arrived at the museum and could leave the bus.

"We rose. We were a forlorn group in our soaked clothes as we got out once more to brave the rain and dash through its downpour.

"The building ahead of us had the austere exterior of

museums everywhere, yet we ran toward it as to a haven. It was very dark inside. There were none of those dramatic spotlights that so many museums have. In fact, there was no illumination of any kind. Hans was ahead commenting, giving facts in a subdued voice as if he were in a church. The stragglers in our group rushed to catch up with him.

"I was about to follow when someone touched my shoulder. I turned to see Mrs. Brown. Her hat shaded her face. Drops of rain splashed from the hat brim to the floor. A strange smile was on her face. I can't describe it—it was a thin, forced smile, and do you know I didn't dare look into her eyes because I was afraid I would discover in them that unbearable sadness I'd seen as we were approaching West Berlin.

"She began to speak. 'Thank you for the fruit,' she said. 'It was delicious. I enjoyed it so very much.' Her voice was a whisper, as if she entrusted me with a secret that no one must overhear.

"I was startled. I was quite put off. I boomed out, 'You're quite welcome.' My voice echoed in the long corridor.

"I was afraid. I felt alone even though Mrs. Brown was beside me. The others had disappeared. I desperately wanted to be with them. I looked to the right. The group hadn't entered that room. I crossed to the left. They weren't there. I rushed ahead and came upon a vast hall. I was relieved to see the others and ran over to listen to Hans talk about the Hellenistic culture of Pergamon.

"Then I paid no attention to Hans. All I could think of was how odd it was that Mrs. Brown had thanked me for the fruit. Why, Mrs. Collins, did she thank me then?"

"It certainly wasn't the first chance she'd had by any means."

"No. She'd sat behind me for hours on the bus. She could have leaned over at any time to thank me. She'd been with me in the bedroom that morning after she'd eaten the fruit and hadn't said a word about it. Why would she have mentioned the fruit there in the museum? Why then?"

"People are unaccountable. Maybe she was suddenly overtaken by remorse that she hadn't thanked you before."

"But don't you agree that it was out of character and very odd?"

"Very odd indeed."

"Well, anyway, the Pergamon Museum was the end of our tour in East Berlin. Hans stayed on the bus with us until we approached the checkpoint. Then he waved goodbye and disappeared in the rain. We all felt sad to leave him in that stricken city. We liked him.

"At the barrier we underwent the same procedure as when we had entered East Berlin, only this time it was infinitely more strict and meticulous. The Vopos or whatever they're called scrutinized our faces and compared them with our passport photographs with greater care. They searched the luggage compartments and beneath the bus even more thoroughly. They conferred with each other, checked, rechecked, then went through the whole tiresome business again.

"Finally the nod was given; we were allowed to cross back into West Berlin.

"Our stay in East Berlin had left us depressed. We were silent, stunned. As we were passing the Kaiser Wilhelm Memorial Church in the swarming traffic of Kurfurstendamm, Mrs. Willoughby spoke for us all. She said, 'I was never so glad to get out of a place in my life. East Berlin is one vast prison now. You see, until last Sunday the inhabitants knew that if things got too bad they could take an S-train or the underground into West Berlin and be free. It was their safety valve. Escape was always possible until Sunday. But there's no hope any longer. Only terrible risk. They'll be shot if they try to leave. Well, it's all too upsetting and doesn't bear thinking about. Once I get out of these wet clothes I'm going to have some strong tea.'

" 'Right you are, Mrs. Willoughby,' Mr. Mauldin said. 'But I'm going to have something stronger then tea as soon as I can make myself presentable.'

"We made a shabby parade across the lobby in our damp clothes as we hurried toward the elevator. By the time I got to the elevator there was no more room in it. I backed away to wait for its return. While I waited I glanced at some newspapers for sale at the front desk. I skimmed the headlines. They were all in German and I could make nothing of them. I sauntered back toward the elevator. By then the indicator was flashing red and descending. I looked across the lobby and saw Mrs. Brown sitting alone on a sofa. Obviously she was quite comfortably settled and in no rush to go upstairs to change. Then the expression on her face startled me—stopped me dead. Mrs. Collins, I believe the word that would best describe her is gleeful—she was, well, smug. Then she gave a great roar of laughter. I couldn't believe it. I knew that no one else in our group would find anything to laugh at so soon after what we'd seen—a whole dead city. I decided that Mrs. Brown must be amused by something in the lobby, but nothing laughable or even remotely diverting was going on there.

"Mrs. Collins, from what I've said of that ghastly afternoon can you think of any reason why Mrs. Brown should have been so deliriously happy?"

Mrs. Collins inspected her bandaged elbow as if it might give an answer. Her brow was ridged by deep thought. "I don't know whether I'm right," she said. "But this may be the answer. You see, people respond in different ways to the same situation. The majority of you were depressed, but Mrs. Brown was happy over her experience in East Berlin, I guess I really mean that she was thankful. She had seen all that misery and realized how fortunate she was. Whatever private sorrow she had known that had upset her so when you were entering West Berlin had seemed of no importance to her once she found out what the people in East Berlin were having to endure."

"Maybe so. Yet I don't think it was gratitude she was showing. She looked triumphant. Why, she was gloating.

"Anyway, our short stay in West Berlin was almost over, and you can't imagine the relief we felt when we drove back to West Germany the next day. We had an enjoyable afternoon and night in Goslar, then we went to Rudesheim. Mrs. Brown was no longer aloof. Twice I sat by her at mealtime and she talked as much as anyone, and she would nod to me when she passed by on her way to the seat behind me on the bus. But in Rudesheim she dismayed me again. I found some beautiful peaches there in a fruit stall. I've told you how fond I am of fruit. I overtook Mrs. Brown on the street. I remembered that she liked peaches, and held out the bag to her.

" 'No, thank you,' " she said.

"I insisted. There were more than I could eat and I knew she liked them. 'Please take some,' I urged.

" 'You're very nice to offer them to me,' she said, 'but I'm allergic to peaches.' I hope I didn't show the amazement I felt. Mind you, she'd eaten the other peaches I'd given her a few nights before.

"Anyhow our tour was ending and there wasn't much more time to be surprised by Mrs. Brown's behavior. After Rudesheim our route lay along the Rhine to Koblenz and then to Bonn. After Bonn we crossed into Belgium and went through Liege to Brussels, our last stop.

"That last night in Brussels, Alex was exuberant. He said we ought to celebrate the end of our tour. We agreed with him and decided to go to a nightclub—that is, everyone except Mrs. Brown and Mrs. Willoughby, who said they were much too tired.

"The floor show wasn't very clever and the champagne was only so-so. No matter, the evening was fun and we didn't want it to end. None of us were likely to meet again and we wanted our farewell to last. Alex was especially mellow. He said it was the first tour he had ever conducted in which there had been a serious threat of danger and he had been frightened when we went into East Berlin. In fact, he had been uneasy all during our stay in West Berlin. Our coming through unscathed called for more champagne. We toasted Alex. Alex toasted us. We were happy and pleased with ourselves.

"And we got back to the hotel very late.

"Mrs. Brown's room was next to mine and there to greet me outside the door were her sensible black pumps waiting to be polished. They reminded me that I should place my pumps outside too. I unlocked my door and went to the closet for the shoes and set them near Mrs. Brown's. Then I went back into my room, double locked the door and got into bed.

"Suddenly something struck me as being very odd.

Something was peculiar. No, it wasn't the champagne that was bothering me.

"I got up and unlocked the door.

"Mrs. Brown's shoes were bothering me. There they were, side by side with my shoes, and they dwarfed mine. But my shoes were *larger* than Mrs. Brown's. I remembered very well that they were *much* larger. In the mixup when we had shared the room in Minden and I had put on her shoes by mistake, my feet had been cramped. I couldn't walk in her shoes.

"I leaned down and picked up Mrs. Brown's shoes. I put them on. They were so loose I couldn't have kept them on if I had tried to walk in them.

"I was startled by a noise in Mrs. Brown's room. I had just stepped out of her shoes and set them back when she flung the door open.

"For an instant the champagne made me see two of Mrs. Brown. Two very formidable twins.

" 'Hello,' I said. 'I hope I didn't disturb you. We've just got back from our party and I was setting my shoes outside so they could be polished.'

"Both Mrs. Browns smiled at me. Both were friendly and polite. 'I hope you had a nice time,' they said. 'Good night.' The door was closed.

"I felt quite dizzy. I managed to get back inside my room. The floor tilted slightly. I grabbed the bed and climbed into it.

"I slept perfectly and woke completely refreshed. Everyone who'd gone to the party felt the same way. The champagne had done us all a world of good. That afternoon the Channel was choppy when we crossed over to England. It didn't bother us at all. A bus waited for us at Dover and we drove to London, talking our heads off about our exciting tour. In the coach station we gathered our bags and souvenirs and lined up for taxis. I had a rather tight schedule to get to London Airport for my New York flight and so Alex and Mr. Mauldin put me into the first taxi available. Then everybody waved one last good-bye to me and the one whose smile seemed warmest and who waved most energetically was Mrs. Brown. I've never seen such a remarkable change in anyone in all my life. You're a psychologist, so please explain it to me. It's been my experience that people don't change."

"You're right, Mrs. Williams. People don't change. Even a person who undergoes the rigors of psychoanalysis doesn't change. He learns more about himself and modifies his behavior, but essentially he's the same."

"All the same, Mrs. Brown changed completely."

"Then there has to be an explanation. However far-fetched something seems to be, it can be understood when all the facts are examined."

"All right. We both say that people don't change, but you have my word for it that Mrs. Brown did."

"Yet you've said that no one else on your tour noticed this change."

"I was the only one who had the chance to notice. I shared a room with her. I saw the despair reflected in her face when we entered West Berlin. I—"

"You stood in her shoes twice."

"I may have been mistaken about her shoes that last night. Remember, I'd had a lot of champagne. But whatever the size of her feet, her *behavior* altered so much that she was as different as day and night. Why she didn't act like the same person at all when we got back from East Berlin. She might have been two different women."

Ellen Williams' statement possessed the room; its impact left a profound silence. The two women looked at each other while the truth shone in Ellen Williams' eyes just as it lighted the eyes of Margaret Collins.

"That's it, Mrs. Williams! That's it exactly. There were two Mrs. Browns. One began the tour in London and stayed with it until you went beyond The Wall into East Berlin. The other Mrs. Brown came out of the Pergamon Museum and completed the tour. One Mrs. Brown had small feet, the other had large feet. One Mrs. Brown liked peaches, the other was allergic to them. One Mrs. Brown knew she was changing places and would have to stay in East Berlin or somewhere else behind the Iron Curtain, and that's why she was so despondent when you saw her face reflected in your compact. The other Mrs. Brown was gloating there in the hotel lobby in West Berlin because she had escaped, and of course she wasn't in any hurry to go upstairs to change her clothes—she wasn't wet. She'd been inside the Pergamon Museum during the downpour, waiting for the other Mrs. Brown to appear."

"But of course," Ellen Williams said. "How stupid of me not to have realized that. If I'd only known what was going on I could have saved the first Mrs. Brown."

"Not at all. There wasn't any possible hope of that. The first Mrs. Brown was beyond your help before you had a chance to notice the differences between them."

"I suppose they were both spies," Mrs. Williams said.

"Of course not," Mrs. Collins replied. "If they had been spies the exchange would have been as smooth as silk and you'd never have been allowed to notice such discrepancies in shoe sizes or tastes for fruit, and the first Mrs. Brown wouldn't have been despondent—if she'd been a spy she'd have been doing a job she relished and was getting good money for."

"Are you suggesting the first Mrs. Brown was kidnapped while we were at the Pergamon and someone else took her place?"

"By no means," Mrs. Collins answered. "It was planned well ahead of time and the first Mrs. Brown was perfectly aware of her fate. It involved some kind of moral blackmail she was forced to pay lest the lives of her family be forfeited, and in carrying it out she had been warned to remain inconspicuous and to form no friendships on the way to Berlin. If she had become friendly with anyone and talked a lot, it would have been obvious on the way back to London that a substitution had been made. That was why she was rude at lunch when you joined her. It was also why she stayed out of the room you had to share, and didn't mix or mingle with anyone. Then in the darkness of the Pergamon just before she changed places she felt there was no longer any danger of her betraying the switchover, and that's why she thanked you for the fruit. She was grateful for your kindness and sorry she hadn't been able to express her gratitude before."

"And I didn't once suspect anything sinister!" Ellen Williams said.

One must always be suspicious, for the world is an evil place, Margaret Collins almost answered, but then she decided if Ellen Williams had reached middle age without grasping that fundamental fact, her naïveté and innocence ought to be preserved.

Besides, the world could be a nice place, too, particularly when it offered a new acquaintance as pleasant as Ellen Williams.

WHAT IF I HAD TAKEN THE TRAIN?

by Robert Colby

I have always been fascinated by the many ways in which fate, with a careless hand, moves us in one direction or another toward the small or important events of our lives, trivial or exciting, happy or tragic. There is a compelling element of mystery attached to the complexities of time and circumstance which lead toward the climax of a dramatic happening.

Take the man who is delayed for some absurd reason beyond prediction and misses his plane by three minutes. The plane crashes and all aboard are killed. Fate dealt him a winning hand, but it could have been just the reverse. He could have missed the plane which arrived safely, catching the one which crashed. Do you see what I mean?

One day you are driving home from work and just as you approach an intersection, there is a fatal accident. You see it happen and if you are morbidly curious, you join the crowd of stunned, gaping spectators. Somehow you get the grim details. A drunk ran a stoplight and slammed broadside into a car in your lane of traffic. The innocent driver was killed, the drunk survived with hardly a scratch.

Thinking back, you begin to wonder. If you had left the office ten seconds earlier, would you now be that dead driver en route to the morgue?

I used to keep track of the crazy twists of fate in my

own life and all of this is simply leading up to that craziest of twists, one violent episode which puts all the others in the shade. In case you should find this one a bit tough to swallow, I've got some very tangible proof which I'll show you later.

It began quietly enough with no ominous clouds, no dark threats of trouble on the horizon of my immediate future. While working out of the L.A. office of a national ad agency as an account exec, I was chosen that spring to take charge of a new TV account, a drama series that would originate in New York when the dull summer repeats were replaced by the fresher, if not duller, offerings of the fall lineup.

I was in no hurry to check in at the New York office since I had a vacation coming first, so I decided to detour and pause in the Miami area to lounge around some palm-strewn, gal-studded beach while recovering from a case of blues evoked by a recent divorce. I was giving the gate to the L.A. beaches because familiarity breeds a certain ennui, if not contempt.

I had planned definitely to take the train in lieu of flight. It seemed to me that with luck and a winning smile, one might meet all sorts of interesting people on a train, including one or two toothsome members of the distaff variety. In three or more days there would be plenty of time to cultivate these little friendships, while a mere five hours aloft offered small promise.

At the last minute, after careful deliberation, I changed my mind. Unless I hit that rare jackpot combination, I revised, three days of rumbling east on a train could be a yawn as wide as the Grand Canyon, so why not charge off on the plane?

Here we have the first switch to a new course of action, with fate moving us toward an entirely different climax. What if I had taken the train? We'll never know, so let's deal with what we do know. However, let's not get on the plane just yet because we haven't even reached the airport and there's a chance we may never get there, let alone board a plane.

When I came to these mighty conclusions about train

versus plane it was past noon on a Friday and I wasn't able to make a reservation on an afternoon flight. Instead, they booked me on a jet scheduled to take wing at nine P.M.—but what if I *had* been able to find space on an afternoon flight? Well, you get the whole point, so let's not belabor it. You can fill in your own what-ifs as we move through this grim accounting.

Since I do not like dawdling around airports, train or bus depots while waiting listlessly to be conveyed somewhere, I usually dash for these forms of public transportation at the last possible moment, but on this occasion, for no reason other than to be in motion, I left with so much time to spare that I alighted at the port an hour before plane time. Slightly ahead of eight o'clock, I believe it was.

After delivering my baggage to the clerk, I bought a paper but couldn't come to terms with it. When my attention began to wander, I went outside. Pensive, I began to circle aimlessly past the glass-enclosed terminals of the other airlines.

I watched the people milling about inside under the lights. Then I caught sight of Marian Lundy, secretary to Harvey Slater, the VP in charge of programming at the TV network of my former employment. She was standing behind the glass, looking almost directly at me in the sightless way of people who are torn by some deeply disturbing, inner emotion.

She was a girl in her late twenties, chestnut-haired, trim-figured and pretty enough to frame. She was also, to the despair of the entire executive wing, very much married. I hadn't seen her in nearly six months, but we had been quite chummy in the tenuous way of office relationships.

I remembered her as a gal with glinting green eyes who had a quick, sardonic wit. With me, at least, she had been delightfully flirtatious, though it seemed only an amusing game she played, knowing she could retreat behind the safe wall of her marriage if I ever took her seriously. Still, there was an undercurrent of excitement in our bantering dialogue, as if there might be real fire beneath the frail smokescreen of words. For my part, with the divorce action already in progress, I had desperately wished that she were available but it had stopped there.

I pushed through the glass doors and stood close beside her. She looked up at me. There was surprise in the readjustment of her pretty mouth, but the aqua-green eyes were lusterless and her look was more a shrug of indifference than a smile of welcome.

"Hello, Mr. Bennett," she said tonelessly.

"Suddenly I'm Mr. Bennett," I quipped. "What happened to good old 'Wayne'? That's what you used to call me."

"I used to know you better—Wayne," she said with barely a smile.

"I'm gone only a few months and already your love has cooled," I told her. "Did you know that I stole your type eraser? And that every night before I place it lovingly beneath my pillow, I kiss it tenderly?"

"Wayne," she said gravely, rebukingly, "at any other time this would be fun. But I—I'm afraid you've caught me in a dreadful mood."

"Problems?"

She nodded, her eyes rolled upward in emphasis. "You just won the annual award for understatement."

"Anything I can do?"

She shook her head as she clutched her lower lip with a row of teeth that would embarrass genuine pearls. Tears sprang from the corners of fetchingly slanted eyes.

"Well, I don't want to intrude, Marian. But if you need a shoulder—"

"No, it's not anything I could discuss, even with a close friend."

There was a silence. I asked her if she were meeting a plane or catching one.

"I'm on the eight-twenty-five flight to Denver," she said, dabbing at her eyes. "I used to live in Denver. I couldn't think of anyplace else to go."

I took her gently by the shoulders and turned her toward me. "Marian, I guess you understand that in back of my office clowning, I always had a big affection for you."

"No," she answered. "I don't have the ego to read special

meanings between the lines, but it is nice to know." Her smile was tremulous.

"Whatever it is you're trying to cope with, Marian, I doubt if you'll find anyone in Denver more ready to help."

"I believe you," she replied, her expression a painful groping for decision. "But I suppose you're flying off somewhere on important business."

"No, I'm beginning a vacation before I transfer to our New York office. I'm on my way to Miami."

"What time do you—"

"At nine."

"And if you missed the plane?"

"I'd simply catch another. I'm in no hurry. Are you?"

"A few hours wouldn't change anything," she said. "Neither would a few years." Then her features became distorted by the wrenching of some secret horror she was trying to dredge up from its hiding place. "You see, Wayne, my husband is dead. It was an accident—but I killed him."

We sat in a circular lounge perched atop a towerlike structure in the center of the airport. My baggage had not yet been put aboard and I had reclaimed it. Marian had not taken with her so much as an overnight case. She had fled impulsively, in terror and panic.

"It was a mistake to run," I said quietly. "Understandable enough, but a mistake. How long has it been?"

"Less than two hours," she answered.

"All right. Did you people have any plans to meet with friends who might be looking for you?" I said.

"No. We weren't going out and we hadn't invited anyone over."

"Good. Then it's not too late. You can tell the police that you delayed because you were in shock and wanted to seek advice. Perhaps you were searching for a lawyer who could inform you of your legal rights, arrange bail and generally keep you from saying or doing anything which might tend to incriminate you."

"That sounds logical, Wayne. Oh, I'm so glad to have

you on my side!" She gulped her drink, spilling some over her trembling hand.

I said, "First, you had better tell it all from the beginning. I know a bit about the law and I'd like to see just how bad it will look to the police on the surface. Did you touch or change anything?"

"No."

"Go ahead, then."

"Well, it was an argument," she began, speaking around her cigarette as I lighted it, exhaling nervous little wisps of smoke. "I wish I could say it was about something momentous or dramatic, but it wasn't that way at all. Just another fight over trifles, except that this one got out of hand.

"Doug, my husband," she went on, "had become more and more critical of me in the last three months or so. He was always a dominant sort. I mean, he knew exactly how he wanted things, down to the smallest details of our life, and he never was very tolerant of my rather casual approach to keeping house, marketing, having something done to the car—things like that.

"He was irritatingly precise and disciplined to doing minor chores *now,* and in just the *right* way, *his* way. And he expected me to keep pace with him, even though I hold a full-time job and often come home exhausted.

"At first, while the aura of the honeymoon lasted, I shaped everything to his exact requirements, but as we settled down to humdrum routine, I became more lax and he became more stingingly sarcastic. He always took for granted everything I did well, never even gave me honorable mention for bringing home a good salary to help out. But one little lapse and he was on my back, snarling.

"At times I actually hated him. But like most of us, he has—had his good points too, just enough of them to keep me from admitting to myself that we were earth and moon apart and that the marriage was a miserable mistake. Then, about three months ago, he lost his job, at the very moment when he was expecting a raise and a boost up the ladder.

"They gave him the usual pat excuse they hand people when the truth is embarrassing; they were cutting down overhead and his particular job was going to become practically nonexistent. He was exceedingly bitter but he didn't say much and I had to figure it out for myself. From observation I knew it had nothing to do with his ability. He just couldn't get along with people. He was disagreeable, maddeningly bossy, and he had that great big sarcastic mouth.

"Well, he got another job, a lesser one. But he was never the same, which isn't saying much. Secretly, I believe he thought of himself as a hopeless failure and, perhaps to compensate by pulling me down, or to make me his whipping-girl, he became not just critical of me, but supercritical. His behavior pattern was borderline insanity. He needed to see an analyst. I told him so in the nicest possible way.

"He took that as an outrageous insult and grew to be more of a tyrant than ever—to the point where I began to find legitimate-seeming ways to dodge him at night; going to a movie with a girlfriend, playing bridge and so on.

"Well, that's a rather necessary slice of background and it—it brings us up to tonight. As usual, he got home ahead of me and the very second I came in the door he asked me why I hadn't done the breakfast dishes, which were still unwashed and egg-faced in the sink.

"I could've told him there hadn't been time because I was running late for work, but it had been a bad day and I was too beat to care how I answered. In any case, I was fairly bursting with too much of him, ready to take out my resignation papers in Nevada. So I said I didn't do the dishes because I damn well didn't feel like doing them. I remarked that I hadn't noticed that his hands were in a cast, and offered to show him where to find all the materials he needed for scrubbing.

"He was furious, of course. He went to make himself a drink and when he found we were out of bourbon he demanded to know why I was so stupid that I couldn't check the supply and pick up another bottle. Then he didn't like what we were having to eat but said it didn't matter because I was the only one he knew who could take an ordinary TV dinner from the freezer, place it in an ordinary oven, and transform it into something that tasted like laundry soap.

"Finally, he expressed his loathing for this new dress I'm wearing, one I just bought with my own money during lunch hour. He said it was gaudy, a cheap, office-girl rag, but typical of my taste.

"That did it! I snapped back that as long as he found me so inadequate, so repulsive in every way, I knew at least one man who would take me off his hands in a hurry, in fact, before the night was over I might be gone . . ."

She paused and I asked her if there had been anyone special she had in mind when she needled her husband with that one?

Her eyelids descended to half-mast when she replied, "Of course not. I was just goading Doug, being vindictive. He dared me to give him a name, so I tossed the first one at him that came into my head—the boss, Harvey Slater. Now you and I know that's absurd because Harvey Slater is old enough to be my father, and if I made a move in his direction he might fall out a window escaping, he's so proper.

"But Doug had never met Harvey and he believed me. I was getting under his skin, so I enlarged on the whole bit, going on about how much loot Harvey had and even insinuating that on certain nights we had been holding hands together, making plans.

"Doug was positively livid. He began to shout accusations. We shot words back and forth. We stabbed each other with the sort of deeply wounding, character mutilating barbs you can never really patch with an apology after the storm, because they're so close to the truth.

"In the end, he called me something too obscene and degrading to repeat, and in a rage beyond thought, I scooped an ashtray from a table and hurled it at him. Well, not at him exactly, not in the sense that you take careful aim. I didn't want or expect to hit him. I just had to send something crashing in his direction to shut him up.

"It was one of those thick, solid-glass ashtrays, heavy and square, with sharp corners. You know the kind, they're practically indestructible."

She paused again and there were fresh tears in her eyes. "By some horrible freak," she continued, "the tray sailed through the air as if guided perfectly by an evil force and struck him in the temple with a sickening thud.

"He clutched at his head and his hand came away covered with—with blood. Then he just collapsed to the floor. I could see that he was dead, it was obvious. This terribly pallid, gray look of death had seeped into his face.

"I sagged into a chair and I sat vacantly for a few minutes in that frightfully silent living room where Doug's booming voice still bounced from the walls of my mind. I reached for the phone but couldn't make the call. After three tries I got a cigarette going and at this time there was a kind of sketchy, fragmentary picture in my jumbled thoughts of what would happen next; the police cars wailing outside, the reporters, the relentless questions, then jail and a long trial ending in—what? The gas chamber? I didn't know.

"The silence and aloneness, Doug there on the floor, only increased my panic. I hadn't a single logical idea, just the one thought—to hide someplace beyond reach where I could think, and where friends and relatives would help me if I ever got the courage to ask them.

"I had just been paid for two weeks and there was enough money, so I left everything behind and I ran out and got a taxi to the airport."

Having come to the end of it, she slumped down in her chair and waited mournfully for my reaction. I didn't say anything for a space because I was groping feverishly for a plan. I can't say that I was sad to hear that Douglas Lundy was dead. Hell, I didn't know the man and it didn't seem as if the world would miss him very much. On the other hand, I did know his widow, and the imprisoned feeling I had for her was being paroled, the gates of hope had opened with a fantastic twist of fate.

At that moment, what I wanted most was to keep Marian Lundy at large and available, on the freedom side of the bars.

"Well, what do you think, Wayne?" she asked in a pale voice close to a whisper. "What should I do now?"

"You should stay here in town and we'll deal with this thing together."

"Oh, Wayne, you really are a friend! And—and much more. I can't tell you how—"

"Double in spades," I said. "But right now let's work out the problem, let's get into high gear. First, it's not quite as bad as I had imagined. The circumstances can be made to work *for* you rather than against you. Just the fact that you're a woman, young and mighty attractive, will be persuasive. After all, in any so-called crime situation where the law is involved, we're confronted mostly with men. Sympathy will flood toward you if we give it a little push."

"Yes, but how? Don't forget, if it goes to trial, there might be several women on the jury."

"It need not go to trial, Marian. In fact, it must not go to trial because you might get a couple of years or so for involuntary manslaughter, which I think is the worst they can do to you. An inquest, perhaps, but no, not a trial."

"Fine. But it sounds so simple the way you put it. How could such a thing possibly be arranged?"

"By a very slight alteration at what is tritely called the scene of the crime," I told her. "Now don't get the impression that I'm completely amoral and that I condone killing people, even accidentally. Still, it *was* an accident, and what can be gained by sending a nice gal like you to prison after a messy trial and all that goes with it?"

"Nothing," she said woefully. "It would break my heart, and my spirit. It might even ruin my life."

"Exactly, Marian. Exactly."

"Then tell me what you have in mind."

"All right, let's suppose that as you relate it to the police, you make only one change in your story—the ending. His hate and jealousy aroused by your fake threat to leave him and go off with the boss, your husband makes a dash for the kitchen and comes back with a knife. 'I'm gonna kill you!' he shouts, and begins to advance toward you. At this point, with no idea but to delay him while you escape out the door, you fling the ashtray at him. And by some chance-in-a-hundred freak, it hits and kills him.

"It was his fault but you are wretchedly sorry and grief-stricken, as anyone can see."

She nodded. "Marvelous. Perfectly believable. Except that he *didn't* have a knife in his hand."

"But he will, Marian, that's the point. When he's found, he *will* have a knife in his hand. At least it will rest near his hand and his prints will be on the handle. Understand?"

"Yes," she said with an undertone of vast relief and excitement. "You couldn't make it much clearer."

I stood. "Then let's go," I said. "Let's hurry."

She lived, I discovered, in one of those apartment buildings sprouting above Hollywood Boulevard, east of Highland. We went wordlessly to the second floor and with a look of awe and dread filling her eyes, she quietly unlocked the door.

The living room was small and not heavily furnished. It took only a glance to note that it certainly didn't contain Doug Lundy's corpse. I was about to voice my opinion that it was a very unfunny gag, when I saw on the carpet a quite large, rusty splotch, and close by, face down, a heavy glass ashtray.

I did not pick it up but I bent down to examine it. One sharp corner was slightly chipped and held a small, dried stain of blood.

Standing, I looked into Marian's startled eyes and said, "Well, unless someone discovered him and had him carted off, which is most unlikely, your boy is still alive."

She gasped, crooking a finger and biting the knuckle. "Do you think he came to and somehow got to a hospital?"

"I don't know what to think," I answered, "except that apparently you didn't kill him after all."

"How sad for you both," said a chilling voice, and I glanced up sharply to see Doug Lundy postured in a doorway left of the living room. At least I assumed it was Lundy. His head was heavily and professionally bandaged. There was no doubt that he had been listening behind the door.

Beyond the fact that his head was bandaged, I can remember little about him, for I was fascinated by the gun in his hand.

"How do you do, Mr. Harvey Slater," he said to me with mock formality, and then quickly to Marian, "So this is the boss, the lover come to take possession of the dead man's widow, even before the body's had time to cool. Right, Marian?"

"Doug!" she cried, "I'm so glad you're alive! But you misunderstand. This is not—"

Well, that was the last word she said to him because at that instant he shot her quite casually, a wry little smile on his face.

As I watched her take a stumbling step, then crumple and fall in a pitiful heap, there was hardly time for one agonized thought before he turned the gun on me and fired again. A hot finger of lead explored my chest with a searing pain and the floor heaved toward me. Then the room vanished.

I remember a sound of distant voices, a vague sensation of movement, the muted keening of a siren, more voices, disembodied faces hovering near, and then nothing at all.

Much later, a solemn intern told me that my life had been saved with half an inch to spare, and that of the three shots fired by Douglas Lundy, the only fatal one was the last, aimed at his own bandaged head . . .

Marian and I are about as happy as we can be in this violent, unpredictable world. We have a charming little house in Westchester, not uncomfortably close to New York City. I disagree with poor dead Lundy—Marian is an excellent cook, and since she no longer has to work, she even helps me with the dishes now and then.

Getting dressed this morning, we were comparing bullet scars, and then at breakfast we got to reminiscing and "what-ifing" again.

"What if you had taken the train?" Marian said as she glanced affectionately across the room at little Wayne Junior in his playpen.

"Yeah, and what if I had been able to get space on an afternoon flight and I missed you at the airport?" I added.

"What if we had never gone back to my apartment but to the police instead?" Marian supplied.

"Try this one," I injected. "Suppose when we got to the apartment, instead of shooting us, Lundy listened to your explanation and we shook hands all around?"

"What if he'd been a better shot and had killed us both?" Marian posed.

"Maybe he did," I replied with a chuckle, "and here we are in heaven."

"Now really," said Marian with a soft smile, "that's pretty sweet. Let's leave it right there."

THE ADVENTURE OF THE INTARSIA BOX

by August Derleth

Solar Pons and I were at breakfast one fair morning only a week after our return from the country and the curious affair of the Whispering Knights, when the door below was thrown violently open, and there was a rush of feet on the stairs that stopped short of our threshold. Pons looked up, his gray eyes intent, his whole lean figure taut with waiting.

"A young woman, agitated," he said, nodding. He flashed a glance at the clock. "Scarcely seven. It is surely a matter of some urgency to her. The hour has only now occurred to her. She hesitates. No, she is coming on."

The sound of footsteps was now scarcely audible, but they came on up the stairs. In a moment there was a faint, timorous tapping on the door to our quarters, and an equally timorous voice, asking beyond the door, "Mr. Pons? Mr. Solar Pons?"

"Pray play the gentleman, Parker," said Pons.

I sprang up and threw open the door.

A sandy-haired young woman not much over her middle-twenties stood there, a package wrapped in a shawl pressed to her breast. She looked from one to the other of us with candid blue eyes, her full lower lip trembling uncertainly, a slow flush mounting her cheeks toward the scattering of freckles that bridged her nose and swept under her eyes.

Then, with that unerring intuition that women especially seem to have, she fixed upon Pons.

"Mr. Pons! I hope I'm not intruding. I had to come. I had to do something. Uncle will do nothing—just wait for whatever is to happen. Oh, it's dreadful, Mr. Pons, dreadful!"

"Do come in, Miss . . . ?"

"I am Flora Morland of Morland Park, Mr. Pons. You may have heard of my uncle, Colonel Burton Norland?"

"Retired resident at Malacca," said Pons promptly. "But do compose yourself, Miss Morland. Let me take that box you're holding."

"No, no!" she cried, and pressed it momentarily closer to her body. Then she bit her lip and smiled weakly. "But that is why I came. Forgive me, Mr. Pons. You shall see for yourself—now."

She threw back the shawl and revealed a box, scarcely as large as a cigar box, made of *kamuning* wood. It was beautifully carved on the top and around on all sides, with curious figures, like a bas-relief. It seemed obviously Oriental in design.

"Open it, Mr. Pons!" She shuddered a little. "I don't know how I could bear to have carried it all this way. I can't look again!"

Pons took the box gently from her. He pushed the breakfast dishes to one side and set the box on the table. He stood for a moment admiring its workmanship, while Miss Morland waited with an apprehensive tautness that was almost tangible in the room. Then he threw it open.

I fear I gasped. I do not know what I expected to see—a priceless jewel, perhaps?—a bibliophile's treasure?—something fitting to the exquisite box containing it. Certainly it was nothing I could have dreamed in my wildest imaginings! In the box laid a mummified human hand, severed at the wrist, affixed to the bottom of the box by two bands of white silk.

Pons's emotion showed only in his eyes, which lit up with quick interest. He touched the dried skin with the fingertips of one hand, while caressing the carved box with the other.

"Intarsia," murmured Pons. "An Italian art, Miss Morland. But this box would appear to be of Oriental origin; the subjects of the ornamentation are all Oriental. Would you care now to tell us how you came by it?"

He closed the box almost with regret, and, Miss Morland having taken the stuffed chair near the fireplace, came to stand against the mantel, filling his pipe with the detestable shag he smoked.

Miss Morland clasped her hands together. "I hardly know how to begin, Mr. Pons," she said.

"Let us start with this fascinating object you have brought us," suggested Pons.

"It was delivered to my uncle three days ago, Mr. Pons. I myself took it from the postman. It was mailed first-class from Kuala Lumpur. My uncle was in his study that morning, and I took it in to him. I recall that his face darkened when he saw the package, but I supposed that it was only in wonder at who might have sent it. It was ten years ago that he left Malaya. He looked for some clue to its origin; there was no return address on the package. He began to take off its wrappings. I had turned away from him to put some books back on the shelves, when suddenly I heard him make a kind of explosive sound, and on the instant he slipped from his chair to the floor. He had swooned dead away. I ran over to him of course, Mr. Pons—and that's how I came to see what was in the box. There was a little card, too—linen paper. I thought, Mr. Pons—I believe such details are important to you. On it was written in a flowing hand a single sentence: *I will come for you.*"

"The card is not now in the box," said Pons.

"I suppose my uncle removed it. I closed the box, Mr. Pons. I couldn't bear to look at what was in it. Then I brought my uncle around. I expected him to tell me what was in the box and what it all meant, but he said nothing —never a word. Seeing that the box was closed, he assumed that he had closed it before or as he fainted, and that I didn't know what was in it. Mr. Pons, I was deeply shocked by what was in the box, but I was even more profoundly disturbed by my uncle's failure to say anything at all of it to me. Since the day he received it, furthermore, he has been very busy, and everything he has done is in the way of putting his affairs in order."

"Did your uncle notify the police?"

"If so, I don't know of it, Mr. Pons."

Pons puffed reflectively on his pipe for a moment before he asked, "I take it you are an orphan and have been living with your uncle. For how long?"

"Ten years," she replied. "My mother died when I was very young, and my father five years after Uncle Burton returned from Malaya. He has been very kind to me. He has treated me as his own child."

"Your uncle is not married?"

"Uncle Burton was married at one time. I believe there was some cloud over the marriage. My father occasionally talked about my aunt in deprecatory terms, called her 'the Eurasian woman.' My cousin Nicholas, who spent the last five years' of Uncle Burton's tenure with him in Malacca, also married a Eurasian woman. My aunt died before my uncle's return to England."

"Your cousin?"

"He returned with Uncle Burton. He's a barrister with offices in the City. His wife is the proprietress of a small, but I believe thriving, importing business in the Strand."

"Your cousin—Nicholas Morland, is it?"

"There were three brothers, Mr. Pons—my father, Nick's father, and Uncle Burton."

"Your cousin, I take it, was your uncle's assistant in Malacca?"

"Yes, Mr. Pons."

"How old is your uncle, Miss Morland?"

"Seventy."

"So he was fifty-five when he retired," mused Pons. "How long had he been the resident in Malacca?"

"Fifteen years. He went out there when he was forty. I never really knew him, Mr. Pons, until his return. I hadn't been born when he was sent out. But Uncle Burton seemed to be very fond of me from the moment he saw me, and it seemed only natural that he would invite me to live with him when Father died. Uncle Burton is very wealthy, he has many servants, and, though he is regarded by some of them as a martinet, they do stay, most of them. And he has a large and secluded home in Chipping Barnet. It seemed the most natural thing to do, to live with him. He sent me to school, and through a small private college. For my part, I am expected to play hostess whenever he has one of his small parties, which are attended chiefly by my cousin and his wife and some other ex-Colonials and their wives. I rather like that now, though I didn't at first. But my uncle is the soul of rectitude. He will tolerate no deviation from proper conduct, so there are never any social problems for me to deal with."

"Your uncle's heirs—who are they?"

Our client looked momentarily startled. "Why, I suppose Nick and I are his only heirs," she said. "I know nothing of his affairs, Mr. Pons. But there is no one else. All our relatives of my uncle's generation are dead, and Nick and I are the only ones of our generation. Nick has no children, so there is no coming generation, either." She took a deep breath and asked impulsively, "Mr. Pons, can you get to the bottom of this mystery? It troubles me very much to see Uncle Burton—well, preparing for death. That's what he's doing, Mr. Pons, it really is."

"Your uncle has no knowledge of your coming here, Miss Morland?"

"None. I left at dawn. He seldom rises before eight o'clock."

"Then you've not had breakfast, Miss Morland."

"No, Mr. Pons."

"Allow me!" Pons strode to the door, opened it, stuck his head out and called, "Mrs. Johnson, if you please!" He turned back to our client. "Pray give me a few minutes to ponder your problem, Miss Morland. In the meantime, Mrs. Johnson will be happy to prepare breakfast for you in her quarters. Will you not, Mrs. Johnson?" he asked of our long-suffering landlady as she appeared on the threshold.

"That I will, to be sure, Mr. Pons. If you'll come with me, Miss?"

Miss Morland, too surprised to protest, allowed herself to be led from the room by Mrs. Johnson.

The door had hardly closed behind them before Pons

was once again at the box, opening it. I was drawn to his side.

"Is this not a unique warning indeed, Parker?" he asked.

"I have seldom seen anything as gruesome."

"It was intended to be. I submit that this severed hand must have a deep significance for our client's uncle. What do you make of it?"

I bent and peered closely at it, examining it as well as I could without disturbing it or removing it from the box. "A man's right hand," I said. "Of probably about forty, not much older, certainly. It is brown-skinned, not only from age. Eurasian?"

"Native. See how beautifully kept the nails are! This man did little work. There are no observable callouses. The hand is smooth even to the fingertips. How long would you say this hand has been severed?"

"Without more scientific apparatus, I should think it impossible to say."

"Could it be as old, say, as Colonel Morland's tenure in Malacca?"

"I should think so. But what could it mean to Morland?"

"Ah, Parker, when we can answer that question we will know why it was sent to him." He smiled grimly. "I fancy it concerns some dark episode of his past. He retired at fifty-five. Is that not early?"

"His health, perhaps, demanded his retirement."

"Or his conduct."

"Miss Morland speaks of him as a model of rectitude."

"And as something of a martinet. Conduct in search of rectitude may be as reprehensible as its opposite." He touched the silk bands. "What do you make of these, Parker?"

"If I may venture a guess, white is the color of mourning in the Orient," I said.

"The bands are new," observed Pons.

"That is certainly elementary," I could not help saying. "I can think of several reasons why they should be. What puzzles me is the reason for being of the hand in the first place."

"I submit its owner kept it as long as he lived."

"Well, that's reasonable," I agreed. "It has been properly mummified. Are we to take it that the owner is not still alive?"

"If he were sufficiently attached to this appendage while he lived, would he so readily have sent it off?"

"Hardly."

"Unless it had a message to convey or an errand to perform."

"Absurd!"

"Yet it did convey a message to Colonel Morland. It may be gruesome, but surely not so much so as to cause a normal and healthy man to swoon at the sight of it. It reminds me of that horrible little trifle of wizard lore known as the glory hand, the bewitched, animated hand of a dead man sent to perform its owner's wishes, even to murder."

"Superstitious claptrap!"

"Colonel Morland, at least, is convinced that his life is in danger, and that the threat to it emanates from Malaya. Let us just have a look at the ship's registry before our client returns to determine the number of ships that have docked from Malaya in the past few days."

We had time to search back five days before our client returned from Mrs. Johnson's quarters; during those five days no ship from Malaya had docked at England's ports, though a freighter, the *Alor Star,* was listed as due within twenty-four hours. At Miss Morland's entrance, Pons thrust the papers aside.

"Thank you, indeed, Mrs. Johnson," said Pons as our landlady turned at the threshold. "And now, Miss Morland, two or three questions occur to me. Pray be seated."

Our client, now somewhat more composed and less uncertain in her manner, took her former seat and waited expectantly.

"Miss Morland, when your uncle came around, did he say or do anything significant?" asked Pons.

"He didn't say a word," she answered. "He was very pale. He looked for the box and seemed relieved to find it closed. He picked it up at once. I asked him, 'Are you all right, Uncle?' He said, 'Just a trifle dizzy. You run along.'

I left him, but, of course, I did watch to be sure he would be all right. He hurried straight to his bedroom with this box. He hid it there, for when he came out again in a few moments, he no longer carried it. He then locked himself in his study, and within two hours his solicitor came. He could only have sent for him, because Mr. Harris would certainly not otherwise have come to call at that hour."

"You evidently found the intarsia box, Miss Morland."

"My uncle has in his bedroom only a cabinet, a bureau, and an old sea chest which he fancied, and which had accompanied him on his journeys. He served a short term in the Royal Navy as a young man, before entering the foreign service. He acquired the chest at that time. I knew that the box had to be in one of those three places, and I found it carefully covered up in the chest while my uncle was closeted with Mr. Harris. Last night, about eleven o'clock, after he went to sleep, I slipped in and took the box so that I might be ready to come to you without the risk of waking Uncle Burton by taking the box this morning."

"Did your uncle mention the box to anyone?"

"I don't know, Mr. Pons. But I should think that, if he had spoken of it to Mr. Harris, he would have shown it to him. Yet Uncle Burton never left the study while Mr. Harris was in the house; so he could not have done so."

"I see. I think, then, Miss Morland, our only recourse is to ask your uncle the questions you cannot answer."

Our client's hand flew to her lips; an expression of dismay appeared in her eyes. "Oh, Mr. Pons," she cried, "I'm afraid of what Uncle Burton might say."

"Miss Morland, I believe your uncle's life to be in great jeopardy. This belief he evidently shares. He can do no more than refuse to see us, and he can certainly not take umbrage at your attempt to be of service to him."

Her hand fell back to her lap. "Well, that's true," she decided.

Pons looked at the clock. "It is now nine. We can take the Underground at Baker Street and be at Watford Junction within the hour. Let us leave the box, if you please."

Our client sat for but a moment, undecided. Then, pressing her lips determinedly together, she got to her feet. "Very well, Mr. Pons. My uncle can do no worse than give me the back of his tongue!"

As we drew near to the home of Colonel Morland in the cab we had taken at Watford Junction, Pons's face grew more grim. "I fear we are too late, Miss Morland," he said presently.

"Oh, Mr. Pons! Why do you say so?" cried our client.

"No less than four police vehicles have passed us—two returning, two going our way," he answered. "I should be very much surprised not to find the police at Morland Park."

Miss Morland pressed a handkerchief to her lips.

Nor was Pons in error. Two police cars stood before the tall hedge that separated the parklike grounds which our client indicated as her uncle's home, and a constable stood on guard at the gate in the hedge.

"Young Mecker," murmured Pons at the sight of him.

As the cab pulled up, Mecker stepped forward to wave it away. Then, his arm upraised, he recognized Pons getting out. His arm dropped.

"Mr. Pons!" he cried. "How could you have learned?" Then he caught sight of our client. "Could this be Miss Flora Morland?"

"It could be," said our client. "Please! Tell me what has happened?"

"Inspector Jamison has been looking for you, Miss Morland. Please come with me."

"Never mind, Mecker," interposed Pons. "We'll take her in."

"Very well, sir. Thank you, sir." He shook his head, frowning. "Dreadful business, sir, dreadful."

Our client stood for a moment, one hand on Pons's arm, trembling.

"I am afraid, Miss Morland," said Pons with unaccustomed gentleness, "that what your uncle feared has come to pass."

We went up a closely hedged walk arbored over with trees to a classically Georgian country house of two and a half storeys. The front door was open to the warm summer morning; just inside it stood the portly figure of Inspector Seymour Jamison of Scotland Yard, talking with another constable. He turned abruptly at our entrance, frowning.

"Mr. Solar Pons, the private enquiry agent," he said heavily. "Do you smell these matters, Pons?" Then his eyes fell upon our client. "Aha! Miss Flora Morland. We've been looking for you, Miss Morland."

"Please! What has happened?" she beseeched him.

"You don't know?"

"I do not."

"Colonel Morland was found murdered in his bed this morning," said Jamison coldly. "The house was locked, no windows had been forced, and you were missing. I must ask you, Miss Morland, to come into the study with me."

"I should like to look into the bedroom, Jamison," said Pons.

"By all means. The photographer is there now, but he should be finished soon. Just down the hall, the third door on the left. Around the stairs."

Our client shot Pons a beseeching glance; he smiled reassuringly. Then she turned and went submissively with Inspector Jamison into the study, which was on the right.

Pons pushed past the police photographer into the late Colonel Morland's bedroom. Before us lay a frightful scene. Colonel Morland, a tall, broad-chested man, lay outspread on his back on his bed, a wavy Malay *kris* driven almost to the hilt into his heart. Most shocking of all—his right hand had been severed at the wrist and lay where it had fallen in a pool of blood on the carpet beside the bed. Gouts of blood had spattered the bed; a froth of blood had welled from the dead man's lips to colour his thick moustache; and the wide staring eyes seemed still to wear an expression of the most utter horror.

The room was a shambles. Whoever had slain our client's uncle had torn it apart in search of something. The Colonel's sea chest lay open, its contents strewn about. The drawers of the bureau, save for the very smallest at the top, had been pulled open and emptied, and the contents of the tall wardrobe cabinet, even to the uppermost shelves, were banked about the hassock that stood before it. The sight was almost enough to unnerve a stronger man than I, and I marveled at Pons's cool, keen detachment as he looked searchingly upon the scene.

The photographer, having finished, departed.

"How long would you say he has been dead, Parker?" asked Pons.

I stepped around gingerly and made a cursory examination. "At least eight hours," I said, presently. "I should put it at between midnight and two o'clock—not before, and not very long after."

"Before our client left the house," murmured Pons.

He stood for a moment where he was. Then he stepped gingerly over to the bed and looked down at Colonel Morland's body.

"The *kris* does not appear to have been disturbed," he said, "which suggests that the murderer carried a second weapon solely for the purpose of severing his victim's hand."

"A ritual weapon!" I cried. "And carried away with him!"

Pons smiled lightly. "Cut with a single sweeping stroke, very cleanly," he observed.

He stepped away from the bed and began to move carefully among the objects strewn about, disturbing nothing. He went straight to the bureau, the top of which had evidently not been disturbed, for what I assumed to be the dead man's watch and wallet lay there. The wallet was the first object of Pons's attention; he picked it up and examined its contents.

"Twenty-seven pound notes," he murmured.

"So the object of this search could hardly have been money," I said.

Pons shook his head impatiently. "No, no, Parker—the murderer was looking for the intarsia box. The top of the bureau was not disturbed because, had it been there, the box would have been instantly apparent; nor have the top drawers been opened because they are not deep enough to hold the box."

He moved cautiously to the side of the bed, avoiding the

pool of blood which had gushed from Colonel Morland's cleanly severed wrist. "The murderer must have stood just here," he said, and dropped to his knees to scrutinize the carpet intently. He was somewhat hampered by the presence of bloodstains, but I could see by the glint in his eyes that he had seen something of significance, however invisible it was to me, for he gave a small sound of satisfaction, as he picked something from the carpet just back from the edge of the great bed and put it into two of the little envelopes he always carried.

Just as he rose from his position, Inspector Jamison came into the room, wearing a patent glow of confidence.

"Nasty little job here, Pons," he said almost cheerfully. "You'll be sorry to learn I've sent Miss Morland off to the Yard to be put through it."

"Indeed," said Pons. "What admirable—and needlessly precipitate dispatch! You have reason to think her involved?"

"My dear fellow," said Jamison patronizingly. "Consider. Every window and door of this house was locked. Only four people had keys—Colonel Morland, whose key is on his ring; his valet, who was his batboy in Malacca and who discovered his body; the housekeeper; and Miss Morland. All of their keys are in their possession. Nothing has been forced. Miss Morland, I am told by Mr. Harris, the Colonel's counsel, stands to inherit sixty percent of a considerable estate, considerable even after the Crown duties."

"It does not seem to you significant that on so warm a night this house should have been locked up so tightly?" asked Pons.

"You're not having me on that, Pons," retorted Jamison, grinning. "We know all about that intarsia box. Morland was in fear for his life."

"You are suggesting then that Miss Morland slipped into the room, stabbed her uncle, cut off his right hand, searched the room until she turned up the box, and then made her way to Number 7B to enlist my services?"

"Hardly that. She is hardly strong enough to have driven that *kris* into him with such force."

"Hardly," agreed Pons dryly.

"But there is nothing to prevent her having hired an accomplice."

"And what motive could she possibly have had for cutting off her uncle's hand?" pressed Pons.

"What better way could be devised to confuse the investigation into the motive for so gruesome a crime?"

"And Miss Morland seems to you, after your conversation with her, the kind of young lady who could lend herself to such a crime?"

"Come, come, Pons. You have a softness for a pretty face," said Jamison.

"I submit that this would have been a most fantastic rigmarole to go through simply to inherit the wealth of a man who, by all the evidence, granted her every whim. No, Jamison, it won't wash."

"That intarsia box—she tells me it is in your possession. We shall have to have it."

"Send 'round to 7B for it. But give me at least today with it, will you?"

"I'll send for it tomorrow."

"Tell me—you've questioned the servants, I suppose? Did anyone hear anything in the night?"

"Not a sound. And I may say that the dog, which habitually sleeps at the front door of the house, outside, never once was heard to bark. I need hardly tell you the significance of that."

"It suggests that the murderer entered . . ."

"Or was let in."

"By the back door."

Jamison's face reddened. He raised his voice. "It means that since the dog did nothing in the nighttime the murderer was known to him."

Pons clucked sympathetically. "You ought to stay away from Sir Arthur's stories, my dear chap. They have a tendency to vitiate your style."

"I suppose you will be telling us to look for a giant of a man who can charm dogs," said Jamison with heavy sarcasm.

"Quite the contrary. Look for a short, lithe man who, in this case at least, probably went barefooted." He turned and pointed to the scarcely visible hassock. "Only a man shorter than average would have had to use that hassock to look at the top shelves of the cabinet. The indentations in the carpet indicate that the hassock's usual position is over against the wall beside the cabinet."

Jamison's glance flashed to the hassock, and returned, frowning, to Pons.

"If you don't mind, Jamison, I'll just have a look around out in back. Then perhaps you could send us back to Watford Junction in one of the police cars."

"Certainly, Pons. Come along."

Jamison led the way out and around the stairs to a small areaway from which doors opened to the kitchen on the right, and a small storeroom on the left, and into the backyard. A maid and an elderly woman, manifestly the housekeeper, sat red-eyed at a table in the kitchen. Jamison hesitated, evidently of the opinion that Pons wished to speak with them, but Pons's interest was in the back door, where he crouched to look at the lock. He really inspected it.

"We've been all through that, Pons," said Jamison with an edge of impatience in his voice.

Pons ignored him. He opened the door, crouched to examine the sill, then dropped to his knees and, on all fours, crawled out to the recently reset flagstone walk beyond it. From one place he took up a pinch of soil and dropped it into one of his envelopes. At another he pointed wordlessly, beckoning to Inspector Jamison, who came and saw the unmistakable print of human toes.

Then Pons sprang up and went back into the house, Jamison and myself at his heels. He found a telephone directory, consulted it briefly, and announced that he was ready to leave, if Jamison would be kind enough to lend us a police car and driver.

Once again on the Underground, I asked Pons, "We're not going back to 7B?"

"No, Parker. I am delighted to observe how well you read me. I daresay we ought to lose no time discovering the secret of the intarsia box. Since Colonel Morland is dead, we shall have to ask Nicholas Morland whether he can explain it. You'll recall that he spent the last five years of his uncle's residency with him. He has an office in the Temple. I took the trouble to look him up in the directory before we left Morland Park."

"I followed the matter of the murderer's height readily enough," I said, "but how did you arrive at his being bare-footed?"

"There were in the carpet beside the bed, just where a man might have stood to deliver the death blow, three tiny files of soil particles, in such a position as to suggest the imprint of toes. The soil was quite probably picked up among the flagstones."

"And, you know, Pons—Jamison has a point about the dog."

Pons smiled enigmatically. "The dog did nothing. Very well. Either he knew the murderer—or he didn't hear him, which is quite as likely. A barefooted man could travel with singular noiselessness. And Morland Park is a paradise for prowlers!" He looked at me, his eyes dancing. "Consider the severed hand. Since you are so busy making deductions, perhaps you have accounted for it."

"Now you press me," I admitted, "that seems to me the most elementary detail of all. I suggest that an indignity the late Colonel Morland committed in the past has now been visited upon him."

"Capital! Capital!" cried Pons. "You have only to keep this up, my dear fellow, and I can begin to think of retiring."

"You are making sport of me!" I protested.

"On the contrary. I could not agree with you more. There are one or two little points about the matter that trouble me, but I have no doubt these will be resolved in due time."

For the rest of the journey Pons rode in silent contemplation, his eyes closed, the thumb and forefinger of his right hand ceaselessly caressing the lobe of his ear. He did not open his eyes again until we came into Temple Station.

Nicholas Morland proved to be a somewhat frosty man in his early forties. He was dressed conservatively, but in clothes befitting his station. Save for the difference in years, he was not unlike his late uncle in appearance, with the same kind of moustache, the same outward thrust of the lips, the same bushy brows. His frosty mien was superficial, for it collapsed as he listened to Pons's concise summary of events, and little beads of perspiration appeared at his temples.

"We must rely upon you, Mr. Morland," concluded Pons, "to explain the significance of the intarsia box and its contents."

Morland came shakily to his feet and walked back and forth across his office, biting his lip. "It is something I had hoped never to have to speak about," he said at last. "Is it really necessary, Mr. Pons?"

"I assure you it is. Scotland Yard will expect to hear about it before the day is out. I am here in advance of their coming because I am acting in the interests of your cousin."

"Of course. I quite understand."

He took another turn or two about his office, and then sat down again, dabbing at his forehead with a handkerchief.

"Well, Mr. Pons, it is a matter that does not reflect at all well upon my late uncle," he began. "As Flora may perhaps have told you, Uncle Burton married a Eurasian woman, a very fine, very beautiful woman some ten years his junior —perhaps as much as fifteen, I cannot be sure, though I suspect my wife would know. I am sure you are aware that matters of moral conduct among the ethnically mixed peoples of the Federated States of Malaya are considered lax by British standards, and perhaps it was true that my aunt engaged in improper conduct with Bendarloh Ali, an uncle of my wife's, who belonged to one of the better native families in Malacca. My uncle thought he would lose face, and he set about to prevent it. My aunt died; there is some reason to believe that it was by poison at my uncle's hands. Her lover was arrested. Some valuable items belonging to my uncle were found in his home. He was accused of having stolen them, on no stronger evidence than their presence in his home, and he suffered the indignity of having his right hand cut off at the wrist. That is the sum total of the matter, sir."

"How long ago did this happen, Mr. Morland?"

"Only a month or two before he was sent home. The Sultan of Malacca was outraged—though he had approved the punishment, he was later led to repudiate it—and demanded the recall of the resident. The Governor really had no alternative but to relieve my uncle of his post."

"Over fifteen years, then. Does it seem likely that he would wait so long to take vengeance?"

"Not he, Mr. Pons. My uncle's victim died three months ago. I think it not inconsistent of the Malay character that his son might believe it incumbent upon him to avenge the honor of his house and the indignity done his father."

"I submit it would be an unnatural son who would separate his father's right hand from his remains," said Pons.

Morland shook his head thoughtfully. "Mr. Pons, I would tend to agree. There is this point to consider. The hand sent my uncle may *not* have been Bendarloh Ali's. Even if it were, I suppose the family represents that ethnic mixture so common in Malacca that no standard of conduct consistent with ancient Malay customs could be ascribed to it."

Pons sat for a few moments in contemplative silence. Then he said, "You are very probably aware that you and your cousin will share your uncle's estate."

"Oh, yes. There is no one else. We are a small family, and unless Flora marries, we will very likely die out entirely. Oh, there are distant cousins, but we have not been in touch for many years." He shrugged. "But it's a matter of indifference to me. My practise is quite sufficient for our needs, though I suppose my wife can find a use for what Uncle Burton may leave us, what with the constant innovations at her shop."

The telephone rang suddenly at Morland's elbow. He lifted it to his ear, said, "Morland here," and listened. When he put it down after but a brief period, he said, "Gentlemen, the police are on the way."

Pons got to his feet with alacrity. "One more question, Mr. Morland. Your relations with your uncle—were they friendly, tolerant, distant?"

"The three of us had dinner at Morland Park once a month, Mr. Pons," said Morland a little stiffly.

"Three?"

"My wife's cousin lives with us. Uncle Burton naturally would not exclude him."

"Thank you, sir."

We took our leave.

Outside, Pons strode purposefully along, some destination in mind, his eyes fixed upon an inner landscape. Within a few minutes we were once more on the Underground, and rode in silence unbroken by any word from Pons, until we reached Trafalgar Station and emerged to walk in the Strand.

"Pons," I cried finally, exasperated at his silence. "It's noon. What are we doing here?"

"Ah, patience, Parker, patience. The Strand is one of the most fascinating areas in the world. I mean to idle a bit and shop."

Within half an hour, Pons had exchanged his deerstalker for a conservative summer hat, leaving his deerstalker to be dispatched to our quarters by post; he had bought a light summer coat, which he carried loosely on his arm; and he had added a walking stick to his ensemble, all to my open-mouthed astonishment. He presented quite a different picture from that to which I had become accustomed in the years I had shared his quarters, and he offered no explanation of his purchases.

We continued in the Strand until we came to a small shop modestly proclaiming that antiques and imports were to be had.

"Ah, here we are," said Pons. "I beg you, Parker, keep your face frozen. You have an unhappy tendency to show your reactions on it."

So saying, he went into the shop.

A bell, tinkling in a back room, brought out a dapper, brownskinned man of indeterminate age. He came up to us and bowed. He looked little older than a boy, but he was not a boy. He smiled, flashing his white teeth, and said, "If it please you, gentlemen, I am here to serve you."

"Are you the proprietor?" asked Pons abruptly.

"No, sir. I am Ahmad. I work for Mrs. Morland."

"I am looking," said Pons, "for an intarsia box."

"Ah. Of any precise size?"

"Oh, so—and so," said Pons, describing the size of the intarsia box Miss Morland had brought to our quarters.

"Just so. One moment, if you please."

He vanished into the room to the rear, but came out in a very few moments carrying an intarsia box, which he offered to Pons.

"Seventeenth century Italian, sir. Genuine. I trust this is the box you would like."

"It is certainly exquisite work," said Pons. "But, no, it is not quite what I would like. The size is right. But I would like something with Oriental ornamentation."

"Sir, there are no antique intarsia boxes of Oriental manufacture," said Ahmad. "I am sorry."

"I'm not looking for an antique," said Pons. "I am, of course, aware that intarsia boxes were not made in the Orient before the eighteenth century."

Ahmad's pleasant face brightened. "Ah, in that case, sir, I may have something for you."

He vanished once more into the quarteers to the rear of the shop.

When he came out this time he carried another intarsia box. With a triumphant smile, he gave it to Pons. Then he stood back to wait upon Pons's verdict.

Pons turned it over, examining it critically. He opened it, smelled it, caressed it with his fingers, and smiled. "Excellent!" he cried. "This will do very well, young man. What is its price?"

"Ten pounds, sir."

Pons paid for it without hesitation. "Pray wrap it with care. I should not like any of that beautifully wrought carving to be damaged, even scratched."

Ahmad beamed. "Sir, you like the intarsia?"

"Young man, I have some knowledge of these things," said Pons almost pontifically. "This is among the finest work of its kind I have seen."

Ahmad backed away from Pons, bowing, his face glowing. He retired once again into the back room, from which presently came the sounds of rustling paper. In just under five minutes Ahmad reappeared and placed the carefully wrapped intarsia box in Pons's hands. He was still glowing with pleasure. Moreover, he had the air of bursting with something he wanted to say, which only decorum prevented his giving voice.

Pons strolled leisurely from the shop and away down the street. But, once out of sight of the shop, he moved with alacrity to hail a cab and gave the driver our Praed Street address.

"Did you not have the feeling that Ahmad wished to tell us something?" I asked when we were on our way.

"Ah, he told us everything," said Pons, his eyes glinting with good humor. "Ahmad is an artist in intarsia. I trust you observed the costly antiques offered in Mrs. Morland's shop?"

"I did indeed."

"It suggested nothing to you?"

"That her business is thriving, as Miss Morland told us." I reached over and tapped the package Pons held. "Did it not seem to you that this box is very much like Miss Morland's?"

Pons smiled. "Once the first box is turned out, the pattern is made. The rest come with comparative ease. They are probably identical, not only with each other, but with a score or more of others."

Back in our quarters, Pons carefully unwrapped the intarsia box he had bought and placed it beside our client's. Except for the fact that there was some difference in age between them, they were virtually identical. Pons examined the boxes with singular attention to detail, finding each smallest variation between them.

"Are they identical or not?" I asked finally.

"Not precisely. The box Miss Morland brought us is at least seventy-five years old; it may be a hundred. It is made of the same beautiful *kamuning* wood out of which the Malays fashion the hilts of their weapons. I trust you observed that the handle of the *kris* which killed Colonel Morland was of this same wood. It has been polished many times and waxed; there is actually some visible wearing away of the wood. The other is a copy of a box like this, made by a skilled artist. I suppose there is a demand for objects of this kind and I have no doubt they are to be had in all the shops which have imported pieces from the Orient for sale. Chinese boxes like this are most frequently in metal or ceramic; wood is more commonly in use from Japan down the coast throughout the Polynesians and Melanesians in the south Pacific." He dismissed the intarsia boxes with a gesture. "But now, let us see what we have from the late Colonel Morland's bedroom."

He crossed to the corner where he kept his chemistry apparatus and settled himself to examine the contents of the envelopes he had used at Morland Park. There were but three of them, and it was unlikely that they would occupy him for long. Since I had a professional call to make at two o'clock, I excused myself.

When I returned within the hour, I found Pons waiting expectantly.

"Ah, Parker," he cried, "I trust you are free for the remainder of the afternoon. I am expecting Jamison and together we may be able to put an end to Scotland Yard's harassing of our client."

"Did you learn anything at the slides?" I asked.

"Only confirmation of what I suspected. The particles of soil I found on the carpet beside the bed were identical with the soil around the flagstone, even to grains of limestone, of which the flagstones are made. There seems to be no doubt but that the soil was carried into the house by the bare toes of the murderer. Other than that, there was also just under the edge of the bed a tiny shaving of camphor wood, which is also commonly used by the Malays who work the jungle produce of that country."

"We are still tied to Colonel Morland's past," I said.

"We have never strayed from it," said Pons shortly. "But thus far in the course of the inquiry, unless Scotland Yard has turned up fingerprints on the handle of the *kris,* we have only presumptive, not convicting evidence. It is all very well to know the identity of the murderer; the trick is to convict him. Ah, I hear a motor slowing down. That will be Jamison."

Within a moment a car door slammed below, and we heard Jamison's heavy tread on the stairs.

The Inspector came into our quarters gingerly carrying a small package, which he surrendered to Pons with some relief. "Here it is, Pons," he said. "I had a little trouble getting the loan of it."

"Capital!" cried Pons. He took the package and carried it to the intarsia box he had bought in the shop on the Strand. "I don't suppose you're armed, Jamison?"

"The tradition of the Yard," began Jamison ponderously.

"Yes, yes, I know," said Pons. "Parker, get my revolver."

I went into the bedroom and found Pons's weapon where he had last carelessly laid it down on the bureau.

"Give it to Jamison, will you?"

"I don't know what you're up to, Pons," said Jamison, with some obvious misgiving on his ruddy face. "P'raps that young woman's turned your head."

The contents of the Inspector's package had vanished into the intarsia box, which Pons now took up, having resumed the garb he had bought in the Strand shops.

"Let us be off. I want to try an experiment, Jamison. Frankly, it is no more than that. It may succeed. It may not. We shall see."

Our destination was the antique and imports shop in the Strand, and all the way there Pons said nothing, only listened with a sardonic smile on his hawk-like features to Jamison's weighty discourse on the damning circumstances which made our client seem guilty of arranging her uncle's death.

As the police car approached the shop, Pons spoke for the first time to Constable Mecker, who was at the wheel. "Either stop short of the shop or drive past it, Mecker."

Mecker obediently stopped beyond the shop.

"Now, Jamison," said Pons brusquely, as we got out of the car, "hand on gun, and pray be ready. Try to look a little less like a policeman, that's a good fellow."

Pons led the way into the shop, carrying the carefully wrapped intarsia box he had bought only a few hours previously. An extraordinarily handsome Eurasian woman came forward to wait upon him. She was of indeterminate age. She could have been anywhere between twenty and forty, but certainly did not seem over thirty.

"What can I do for you, gentlemen?"

"The young man who waited on me this noon," said Pons, unwrapping the intarsia box as he spoke. "Is he here?"

She nodded, raised her voice to call, "Ahmad!" and stepped back.

Ahmad came out, a look of polite inquiry on his face. He recognized Pons as his noon-hour customer. His eyes fell to the box.

"Sir! You are disappointed?"

"In the beauty of the box, no," said Pons. "But the interior!"

Ahmad stepped lightly forward and took the box, discarding the wrappings. "We shall see," he said, bowing almost obsequiously.

Then he opened the intarsia box.

Instantly, a dramatic and frightening metamorphosis took place. Ahmad's smiling face altered grotesquely. Its mask of politeness washed away to reveal dark murderous features, suffused with sudden rage and fear. He dropped the intarsia box—and from it rolled the severed hand of Colonel Burton Morland! Simultaneously, he leaped backward with a feline movement, tore down from the wall behind him a scimitar-like *chenangka,* and turned threateningly upon Pons.

For scarcely a moment the scene held. Then Mrs. Morland began to waver, and I sprang forward to catch her as she fainted. At the same moment, Inspector Jamison drew his gun upon Ahmad.

"My compliments, Inspector," said Pons. "You've just taken the murderer of Colonel Morland. I think," he added blandly, "if I were you I should take Mrs. Nicholas Morland along and question her about the profit motive in the death of her husband's uncle. I believe it almost certain that hers was the brain in which this devilish crime was conceived. —Is the lady coming around, Parker?"

"In a few moments," I said.

"Call Mecker," said Jamison, finding his voice.

Pons stepped into the street and shouted for the constable.

"It was not alone the fact that no ship had docked recently from Malaya that made an avenger from the Orient unlikely," said Pons as we rode back to Praed Street on the Underground, "but the same aspect of the matter that so impressed Jamison. The murderer clearly had prior knowledge of Morland Park, something no newly arrived foreigner could have had, and he must have been someone who had ample opportunity to take an impression of the back door key, since he would prefer to enter by that door not guarded by the dog. Nothing in that house was disturbed, save Colonel Morland's room. Not a sound aroused anyone throughout the entry into the house and the commission of the crime.

"Yet it was evident that the murderer also had knowledge of the indignity done to Bendarloh Ali. Miss Morland had no such knowledge. Her cousin Nicholas had. Presumably, since his wife was of Bendarloh Ali's family, and had been in Malacca at the time Ali was so brutally punished, she knew as much as her husband. It is not too much to conclude that her cousin, who was therefore also of Bendarloh Ali's family, knew the circumstances also. Ahmad, of course, is that cousin. Ahmad had been as frequent a visitor at Morland Park as his employer. He knew the grounds and the house. The shaving of camphor wood, as much a product of Malaya as *kamuning* wood, places Ahmad indisputably in the late Colonel Morland's bedroom.

"Manifestly, the preparations were made with great care. Mrs. Morland directed her relatives to send the hand of Bendarloh Ali to Colonel Morland in the intarsia box which she forwarded to Malay for that purpose. That the box had served as a model for Ahmad's carefully-wrought imitations did not seem to her important, since Ahmad had been instructed to bring the box back from Morland Park. Ahmad undoubtedly killed Colonel Morland to avenge the family honor after Bendarloh Ali died, but I think it inescapable that his desire for vengeance was planted and carefully nourished by Mrs. Nicholas Morland, whose real motive was not vengeance, but the control of the unlimited funds which would be at her disposal when her husband came into his share of his uncle's estate.

"One of our most sanguinary cases, Parker. And though we have taken the murderer, I suspect that the real criminal will go free to enjoy the expansion of her shop according to her plan. It is one of life's little ironies."

BESIDE A FLOWERING WALL

by Fletcher Flora

Having become a creature of habit, the stale protagonist of a domestic regimen, Ruth awoke that morning, as usual, at almost precisely eight o'clock. The odd thing about her regimen, including the precision schedule of waking, was that it was, and had been from the beginning, entirely unnecessary. So far as her commitments were concerned, her obligation to be here or there at this hour or that, she might as well have awakened anytime and at her discretion have gone anywhere.

Yet, commitments aside, the regimen was, for its own reasons, essential. It gave order and stability to a life that would have, without it, blown apart in an explosion of centrifugal pressure or, even worse, have diminished and died in the dust of abandoned hopes and sustained frustration. She was, indeed, like the compulsive alcoholic who must adhere to the discipline of abstinence or submit to the anarchy of excess.

This particular morning, however, although it began for her at the time and in the place of other mornings, was in fact the morning of such a day as she had never lived and would never live again. It was, in prospect, the culmination of all the years of days that had gone before it, and it would be, before it was over, the end of them. It would be, by the terms of a kind of destined and dreadful rationale, the end of all that had never been done, the suffix of all that had never been said.

She had planned the day, insofar as she was able, quite carefully. It was characteristic of her, as she had become, that even her aberrations, the willful departure from accustomed ways and normal expectations, must somehow sustain the quality of habit, every strange effect of every disturbing cause somehow anticipated and rehearsed, as if she would otherwise be lost and impotent in a confusion of wanton reactions. The planning had begun, in fact, late in the afternoon of the day before; a few minutes after five o'clock, to be as precise as possible.

Ruth always had two very dry martinis at five o'clock, or rather in the half hour following the hour, and Mrs. Groat, who came in days to clean and cook, had just brought in the little silver tray with the silver shaker and the delicate long-stemmed glass of shining crystal. The telephone in the hall had begun to ring at that instant, and Mrs. Groat had gone to answer it, leaving Ruth to pour the first martini for herself, in itself a deviation from the normal that now seemed, in retrospect, to be darkly prophetic. Ruth had just taken her first sip from the delicate glass, when Mrs. Groat returned with news that was, if not revolutionary, at least unusual enough to excite her curiosity.

"Someone for you," Mrs. Groat said. "A man."

Ruth had experienced no sudden and mysterious intuition about the call. After all, she was still called occasionally by men, almost invariably on matters of business, and there was no reason why she should have expected this particular call to be in any way unusual. Putting her glass on the little table beside her chair, she went past Mrs. Groat into the hall, picked up the phone and said, "Hello."

"Ruth?" the man's voice queried.

Then, of course, she knew. The single syllable of her name was spoken as casually as if it prefaced a response to something she had said a decade ago, and she stood mute for a moment, her brain scalded with remembrance. After the mute moment, because it was imposed by a fierce pride, she answered with a voice that was miraculously contained.

"Yes. Who's speaking, please?"

"It's Pat. Pat Brady."

"Pat!" She permitted an inflection of surprise to enter her voice. "Where in the world are you?"

"I'm in St. Louis."

She had assumed that the call was local, and she felt an irrational anger at the electronic marvel of direct long-distance dialing. Previously, you would at least have had the intermediate operator to warn you of the unexpected, so that you would have an instant to prepare the reaction of pleasure or excitement or shock, or to disguise, as she was disguising now, the sickening ambivalence incited by what had been and what was.

"That's too bad," she said. "I'd enjoy seeing you again."

"That's why I called. I'm at loose ends tomorrow, and I'd like to see you again, too. Would it be convenient if I came? I'd have only a couple of hours in town at the most."

"Are you sure you want to come all the way from St. Louis for just a couple of hours?"

"Nothing to it. I'll hop a jet in the morning and be there in a flash. I'll take another jet out in the afternoon."

"What time should I expect you?"

"You name the hour, and I'll be on your doorstep."

"Would two o'clock in the afternoon be all right?"

"Fine. Expect me then. Same old place?"

"Same old place. Mother and Father are both dead now. Perhaps you'd heard."

"I hadn't. I'm sorry."

"Well, one adjusts after a while."

"Of course. Nothing else to do. Until tomorrow then, Ruth."

"Until tomorrow. Good-bye, Pat."

It was miraculous, truly miraculous, how calmly she had spoken his name. She was exorbitantly proud of herself, of her miraculous control. To demonstrate to herself that it was secure, not just something she had achieved briefly by a great effort, she repeated the name three times to herself with a kind of deliberate and lilting cadence: *Pat, Pat, Pat.* She cradled the telephone and returned to the living room where Mrs. Groat, who had eavesdropped, was clearly torn between an uncertain respect for Ruth's privacy and her own agitated curiosity. Leaning toward the latter, she hovered in hope. Ruth, aware of this, sat down in her chair and picked up her glass from the silver tray. How steady her hand was! The glass, on its way to her lips, did not shake in the least. Not a drop of the precious pale liquid was lost from it. And how good the strong martini was! It slipped smoothly down her throat and gathered in her stomach in a warm little puddle.

"That was an old friend," she said. "I knew him quite well a long time ago. His name is Pat Brady."

"How nice." Mrs. Groat, whose experience with men had confirmed her mother's warnings, sounded vaguely belligerent. "Will he be coming to call?"

"Yes. Tomorrow afternoon."

"Will you want me to prepare something special? Tea or early cocktails or something?"

"No, thank you. As a matter of fact, you may plan to have the afternoon off. Pat and I will have so many things to catch up on. We'll manage quite well, I'm sure."

Mrs. Groat's open face suddenly closed. Uncertain whether she should rejoice in her unexpected half-holiday or take offense at what might be her peremptory exclusion, she retreated to the kitchen to analyze the development.

Ruth, lifting her glass to her lips again, discovered with a slight shock that it was empty. She had drunk the martini much too fast. Really, she must try to restrain herself. Two martinis between five and five-thirty were her quota, her absolute limit except on those rare occasions that might be called special, and she always paced her consumption of them to last the full half-hour. Having drunk one already, at barely ten minutes after the hour, she would simply have to pace more slowly for the next twenty minutes. Or could this occasion, perhaps, be called special? Well, hardly. Tomorrow, however, was another matter. Tomorrow would be special. Tomorrow she would have her martinis earlier, and it was entirely possible, even probable, that she would have three, or even four.

Already she was making plans. In fact, although she was not consciously aware of it, she had begun planning the moment she cradled the telephone. That was evidenced by her prompt and rather ruthless exclusion of Mrs. Groat, who would only be in the way. *Three's a crowd, Mrs. Groat. Extras are unwelcome on special occasions, Mrs. Groat. So sorry, Mrs. Groat, but you are not wanted.*

She emptied the silver shaker into the delicate crystal glass and took the first sip of her second martini in her disciplined drinking. She was tempted by her growing excitement to drink with reckless haste, but she managed, by a stern exercise of will, to stretch the martini over the remaining twenty minutes, and it was just five-thirty when she got down to what would have been the olive if she ordinarily bothered with olives, which she did only on special occasions. Like tomorrow, for example; tomorrow she would have olives.

Leaving her glass beside the shaker on the tray, Ruth went upstairs to her room. The room was large and light, at the front of the house. It had once been the room of her parents, but now her parents were dead; dead and buried side by side in the cemetery east of town, and the room was hers. She crossed the room to a window overlooking the front yard and stood staring out across the yard and the street to the house directly opposite. In other years there had been no house there, only a beloved and beautiful vacant lot, beaten bare by the neighborhood kids who had gathered to play baseball and shinny on fair days, and Pump, Pump, Pull Away in the soft interminable dusks of summer. Next to the house that now stood where the lot had been, was the house in which Pat had been born and had lived out the years of his boyhood. Shifting the direction of her gaze, looking across the street obliquely, she could see the house.

Oh, he had been a beautiful boy! Swift and strong he had been, and good at games, and later adept in love. It was no wonder she had loved him desperately all those years. The wonder was that he had loved her, for she had been a plain girl, as she was a plain woman, with an odd faded look as if she had been laundered too many times in boiling water. Of course, a girl's looks are not important to a boy when he is very young. What is important is her steadfast loyalty and her readiness to do what a young boy wants to do. And he *had* loved her. He *had*. His love had survived puberty, and the years after, and it had survived in the after-years the trials of abortive expression in this private place or that, at one fearful and ecstatic time or another.

Then, in the end, it had come to nothing. That was the shame of it, the terrible degradation. If only it had ended, if it had to end, in an explosion of fury or a flash of tragedy. If only it had ended in a way that was worthy of the quality of her love—but it hadn't. Instead, it had expired with a whimper. For him, it had died of apathy. It had simply come to *nothing*.

Turning away from the window, she went into the bathroom. In the mirror above the lavatory, she saw the reflection of her face and paused deliberately to study it dispassionately. Her face was another shameful thing. It was not so much that she minded being plain, or even ugly. She would have preferred, in fact, a distinctive ugliness. What she minded was the faded effect of anemia—the *nothingness*. It was a lie, that's what it was. Her face was a *lie*. It denied the fierce intensity of her heart and brain. It obscured the history of her total commitment to love in her early years, and of her love's cruel mutation in the desolate years afterward.

She evaded the lie by opening the medicine cabinet door. Reaching behind a screen of bottles on the top shelf, she removed a small box. There was no label on the lid of the box. Removing the lid, she stood staring at the white powder the box contained. She could not recall the name of the powder, and made no effort to do so, but she knew well enough its potential. In her hand, in the small box, she was holding sudden death for at least a dozen people. Her father had been a pharmacist and a successful businessman. He had owned three drugstores when he died, two years after her mother's death, and she had gone the day after his funeral to one of the stores, which had since been sold, and had taken this powder from behind the prescription counter. In the bleak newness of being utterly alone she had thought she would like to die. It was not that she had loved her parents so much, or that she even missed them excessively for themselves when they were gone. It was just the loneliness. If she had married Pat, as she had expected and planned, the death of her father would have meant little more to her than a minor adjustment and a large inheritance.

Anyhow, she had decided not to die; not yet. As she had once lived for her only love, she continued to live for the love's mutation. The day would come, would surely come, when she would have the chance to make right what had all these years been wrong. If she could not recover the love, she could at least remove its shame. She could give to her love, the truth in her heart behind the lie in her face, the proud and star-crossed ending it deserved.

Staring at the snowy powder in the little box, she formed with her lips the shape of a word: *Tomorrow*.

Today—today was yesterday's tomorrow—and now that it had begun, it was necessary to get through it, from minute to minute and hour to hour, until it was spent, ended, at whatever time the ending came. Ruth got out of bed and showered and dressed in sweater and slacks, and then she sat down in front of her dressing table and began to brush her light brown hair a hundred strokes. Her head canted first this way and then that, according to which side of the part she was brushing on, and when she had finished the hundred strokes exactly, fifty on each side of the part, she laid the brush on the table, avoiding her image in the mirror, and went out into the hall. With the door closed behind her, she could hear Mrs. Groat, who carried a key to the back door, at her work in the kitchen below. Mrs. Groat was a noisy worker, seeming to *attack* every task as if she feared a counterattack, and it was a constant wonder to Ruth that she did not leave behind her a litter of damaged pots and shattered glass and china. Even the vacuum sweeper, operated by Mrs. Groat, assumed a kind of roar, as if it were powered by a miniature jet engine.

Having descended the stairs, Ruth found her place set as usual on the table in the dining room, the electric percolator giving off the good, rich smell of coffee on the server near at hand. She poured a cup of coffee and sat down at her place, and Mrs. Groat, hearing her arrive on her usual schedule on this unusual day, came in from the kitchen with a glass of orange juice.

"Good morning," Mrs. Groat said.

"Good morning."

Ruth, leaning slightly forward over her cup, inhaled the rich vapors. Mrs. Groat lingered, sensing the day's difference and anticipating some kind of minor revolution.

"The usual breakfast?" Mrs. Groat asked, her voice brusque.

"Yes," Ruth said. "The usual."

The usual, in addition to coffee and juice, was one slice of buttered toast, two strips of crisp bacon, and one egg over easy. Mrs. Groat, vaguely disappointed in the failure of revolution to develop, returned to the kitchen, and Ruth began to drink her steaming coffee. She had just finished the cupful when Mrs. Groat came back with her plate. Ruth was, surprisingly, quite hungry. The excitement within her, contained and growing, nourished by her expectations, had given an edge to her appetites and senses.

She finished her breakfast, and then, because it was a fair day, and because she was too large for the house with the excitement growing and growing within her, she went out into the yard and cut flowers and brought them in and arranged them in a vase, which she placed in the living room. Then she went back out into the yard and pruned and dug and watered and did a dozen things that did not need doing at all, or could have been done later, because it was essential, absolutely essential, that the hours of the morning be filled, the time passed, and somehow the hours were and time was.

At noon, she went back into the house and washed her hands and face and had her lunch and went upstairs to her room. She lay down on her bed, neatly made by Mrs. Groat, and she wished that she could sleep, could close her eyes and know nothing and open them again just in time to do what must be done before it was too late for doing anything. It was, of course, impossible to sleep with her excitement now monstrous and pulsing and scarcely containable, and it would hardly have been worthwhile anyhow, even if it had been possible, because Mrs. Groat clumped upstairs just before one o'clock and knocked on the door and came in uninvited. She was wearing her hat with an effect of belligerence, and she was clutching her purse like a primitive weapon.

"If you have no further use for me," she said, "I'll be leaving now."

She made it sound as if, after faithful service, she were being discarded. Ruth sat up on the edge of the bed. She wondered if Mrs. Groat could sense her excitement, could feel it in the air or hear it in her voice or see it seeping through her skin like a vapor, and it seemed incredible that Mrs. Groat could not.

"That's fine," Ruth said. "Enjoy your afternoon."

"Thank you." Mrs. Groat did not sound optimistic. "I'll see you in the morning."

"Yes, as usual. In the morning."

Ruth pronounced the word with no sense of reality. A word is what it was. Morning was a word, a sound, without substance or prospects. What was real, real and here and suddenly demanding, was this afternoon, two o'clock this afternoon, and now she would have to hurry, having waited so long, to do in advance what needed doing. She undressed and took another shower and stood for a minute or two in front of the long mirror on the inside of the bathroom door to look at her lean body, so much more beautiful than her shameful nothing face, and she felt all at once a great pity and regret for the terrible waste of her beautiful lean body. In the bedroom she dressed carefully, putting on at last a pale green sleeveless sheath. By that time it was one-thirty, a little past, and she went back into the bathroom and took the small box of powder from the medicine cabinet and carried it downstairs. In the kitchen she made a shaker of martinis and put the shaker in the freezer compartment of the refrigerator. When martinis got crackling cold, she had discovered, they became just slightly thick and exceptionally good. Next, she set the silver tray on the cabinet beside the sink and placed on the tray a small bowl of olives and a pair of crystal glasses. Beside the tray she placed the small box of powder.

It will only require a little, she thought. *A pinch apiece for the two crystal glasses.*

The thought did not depress her. On the contrary, it was exhilarating, a lyric expression of her sustained excitement. The exhilaration cried out for accompaniment. Turning away, she went into the living room and looked among the recordings in the cabinet of her stereophonic phonograph. There! That was just right. That was just what she needed, what her mood needed, at once gay and grave and exalted. She put the recording on the phonograph and stood listening to the first movement of Mozart's Jupiter symphony, and the first movement ended, and the second movement began, and then, halfway through the second movement, the front doorbell rang.

How assured she was! How fully in control of the terrible excitement that tried to rise from her breast into her throat and strangle her! She was proud of her assurance, her quiet command of her furious heart. Leaving the Jupiter to play itself out, she walked into the hall and opened the door. At that instant, as the door opened and she saw the man standing outside with his hat in his hands at the far end of a decade gone, her mind was trespassed by a scrap of verse, a strange and perverse lyric culled from a litter of odds and ends for some reason remembered:

I saw my dear, the other day,
Beside a flowering wall;
And this was all I had to say:
"I thought that he was tall!"

How many years ago had she read that? Oh, years and years, in a book of poems by Dorothy Parker. But why had it lain intact and dormant so long in her mind to be remembered at this instant? Was it just that the man outside her door seemed in the instant, whatever he had been and still was, somehow deficient? That was nonsense. The deficiency was not in him, but in her immediate *response* to him, because her anticipation and excitement had tricked her into expecting too much too soon. Closing her eyes, she saw him suddenly, at once reduced and enlarged, growing in a vision from a boy to a man, and her contained excitement was restored with the vision.

"Pat," she said. "How nice to see you again."

"Hello, Ruth. You look the same as ever."

"You know better. I'm ten years older, and I'm sure I show them all. Come in, Pat. We have so much to say to each other."

He left his hat in the hall and followed her into the living room. The Jupiter was still playing. She turned it down and sat beside him on the sofa, the interval between them suggesting to her the separation by scale, as on a map, of what they had been and what they were.

"I'm afraid I won't be able to stay as long as I hoped," he said. "An hour at the longest. My schedule's tighter than I thought, and it will take me the better part of an hour to get back to the airport."

Small matter, she thought. *It will be better to end quickly, now that the time is here, what has taken far too long already.*

"Then you must tell me all about yourself at once," she said.

"There isn't much to tell." His voice struck a note of false humility which she felt uneasily was a kind of inverted pretension. He was too well preserved, too immaculately groomed, even after a long taxi ride, in clothes that were too obviously expensive. "After college, you remember, I went to San Francisco. After a year I dropped down to Los Angeles, and I've been there ever since."

"I didn't know. I've had no word from you all this time."

"I'm sorry. I intended to keep in touch, but you know how these things are. A man gets involved, he doesn't have much time for old friends and places."

"I must say that you seem to have done very well," Ruth said.

"I've been able to get my share, I guess."

"What do you do?"

"I'm in real estate. Real estate and insurance."

"Oh? You used to want to paint. We used to talk about it."

He laughed, and she listened intently with fierce longing for a suggestion of wistfulness in the sound, the merest whisper of sadness for old hope abandoned and limitations enduring—but there was none. His laughter was brief and untroubled, an expression of indifference tainted with disdain.

"I soon had that fantasy knocked out of my head, once I was out on my own. Business is the thing for me. There's where you're up against the real competition. There's where you find the men with drive and vision. Believe me, you have to stay alert if you hope to stay up front."

"Are you up front?"

"Well, I don't like to blow my own horn, you know, but I manage to hold my own. Maybe I've had some luck, too. You have to get a few breaks as you go along. Still, in the long run, you make your own breaks. The secret is in cultivating the right people. Profitable associations, you know. I've been put next to some great opportunities by men in position to do me a good turn, not by chance."

"I'm delighted. I've often wondered what you were doing. It's comforting to know that you have done well."

"Oh, never worry about old Pat. I have a way of taking care of myself. Right now, as a matter of fact, I've got a show on the road that stands to make me a mint. Would you like to hear about it?"

"Please tell me. You can't imagine how fascinated I am."

"Nothing to it, as I implied, if you know a few people in the right places. I was handed a bit of advance information, very confidential, that a certain area is due for fast promotion and development, a kind of crash program I was able to get in on the ground floor; to buy up a big tract of land at a very good price, you understand. Next month I start building. Modern, medium-priced houses, a classy little residential area with a lot of eye-appeal, you know; variety of construction, nice landscaping and a community club and pool—all that. It represents a big investment, but it'll pay big dividends. You wait and see."

"I hardly can. You must let me know immediately."

"Yes, sir! Business is the thing. Old Silent Cal was dead right years ago. The business of this country is business. He was before our time, of course, but I remember reading that remark. I think I've got it right. Didn't Calvin Coolidge say that?"

"I don't know. I read so little about Calvin Coolidge."

"If you're interested in my opinion, he was a great man, a great president. He was smart enough to put first things first and then leave them alone. There's too much meddling nowadays by the government—all these left-wing fellows. That's the trouble with most of your writers and artists and professors—so-called intellectuals, radicals, people like that. They'll wreck the country if they aren't stopped."

"Perhaps it won't matter in the end. Perhaps all together we will wreck the whole world, and then nothing else will matter."

"What? Oh, you mean The Bomb. In my judgment, there's far too much loose talk about that. What we'd better be worrying about is all this creeping socialism that's taking over everything. But you don't want to get me started on that subject. I might forget the time and miss my jet."

"Yes. You mustn't forget your jet."

"Right." He shot a sleeve and looked at his watch. "Plenty of time however. How did we get started on business and politics, anyhow? We ought to be talking old times. I passed one of your father's old drugstores downtown. It's changed names."

"After my father died I sold the stores."

"You shouldn't have done it. You should have run them yourself. A clever woman like you could have done wonders with them; branched out in other towns, developed a chain."

"I am not a pharmacist."

"No matter. You can hire pharmacists by the dozen. Your father was realistic enough to understand that."

"I was not interested. Perhaps I have no drive or vision."

"Too bad. Do you live alone here?"

"Yes. Alone."

"You haven't changed things much."

"Very little. Are your parents well?"

"Father's dead. Mother's still around. Quite a problem sometimes, Mother is."

"Does she live with you?"

"Hardly. Living with Mother would be impossible. Evelyn and I agreed on that before we were married. Families don't mix."

"You're married? I didn't know."

"Wrong tense. *Was* married. It didn't work, and it didn't last long. Couple of years. Since then, I've carefully preserved my independence."

She thought of something then a possibility that she had not considered before, and she couldn't for the life of her understand why she had not.

"Do you have children? A child?"

"Fortunately, no. Evelyn saw to that, I'm happy to say. It was, I believe, the only sane position she ever took on anything."

"You sound as if your marriage was unhappy. I'm sorry."

"Don't be. It was a mistake from the beginning, a sick sort of joke, and I was lucky to get out of it. How about you? Have you made the big mistake?"

"I've made mistakes, but not that one. I haven't married."

"Remember when we were kids? *We* were going to get married someday. Remember?"

"I remember."

"Well, things change; plans and people and things. As I came down the block I saw that the old vacant lot across the street is gone. We had great times on that lot."

"Yes. Great times."

So he came to them at last, after real estate and insurance and creeping socialism and birth control and divorce and Calvin Coolidge. The great times. The early days, the sweet, fierce days of total commitment before the mutated bitter aftermath—his voice went on and on, assaulting the fragile past, evoking and evading the holy places of their adolescent intimacy, and she sat and listened mutely in the cold and arid climate of her private wasteland. She was drained of pride and soiled with shame. She was dying, dying. She was a religious dying in the terrible conviction that there was, after all, no God. Fool that she was, she had wasted her love, and her hate after her love, on an absurd lie.

Why couldn't he have become a magnificent failure or a fanatic or even a splendid rogue? The wild, silent crying of her mind was her elegy and his epitaph. *Why couldn't he have become anything but a bore?*

He looked again at his watch, and she was, she discovered, suddenly standing.

"It must be almost time for you to leave," she said. "I have martinis made. Will you have one before you go?"

"Thanks," he said. "One for the road. I'll just call a taxi while you're getting it."

She went into the kitchen and removed the shaker from the freezer. She poured martinis into the two delicate crystal glasses on the silver tray. She dropped olives into the glasses and took up the small box of powder. For a moment she held it in both hands below her breasts in what was almost a gesture of love, and then she threw it with a gesture of violence across the kitchen. The box struck a cabinet on the opposite side and fell to the floor. The lid flew off, and the powder spread like a skim of snow on the bright tile. Lifting the silver tray, she carried it into the living room.

"They are quite dry," she said. "I like my martinis quite dry."

He took a glass, and she, after placing the tray on a table, lifted her own.

"Old times," he said.

"Yes. Old times."

The horn of the taxi sounded as they finished drinking, and she walked with him to the front door, but she did not linger to watch him go down to the street where the taxi was waiting. When he paused once to turn and wave, the door was closed and she was gone.

In the living room, sitting on the sofa, she drank slowly over a period of half an hour the three martinis that were left in the shaker.

I'm free, she thought. *Now I am free.*

In the terrifying emptiness of her freedom, with nothing left to live for and nothing worth dying for, she sat and drank the martinis.